# The Games She Played

# Books By Meredith Bond

**The Merry Men Series**
*An Exotic Heir*
*A Merry Marquis*
*A Rake's Reward*
*A Dandy in Disguise*
*My Lord Ghost*
*My Gentleman Thief*
*Under the Mango Tree*
*When Hearts Rebel*
*A Spanish Dilemma*

**The Storm Series**
*Storm on the Horizon*
*Bridging the Storm*
*Magic in the Storm*
*Through the Storm*

**The Falling Series**
*Falling*
*Falling for a Pirate*

*Chapter One: A Fast, Fun Way to Write Fiction*
*Self-Publishing: Easy as ABC*
*"In A Beginning"*, a short story featuring Lilith

# THE GAMES SHE PLAYED

## The Ladies' Wagering Whist Society

### Book Three

**Meredith Bond**

# Chapter One

~June 1~

"It's a bet!" Lord Swindon said with a laugh and a greedy glint in his eye. He held out his hand. The Viscount Rivers gave the man a tight smile as they shook on the deal.

Epsom Downs was unusually quiet, with only maybe a hundred people milling about or chatting from their carriages. The Derby Stakes, one of the biggest races of the season, would not be held for another few weeks. This made it a perfect day for the private relay race, which had been arranged by Lord Bunbury to hold over eager race-goers as they awaited the big day.

Rivers had been thrilled to hear of the race, which was to be ridden not by jockeys but by anyone at all who wished to enter. He'd signed himself and his daughter, Diana, up immediately.

"And here I thought you were an intelligent man," Swindon said with a shake of his head. "Clearly, looks are deceiving."

"I beg your pardon?" Rivers asked, lowering his eyebrows.

"It's one thing to bet on a race you're riding in," Swindon said, dipping his thumbs into his waistcoat pockets, spreading apart his open double-breasted coat of blue superfine, "but a relay where half the race is being ridden by a girl?" He quickly held up a hand, "Now, don't misunderstand me, your daughter is a pretty little filly, but there's no possible way she can ride well enough to win you this race."

The man, oblivious to the stupidity of his words, turned to look at the young woman in question. She was standing some ten feet away talking with her cousin, Lord Audley. "I might like her to ride my..." He gave a little chuckle and wisely chose not to finish that sentence. "But I doubt her ability to ride a horse well enough to win a race."

"Did we say five hundred?" Rivers ground out between his clenched teeth. He gave the man a hard smile. "I meant five *thousand*."

Swindon's eyebrows rose to the top of his forehead. "Do you have that sort of money at hand, old man?"

"Do you? Do you have the guts to make the wager?"

Swindon lifted his nose into the air. "I want it in writing."

"Fine. Get some paper."

Swindon's lips quirked up to one side as he gave Rivers a little nod. "I'm sure someone has some about." He turned and headed off to find the required implements, assuming Rivers would follow. He wasn't wrong.

~*~

Diana Hemshawe, allowed her mare, Nike, to start off the race toward the back of the pack in order to gauge the strengths of each rider and mount. Slowly, as she watched other horses fall away behind her and Nike, she was certain they wouldn't have any difficulty winning. The race had been open to the first ten people to sign up, as long as they weren't professional jockeys, so she'd worried a bit that there could be some serious competition. Happily, it didn't seem as if there were too many here who had the skill and experience of her and her father.

They'd been racing throughout Europe for the past nine years, traveling from course to course, town to town. It had been an incredible way to spend one's adolescence. She'd learned more about the world and its people than she ever would have from the comfort of her father's estate.

Her mother had implored her not to go with her father. When he'd invited her, she was only ten-years-old. Her mother had promised Diana she could learn as much about the world as she wanted—through books. Diana nearly laughed as she recalled her mother's earnest, if futile, arguments.

No, Diana had eagerly gone with her father, and she'd never once regretted the decision. She loved the thrill of the race, the camaraderie of the racing set, even the parties afterward. Today when they won this race, she would celebrate with him as she had after every race, sitting comfortably among the men and women of the racing world in the local pub or inn. Of course, now everyone they sat with would be speaking English—something Diana was still getting used to after so many years of living in France and Germany.

Her father had insisted they return to England when Diana turned nineteen so she could find a husband. She was yet to be convinced of the necessity, but she did admit she was enjoying London. They'd been here for nearly three months, and she'd even managed to make friends, which wasn't something she'd ever done very much of. It was simply too difficult to maintain when one traveled so frequently. Now, as a member of the

Ladies' Wagering Whist Society, she knew what true friendship was.

From the corner of her eye, Diana spied two competitors who might actually provide her with a challenge. They were both men on thoroughbreds and clearly as eager to win as she. But despite the fact that their horses were bigger than hers, the riders themselves were both much heavier. She clearly had the advantage.

Leaning forward, she whispered in Nike's ear, "Good girl, Nike, just a little faster now. Not too much, though; we don't actually want to show these men what we can really do yet." She loved seeing the shocked expression on gentlemen's faces when they saw just how fast she could ride. But she would hold off on that for a later race. A slight tightening of her knees against the horse's flank gave her mare the signal to increase her speed just enough to edge out her two competitors. She approached Tattenham Corner, where her father would take over the race.

Once her father had taken over, Diana rode her slightly heaving horse into the center of the field to watch her father easily win the race. She'd gotten only about halfway across when her father's body jerked upward as if he'd been shot. He dropped the reins, his right hand going to his left shoulder. Diana jolted with shock as he tumbled from his horse. Thank God he was on the inside of the track and tumbled into the center, away from the deadly hooves of the other horses.

Within seconds, she was galloping toward him and frantically looking around to see who'd shot him. Why would someone do that? Had he crossed someone? Could her dear, sweet, charming father have an enemy who'd followed them to England?

She jumped from her horse when she was barely a few feet away and ran to his disturbingly unmoving body.

"Papa! Papa!" she screamed.

He lay there, his face gray and still—too still. He wasn't conscious! His leg was bent at a terrible angle, and it was clearly broken.

"Doctor! Is there a doctor?" she screamed out over the thundering of the horses still racing.

A man came running, ducking under the rail on the other side of the racetrack. "Is he all right?"

"Are you a doctor?"

"No, I'm Bunbury. I organized the race." The man knelt down and put a hand over her father's mouth to see if he were still breathing.

"Didn't you hire a doctor to be present should there be an accident?" Diana asked.

The man's worried eyes met hers. "No, I didn't think of it."

"Is he all right?" asked Audley, Diana's cousin, dropping to the ground next to her.

"No. We need a doctor immediately," Diana answered.

"He's breathing, but barely," Lord Bunbury said. "I'll get a wagon and send for a surgeon. We'll take him to the King's Head. It's not far." He took off running.

Tears pricked Diana's eyes as she reached out and brushed her father's dark brown hair from his forehead. "It's all right, Papa. It's going to be all right," she whispered, praying he could hear her.

An agonizing twenty minutes later, he was lying on a bed at the King's Head Tavern. The surgeon had just come in and been appraised of the accident. Diana stood off to one side of the room, watching intently. Never had she seen her father fall from a horse. She was certain he didn't know how.

"Look for a bullet hole in his shoulder," she directed the surgeon, who'd started with the most obvious thing, her father's leg.

The man stood up from where he'd been bent over her father's lower limbs and turned to look at her. "He was shot?"

"That's the way it looked. It's what made him fall," she answered.

The surgeon immediately examined both of her father's shoulders. "Are you certain? There's no bleeding, no broken skin. Nothing," the man said.

"That's... That's very strange. I distinctly saw him sit up and put his hand to his shoulder. It was then that he fell," she said.

"I saw it too." Audley nodded.

She tried to give her cousin a smile to thank him for his support, but she couldn't get her lips to cooperate. There just wasn't a smile in her.

"No. There's no wound here at all," the doctor confirmed. He felt along his body. "He's got some broken ribs, which isn't surprising. But it's his leg I'm most worried about. It needs to be set immediately. Good thing he isn't conscious, because this is going to hurt."

Diana turned away as he got to work cutting away her father's boot and stockings to reveal his leg.

Unfortunately, it must have been the pain that actually made her father come to. He inhaled sharply as the doctor set the broken bone. Once again, his hand flew to his shoulder.

"Papa!" Diana flew to his side. "It's all right, Papa. The surgeon is here. He's seeing to you. You're going to be fine."

Her father's pale blue eyes shimmered from his too-white face. "Diana, my sweet... You shouldn't be here," he whispered, his voice hoarse. He seemed winded, even though she knew that couldn't be the case.

"Of course I'm here. I will always look after you. You know that. I've always done so, haven't I?"

He gave her a weak smile and a feeble pat on her arm. "You have. I don't know...what I would do...without you. Please don't mourn...for me when I'm gone...my sweet. Ride. Ride another race...to celebrate my life."

Diana gave a strained laugh. "Papa, what a goose you are! You're not going to die."

He took in a shallow breath and winced.

"It's just your ribs. Some are broken. The surgeon said so. He'll bind you up and you'll be good as new in no time," she said, wishing she could believe her own words.

Her father shook his head from side to side. "No..." A tear slowly leaked from one eye and slipped down his temple into his hair that in the past year had begun to turn gray.

"Ah, well now," the surgeon said with forced cheer, "you're awake, I see. Good, good. We'll get you wrapped up and patched up in no time. You'll have to stay off that leg for a good six weeks or more, but your ribs should heal in a much shorter time." He came up the other side of the bed and smiled down at his patient.

"Doc, I..." Lord Rivers started.

"Now, now, no talking. Just take shallow breaths to ease the pain for the moment, and then I'll give you some laudanum to let you sleep." The man went back to splinting Lord Rivers' leg. Diana held his hand and tried to force herself to be as upbeat and optimistic as the doctor seemed to be.

~*~

Andrew Crowther sat back in the post chaise he'd hired to transport himself and his valet from Dover to London. The crossing from Calais had been easy enough, but sadly, Michel didn't do well on the water. The valet had been hanging over the side rail, sick as could be, for much of their time aboard. If Andrew had known he had that problem, he could have brought some ginger tea to calm his stomach. It had just never occurred to him, being a strong-stomached traveler himself.

"What use is having a physician for an employer," Michel had cried in his native French.

Andrew had felt bad, but there'd been nothing he could do for the fellow.

Even now, Michel still looked a little pale and gray. Andrew handed him another piece of sugared ginger.

The man took it with a nod of thanks. "It is very green, your English countryside," he said, practicing his English.

"It is. Not so very different from France, no?"

"Perhaps. I do not much go outside the city."

"Well, you'll feel right at home in London, I assure you," Andrew said, giving him a reassuring smile.

"If I survive the journey," the man groaned, leaning his head against the side of the carriage.

"Keep your eye on the passing scenery. It will help."

Michel nodded. "Oui, c'est vrai."

They sat for a few minutes in silence, each watching through the window. Andrew did his best to keep his worries at bay. It had been nearly three years since he'd last seen his parents. They'd been momentous years for him—studying and learning all he could at the feet of the great French physician René Laennec. Laennec's new discovery, which he called the stethoscope, was going to revolutionize coronary medicine, Andrew was certain of it. Already, it had saved the life of a number of patients. Andrew was excited to bring this new tool with him to London. He didn't know if he would be the first, but he would certainly be one of the only physicians there with one.

What worried him, however, was how his parents were coping with the death of his brother in a riding incident. It was a terrible thing to think, but Andrew had been relieved to learn he'd died that way and not by a disease that Andrew might have been able to prevent. Still, now Ian was gone, it would be Andrew who would have to take over the role of heir to his father—not something he was looking forward to at all.

The one thing Andrew was absolutely certain about, however, was that no matter what his father said, he would not be giving up his medical practice. He'd worked too long and too hard to give it up now. He was still a little new, a little green in the field, but he had great ambitions—and nothing, not even an earldom, was going to convince him to give it up.

# Chapter Two

"We will go directly to the tailor," Michel announced suddenly, pulling Andrew from his thoughts.

"What? To the tailor? No, of course not. I must go home and see my parents."

"Not looking like that," Michel said, looking Andrew up and down.

"Michel, I could be dressed in rags and I would still go to my parents first. But..." He held up his hand to stop his valet from screaming out in horror. "I am not. These clothes are perfectly fine."

"You are not dressed the part of the heir to the count," Michel argued.

"My father is an earl, not a count, and it doesn't matter. I can attend to my clothes later—or you can do it for me. You have my measurements."

Michel's mouth opened and closed in dismay. "It is how all of your clothes have been purchased. You need to go yourself and see the fabrics. Feel them. Decide on the color."

"I have full faith in your expert opinion. If you remember, that is why I hired you," Andrew said.

"Oui, Docteur, but..."

"No, Michel, I will not change my habits just because I am now my father's heir."

"But..."

"It is not open for discussion. We will talk about it further when it becomes necessary, but for now, I simply need to see to my parents. They are grieving, Michel, they won't care what I'm wearing." If only he was certain what he said was completely accurate. He did not, in fact, *want* to see his parents, but he knew he *should*. That he had to do so.

Their favorite son had died, and they were left with number two, the disappointment. Oh, he didn't feel bad about being the less favored son. In fact, it had allowed him to do exactly as he'd wanted—follow his passion and go to medical school. Poor Ian had had no choice in what he did with his life. He'd been the heir. He'd had to behave with impunity, follow their father's dictates, and in short, be the perfect son whether he wanted to or not. No, Andrew had felt no malice toward his brother at all. Happily, Ian had seemed to enjoy his lot in life—what a shame it had ended too soon.

What pained Andrew more was the fact that he and his brother hadn't had much of a relationship. One would think that brothers, close in age, would have been friends, companions, playmates, but he and Ian had had very little of that. Their father had seen to it that even in play, Andrew's brother had been directed more toward his eventual role as the marquess. Andrew had mostly been left to his own devices, and now he would never have the opportunity to truly know his brother. That was what hurt more than anything.

~June 2~

"No! I said no," Lord Rivers raised his arm and threatened to knock the glass of laudanum out of the surgeon's hand.

"But, my lord, it's going to be a very painful journey," the man protested.

"I understand that...but I will not...take any more of that...vile stuff. Now...see to...the footmen...who will carry...me down...the stairs," Rivers commanded and as forcefully as he could, given his weakened state. Just this small argument had him gasping for breath.

"Go and do as my father says," Diana said, intervening on her father's behalf.

"Thank you...Diana...my dear...sweet girl," her father said. He was clearly trying to take slow shallow breaths. His ribs must be causing him a great deal of pain. Poor Papa! How he was going to survive the nearly two-hour journey back to London, she just couldn't imagine.

"It's all right, Papa. It's all right. If you don't want the laudanum, you shan't have it," she said, brushing a wisp of hair that always fell onto his forehead.

He breathed a little easier and closed his eyes, now satisfied his wishes would be seen to.

He didn't open them again until he'd been conveyed down the steep stairs of the tavern and into the wagon on a stretcher. The doctor wanted him to remain flat on his back due to the breaks in his ribs and his leg. Of course, at first, the surgeon had protested vehemently at Lord Rivers being moved at all this early in his recuperation, but Diana's father had insisted. He wanted to be at home, in his own bed, tended by his own people. Nothing anyone could say would dissuade him from this course of action.

Diana climbed up into the wagon and sat down on the hay-strewn floor, heedless of her dress. It wasn't a particularly fine dress, just a simple blue cambric, which made it perfect for traveling. Within minutes, they were going along at a smart pace. Both she and her father, however, could feel every bump and dip in the road.

"It should get easier the closer we get to London," Diana reassured her father. She held tightly onto his hand as they traveled over the rough roads, leaving the racecourse area.

Lord Rivers gave a short nod. He managed to open his eyes and look up at his daughter. "Diana," he whispered through clenched teeth.

She leaned down closer to hear what he had to say.

"I tried...to tell...that idiot doctor... yesterday... but he... wouldn't listen..." he ground out.

"What, Papa?"

"The reason...I fell..."

"Yes! I have never in my life known you to fall from a horse. At first, I'd thought you'd been shot. It was the only explanation I could find. But the doctor checked and you had no bullet wounds."

He shook his head a bit. "Not...not a bullet... My chest...a pain...in my chest."

"You had a pain in your chest?"

"So sharp...I couldn't hold...on...to the...reins."

"Oh, my goodness!"

He opened his eyes, which had closed again with the pain of the jostling road. His blue eyes, so very much like her own, looked up at her with a wisdom and determination Diana feared she would never have. "You...must marry...Diana. No...no more dawdling... looking for...the perfect man. I want... I want to see...you married...before I...die."

"Die! Papa, don't be ridiculous! You're not going to die."

Her father managed to tilt his head just a touch and raise one eyebrow. He didn't believe her. "Promise," he whispered.

Diana sat up and huffed out a breath.

"Diana!" Her father's voice grew slightly stronger, but it was clearly taking him a good deal of energy to make it so.

"Fine, Papa. I will stop being quite so picky and truly look around for a husband if it will make you happy. But no more talk of dying!"

He gave her a small smile, which lingered on his lips until the wagon hit another rut in the road.

This was going to be a very long, very painful journey.

It felt like ten hours later, but finally they reached their townhouse. The two Rivers footmen each took an end of the stretcher and carried their master up to his bedchamber. As they did so, Diana was waylaid by a man in a slightly threadbare gray coat.

"I beg your pardon, but are you Miss Rivers?" the man asked. He carried a leather medical bag in his right hand.

"Yes," Diana said, stopping her ascent up the three steps into her home.

"I am Mr. Wheat, Lord Audley sent me. I'm the surgeon."

"Oh! Yes, of course. Thank you so much for meeting us, Mr. Wheat. Please come in."

"Thank you." He followed Diana into the house. "I just want to check on your father and see if there's anything else I can do for him. I understand he's already been seen by a surgeon?"

"Yes, but I wanted another opinion. Thank you so much for coming. Please, this way." She led him up the stairs to her father's bedchamber. Susan, the chambermaid, came out of the room just as they reached the top of the stairs.

"Oh, Miss Rivers. If you would just give your father a moment before you go into see him. Mark and Harry are just getting him changed and into bed."

"Of course," Diana said. She and the doctor stood out in the hall for the few minutes until the footmen came out to inform them that Lord Rivers was ready.

The doctor made quick work of examining what the other surgeon had done. He rewrapped his leg in its bindings, which would keep it steady while the bone healed, but other than that, he declared the man had done a fine job.

"There is one thing, Mr. Wheat," Diana said, stepping forward as he was putting his things back into his medical bag. "My father said the reason he fell from his horse was because of a sharp pain in his chest. Might you be able to do something... know, perhaps, a reason for this?"

The doctor stopped and looked back at his patient, who was resting as well as possible. His chest rose and fell quickly with his short breaths.

"I would recommend a physician see him. I'm afraid I am a surgeon. Broken bones and wounds I can manage. Chest pains?" The man scratched his head. "They're out of my purview. I'm sorry."

"Do you know of a good physician?" Diana asked.

"Dr. Beaumont is quite popular. He'll be able to come and cup Lord Rivers. Bleed out any bad humors that might be lurking."

"Bleed?" Diana shook her head vigorously. "Oh, no. I don't want him bled. I'm sure that wouldn't be the right treatment."

The man smiled down at her condescendingly. "And what would you know of chest pains and medicine, Miss Hemshawe?"

Diana opened her mouth for a moment, wishing she could say something clever, but unfortunately, he was absolutely correct. She knew nothing. Perhaps bleeding would be the best thing for her father, but she wanted to explore all the possibilities before committing to the first treatment at hand. "Thank you for your advice, sir. I will speak with my cousin, Lord Audley, and decide on our next step."

The man gave a nod and headed out the door.

"Don't... Don't let...them...bleed me. Hate those bloody leeches," her father whispered from the bed.

Diana rushed over and took hold of his hand that had been resting on his chest. "I promise, Papa, I won't."

~*~

"Well, it's about time!" Lord Darby said, coming out of his study at the commotion being caused by Andrew's arrival.

Andrew stopped short just inside the door. His father looked as if he'd aged twenty years. Lines crossed his forehead and radiated from his eyes. His face was still strong, however, his eyes still piercing in their disapproval, and his hair was still the same pale blond as Andrew's own. "Father." Andrew bowed before coming forward. "Please accept my most sincere condolences."

His father's mouth pinched together, but he gave his second son a quick nod of acknowledgement. "What took you so long to get here?" the earl asked, turning and leading the way into his study.

"Er, nothing, sir. I came as quickly as I could, as

soon as I received your letter." Andrew was a touch confused. "I resigned my position, packed all my belongings—"

"Why the hell didn't you leave that to your man? You could have come right away and left him to deal with all that." He waved his hand in the air. "Nonsense," he finished, "you were needed here."

"What was the emergency? When I received your letter, it said you'd already had the funeral." He paused when his father winced. "I'll travel to Darby as soon as I can to pay my respects."

"Don't bother," his father growled. "Your...your mother..." He turned and looked out the window. "She's not been well." He spun around to face Andrew, pointing an accusing finger at him. "I paid a small ransom to that medical school, and you dawdle, taking your sweet time to come here when she is in desperate need of a physician."

"What? Why didn't you say so in your letter? Why hasn't she been seen by someone already here?" Andrew exclaimed. "Where is she? Is she still unwell?"

"Of course she's still unwell! You think these things just go away on their own?" his father bellowed.

Andrew took a step backward, his spine straightening. "I will go and see her, then. Excuse me." He spun on his heel and left the room.

Patience, he reminded himself. He would need all the patience in the world in order to deal with his father. He'd never been an easy man, but now—grieving and obviously upset about his wife's health—he would be even more trying.

Taking the stairs two at a time, he went to his own room, where his luggage had been taken, to find his medical bag before going to his mother. His knock on her door was answered by her maid.

She curtsied briefly as she let him into the room. "Lord Colburne, my lady," she said, announcing him.

Andrew nearly stopped her—Colburne was his brother—but no, now it was him, he supposed, assuming his father would transfer his lesser title from one son to the other. With the greeting his father had just given him, Andrew wasn't sure this was a certainty. He set these thoughts aside to focus on his mother and her health.

"Andrew," his mother said on a sigh. Her voice sounded weak and breathless.

He drew up to her bedside and lifted his lips into a smile. "Mother. How are you feeling?" Like his father, she too had aged more severely than she should have. Her skin hung from her cheeks, softened with age, and her green eyes, always so full of life and vigor, had dulled. Andrew felt for his parents. Clearly, their grief was taking a toll on them both.

She gave a weak cough as she shook her head. Her hair was in a long braid resting over her shoulder. It had been a mix of light brown and blonde when Andrew had left for France, but now there was more silver than anything else. "Well enough, considering..."

"It doesn't sound that way to me." He set down his medical bag at the end of her bed. "May I have a listen?" he said, opening it and reaching for his new stethoscope.

She held up her hand. "It's nothing, Andrew... I'll be fine."

He stopped. "Please?"

She shook her head. "No. It's simply... simply the shock. That's all."

She seemed to be having problems breathing. He didn't like this. "If you allow me to listen, perhaps I can prescribe something to make you feel better more quickly."

"I said no," she repeated more forcefully this time. She fell into a fit of coughing.

Andrew rushed to her side and helped her to sit up so she could breathe more easily.

"Thank you," she whispered.

He gently propped her onto her pillows. "Father is insisting—" he began, hoping he could convince her to allow him to see to her health.

"Your father is making...a big deal of nothing.... He is overthinking everything now...seeing illnesses where there are none," she managed. It was the longest speech she'd said since he'd come in.

"But Ian didn't die of an illness—at least, not according to the letter Father sent me. He said that he'd fallen off his horse while hunting," Andrew pointed out.

Lady Darby lifted a shoulder. "Still..."

"Please, Mother," Andrew made a move toward his medical bag once more.

"If you dare take anything from that bag... It had best not be for me," she said, her voice hardening ever so slightly. Well, at least she was beginning to sound like the mother he knew.

He sighed and closed his bag again. "Very well. I can't force you to allow me to examine you."

"No, you cannot...and you will not do so." She winced as she coughed violently before glaring at him. "How was your journey?" she asked.

"It was fine, thank you."

"And Paris?"

He gave her a little smile. "Lovely, as it always is in the spring."

"From your letters, I wouldn't think..." She paused to cough again into her handkerchief. "...you'd seen much of it," she finished.

He gave a little chuckle. "Well, I have been spending long hours in the hospital tending to patients, but happily, we had to travel to some patients. That meant going outside, so I did get a chance to get some fresh air every so often."

She gave an understanding nod.

"For how long have you been unwell?" he asked, thinking that at least he could get a feel for what might be ailing her, despite not being allowed to examine her.

"Since Ian... Since we got the news," she said softly, her eyes filling with tears, "I wasn't... I wasn't able to attend..."

"Well, perhaps that was for the best," he said.

She gave a little nod and wiped at the corners of her eyes. "That's what your father said."

"So that was over a month ago."

"I suppose so."

"And you're having problems breathing?" he asked.

"Have you eaten?" she countered, clearly catching on to his line of questioning.

"Er..." He had to think of whether he'd eaten or not. He had a tendency to forget to do so.

"Why don't you go downstairs. I'm sure the cook...has some cherry tarts," she finished after a brief cough. "I think I'd like to rest."

She was looking terribly pale and worn out—even more so than when he'd come in.

"Of course. An excellent idea. I'll go do that." He came over and placed a kiss on her forehead. She wasn't feverish, he was happy to discover. "I'll be by later to check on you and perhaps then you'll—"

"No," she interrupted him, "I won't."

# CHAPTER THREE

**~June 4~**

Diana was sitting with her father as he attempted to eat a little breakfast when there was a knock on his door.

"I beg your pardon," Mark, the footman said, holding a salver out in front of him.

"If that's today's mail, please put it on my father's desk in his study," Diana said, beginning to turn back toward her father.

"Now, Diana—"

"No, Papa, you are not going to be bothered by business for at least the next week or so. If there is anything of urgency... Well, it can just wait until you've had a chance to see a physician and get some much-needed rest."

"It's a note for you, Miss," Mark interrupted. "I would have waited to give it to you, only there's a man downstairs waiting for a reply."

"Oh!" Diana stood up and took the note.

"What is it?" her father asked. His breathlessness was a little better now that his ribs were properly bound, but he still kept his sentences short, Diana noticed.

"It's from Lady Norman. She needs to know if

I'll be able to come a little early to the Ladies' Wagering Whist Society meeting today." She started to refold the note. "Well, this is fortuitous. It gives me the opportunity to inform her I won't be attending at all."

"What? Why not?" Lord River's asked.

She turned back toward him. "I'm not going to leave you alone all afternoon while I go and play cards. Don't be ridiculous!" She gave a little laugh.

"I'm not. And, yes you are," he answered.

"No, Papa. I couldn't possibly—"

"Maybe they'll know of a physician," he said.

That stopped her, though. "I was going to ask Audley, but that's not a bad idea. There are a number of older ladies who are part of the group. I'm sure they know the best physicians in London."

Her father just nodded, perhaps still too winded to speak further.

"All right. I'll go see Audley this afternoon, and then go to my Society meeting but just for a short time." She wagged a finger at him, adding, "You need to eat some more. I'll respond to Lady Norman's note while you do so. I want to see at least half that plate empty when I return."

He gave a little chuckle but said, "I wish I had the appetite you demand." She shook her head before going off to write her note.

~*~

At two that afternoon, Diana set out for her cousin's home. She hoped he'd be up by now. With a fellow like Audley, you never knew.

Indeed, she found him eating something that looked suspiciously like breakfast.

"Good afternoon, Audley," Diana said, coming into the dining room unannounced.

Her cousin looked up from his plate, his knife and fork momentarily stilled. His dark, brown hair was carefully tussled—or not so carefully, Diana couldn't tell. He was wearing a very sharp-looking cream banyan with a brown design all over it. The plate in front of him held a substantial repast of eggs, steak, toast, and a scattering of something that might have once been a vegetable.

"Good afternoon. Were there no footmen at the door?" he asked, looking behind her.

"There was. I told him I'd announce myself. Do you mind? I didn't think we stood on ceremony," she said, pulling out the chair opposite him.

"No, we don't, it's just Mama who likes everything to be just so."

"Oh, well, Aunt Audley will forgive me, I'm sure."

"Yes, I suppose. Just don't mention it to her should you see her, all right?"

"Of course. I actually only have a moment to stop, so it's unlikely we'll meet." Diana paused and then said thoughtfully, "She doesn't like me very much, does she?"

Audley removed the fork from his mouth and sat back as he chewed. Once he'd swallowed, he shook his head, "It's not that she doesn't like you, it's just that she's so busy with my sisters—"

"Oh, I wasn't complaining about the fact she won't chaperone me. I don't mind that at all. It was just an off-hand comment. Forget I made it."

Audley gave an easy-going shrug and put more food into his mouth.

"What I actually came to ask was whether you knew of a physician who could come to see my father," Diana said.

Her cousin frowned. "What was wrong with the surgeon I sent?"

"Nothing! He seemed to be a very competent man, but he said Papa needs to be seen by a *physician*. There might be something more wrong with him than just some broken bones," she added more quietly.

"What?"

"I don't know, which is why we need the physician."

"Oh, yes, of course." Her cousin speared another piece of meat from his plate. "Sadly, I don't know of any."

"None at all?"

He shook his head, since his mouth was full.

"Harrumph." Diana sat back and crossed her arms in front of her. "I suppose I will have to ask the ladies of my Wagering Whist Society. I was hoping you would know of someone, but I'm sure one of them will be able to help me."

"Fine idea," he agreed.

She gave him a little smile. "Well, then, I won't disturb your meal any more than I already have—not that you've stopped eating for even a moment..."

"I'm hungry!" her cousin protested.

"It's fine. Not very polite, but fine," she said with a little laugh as she stood. "I'll be off, then, to the ladies."

He gave her a nod, but didn't even make a pretense of standing to say goodbye.

~*~

Many of the ladies were already assembled by the time Diana reached Lady Norman's home.

"Good afternoon, Miss Hemshawe," Lady

Norman said, greeting Diana as she came into the drawing room.

Diana paused to curtsy to the assembled ladies. "Good afternoon." She accepted the cup of tea her hostess poured for her and then sat next to Lady Sorrell. "Is there a reason why we're meeting earlier than usual today?" she asked quietly.

"Yes, but no one but Lady Norman knows what it is, and she hasn't shared yet. Once everyone gets here, I think all will be made clear."

Just at that moment, Lady Blakemore and Mrs. Aldridge with her little dog, Duchess, came in.

"Good afternoon, good afternoon!" Mrs. Aldridge cried happily. She set her dog down on the floor, since Lady Norman had asked her not to allow the dog onto the furniture. Immediately, Duchess's little black nose was sniffing the pastries sitting on a plate on a low table in front of the sofa.

"Ah-ah, Duchess, be a good girl," her owner admonished gently. She put her hand down, and the dog came over to sniff it and then reluctantly sat at her feet, nose still twitching.

Diana smiled. She loved watching the little pup. She was such an endearing little thing, with her long floppy black ears and black and white mottled coat. As if sensing her approval, the dog got up and came over. Placing her forepaws on Diana's knees, she looked up, clearly hoping for a pet. Diana happily complied, running her fingers through the dog's soft fur. She was rewarded with a lick to her hand.

"Well, now we're all here," Lady Norman said, after handing the two newcomers their tea. "Let's get down to business."

Diana looked up from the dog and noticed Lydia hadn't yet arrived. "I beg your pardon, Lady Norman, but Miss Sheffield isn't here."

"Precisely," Lady Norman nodded. "I'm afraid the reason I asked you all here was for your approval to, er, fudge our points just a little."

"What do you mean?" the Duchess of Kendall asked, frowning at their hostess and the founder of the Ladies' Wagering Whist Society.

"Lord Daniel, Miss Sheffield's father, came to ask my assistance in finding out more about his daughter's sudden engagement to Lord Welles," Lady Norman explained.

"Oh my," Lady Sorrell said under her breath.

"He's worried she's hiding something from him, and he has asked if we might try to discover what it is," Lady Norman continued. "I thought the easiest way for us to do that is to tell Miss Sheffield that we have tallied the points and she has, unfortunately, lost our game. With Tina's proposal, we got off schedule. We're just one hand away from finishing our second rubber, and Lydia *is* in last place, but—"

"There is still that hand to be played," Diana finished.

"Why don't we just play the hand and then tell her she's lost?" the duchess asked.

"Two reasons," Lady Norman said. "First, it may take her some time to explain things to us, and second, I can tell you from experience, it's awkward to stop after an hour or so and then have to divulge something that is potentially very embarrassing."

There was silence for a moment while everyone digested this.

The dog wandered from Diana's side, looking curiously at everyone she passed as she returned to her owner, who was helping herself to a piece of cake. Silence was an unusual thing amongst the ladies.

"You are thinking if she tells us her secret, we would learn whether there is anything...unusual about her engagement?" Lady Sorrell asked.

"That is my hope," Lady Norman said with a nod. "I believe a vote would be best. All in favor of informing Miss Sheffield she has lost the game, please say 'aye'." Lady Norman immediately followed her statement with her own 'aye' and then looked around the room at the other ladies.

There were a smattering of 'aye's. The Duchess of Kendall sat silent with her mouth pursed. Lady Sorell stared silently at her hands, clasped in her lap.

"And the 'nay's," Lady Norman prompted.

"Nay!" the duchess said immediately.

Lady Sorrell looked up. "I just don't know if this is right, to lie to her this way simply to satisfy her father's curiosity," she said.

"I'm sure it's not idle curiosity, Lady Sorrell, he is looking out for the happiness and welfare of his daughter," Mrs. Aldridge said, picking up her little dog and placing her on her lap.

"That is the way I see it as well," Lady Norman said.

"Well... Do you truly feel there might be something untoward about her engagement?" Lady Sorrell asked.

"It is not I who feels this way but her father," their hostess answered.

The woman gave a little nod. "Well then, I suppose I must side with the 'ayes'."

"Then it is just you, Your Grace, who does not agree to this idea. I'm sorry, but you are overruled," Lady Norman said, looking to the duchess.

"I don't believe it is anyone's business why or how Miss Sheffield entered into this engagement.

And I don't believe lying to her to get her to spill her secrets is the way to pry information from her," the lady said.

Diana had to agree; when it was put that way, it did seem rather unethical.

"But if there is something bothering the girl which would lead her into a match that shouldn't be, isn't it up to us, her friends, to make sure she is protected?" Mrs. Aldridge answered.

"No," the duchess answered shortly. "She is a young woman of good sense. If she needs help, I would expect her to ask for it, not have it forced upon her."

"But what if she doesn't know how to ask?" Mrs. Aldridge responded, clearly becoming agitated.

"Ladies, I believe the point is moot. We have taken a vote and decided upon this course of action," Lady Norman pointed out. "Miss Sheffield will be here—"

There was a brief knock on the door before the footman opened it to reveal the young lady in question. "My goodness, am I late?" Miss Sheffield asked, coming into the room.

Lady Norman stood and nodded to her. "No, not at all. We were just enjoying some tea. Would you care for some?"

Lydia relaxed a touch. "Oh, yes, thank you." She came forward and accepted the cup their hostess had poured.

"I'm terribly sorry, but I have bad news for you," Lady Norman said as she sat on the sofa again.

The duchess watched disapprovingly. Mrs. Aldridge was having some difficulty keeping her dog's nose from the now-empty cake plate in her hand while also lending her silent support for Lady

Norman.

"We were tallying the points, and it seems you have the fewest," Lady Norman said, with a slight hesitation to her voice. It seemed now that the matter was right in front of her, and she too was having some second thoughts.

"Me?" Lydia started. "But surely that can't be right. I won one of the hands we played last week."

"True but sadly, it wasn't enough," Lady Norman said, turning her face away.

"I'm afraid it's your turn to reveal a secret," Mrs. Aldridge said, as Lady Moreton removed the empty plate from her hand and put it on the table out of the dog's reach. "Oh, thank you."

"Perhaps there's something—" Mrs. Aldridge started but then stopped abruptly.

"It's extremely annoying, we are aware," Lady Moreton said, "but we did all agree to abide by the rules. Lady Norman told us about Tina. Today, it's your turn."

All eyes turned to Lydia who looked wide-eyed back at them. Her teacup rattled in its saucer as she gently set it back down after taking a bracing sip. She paused, seeming to think through her words before starting. "Well, you all know, I'm sure, that I've recently become engaged to marry Lord Welles."

"Yes, of course," Lady Norman said.

"Congratulations," Diana put in, hoping to relieve some of the tension she could see in her friend's eyes.

"Thank you. It's not a real engagement, however. I've promised Lord Welles I would call it off at the end of the season."

# Chapter Four

"But why?" Lady Blakemore asked, appropriately shocked.

Diana could only hold her breath, waiting for Lydia's answer, and she suspected she wasn't the only one.

"Because I don't want to marry—ever," Lydia admitted.

"Has your father been pressuring you to become engaged?" Diana asked. She too was feeling the weight of her father's insistence she marry as quickly as possible.

Lydia gave her a hesitant little smile. "He has, but it's not that. I simply don't want to ever get married."

There was silence all around the room until Lady Moreton asked gently, "Did your parents have a difficult marriage?"

"No! They were very much in love," Lydia answered.

"Then why don't you want to marry?" Lady Norman asked.

Lydia turned her head away for a moment. This was clearly a very difficult conversation for her. "I watched my mother die in childbirth. I am never going to go through that. And the only way to ensure I don't, is to not get married."

"Oh, you poor child!" the duchess said with feeling.

"How awful," Mrs. Aldridge agreed.

"That must have been very difficult," Lady Blakemore said.

"It was," Lydia admitted. "So, you understand now. My father has insisted I become engaged this season. He wants me to marry, but... I can't. I just can't."

With the mention of Lydia's father, Diana's mind went back to her own. Her eyes strayed to the clock sitting on top of the mantle to her right. It was well past three. She had left him nearly two hours ago. Truly, she hadn't meant to stay away from him for this long, and she worried he might need her.

But the conversation flowing around Lydia and her difficulties was impossible to break into with her own problems. It just wouldn't be right and poor Lydia... Her poor, dear friend, living with this fear... Going so far as to have a fake engagement just so her father would think she was doing as he'd asked. It was really incredible, and yet Diana was certain Lydia's fears, while definitely well founded, were excessive.

Diana continued to participate in the conversation the best she could but was relieved when Lady Norman finally stood up and said, "Well, while you think on all that we have said, Miss Sheffield, perhaps it would be best if we got started on our next game?"

This was her moment. "Before that, my lady," Diana said, standing up before anyone else had an opportunity to do so. "Ladies, if I could beg for your advice..."

"What is it, Miss Hemshawe? You've been rather quiet this afternoon," Lady Sorrell said, as perceptive as ever.

"My father... He fell from his horse a few days ago while racing. I'm afraid he's not doing very well—"

"Oh, no!"

"I am so sorry to hear that!" various ladies exclaimed.

Diana clasped her hands together. "I almost didn't come today, but I needed to in order to ask if any of you know of a physician who might see him."

"I believe it is a surgeon who you need, Miss Hemshawe, to see to any bones that might be broken," Mrs. Aldridge said.

"He has been seen by a surgeon, ma'am. Two, in fact. But the reason for his fall was because of a sharp pain in his chest. We need a physician," Diana explained.

"*Angina*," the duchess said, knitting her eyebrows together. She blinked a few times as she added, "My husband died of *angina pectoris*. If only we'd known... It is a sudden and horrid malady."

"I am so sorry, Your Grace. I'm sure you understand, then, how urgent it is that I find a well-qualified doctor," Diana said.

"I don't know how good he is," Lady Blakemore began, "but I would imagine that he is very well qualified..."

"Who is that?" Diana asked, her heartbeat picking up at the possibility of actually getting a name.

"My husband was telling me this morning that a friend of his, Lord Darby, was complaining about his son last night. Apparently he's been studying and working in Paris at a hospital there. He specializes in problems of the heart," Lady Blakemore said.

"And he's a physician?" Diana clarified.

"Yes. Lord Colburne is his name. He's Lord Darby's new heir—having recently lost his older son in a riding accident. I can give you his direction," Lady Blakemore said.

"That would be wonderful, my lady! I can't thank you enough," Diana said, trying not to allow her intense relief to show.

~June 5~

Lord Darby had been as surprised as Andrew that his complaining at his club had actually resulted in a consult for a new patient.

"Well, don't kill him!" were his father's encouraging words when Andrew had told his father about the request to pay a call on Lord Rivers.

Andrew held his tongue and his sigh and simply went off to meet the man.

"I am Dr, er, Lord Colburne," he told the footman answering the door. "Here to see Lord Rivers."

The man bowed him into the simple gray marbled foyer. Unlike his father's house, there were no ancient Greek statues or ornately painted ceiling complete with cherubs roaming through the clouds. No, this home seemed to be very simple and understated. Andrew felt at ease immediately.

"If you would follow me to the drawing room, my lord, Miss Hemshawe requested an interview with you before you go in to see her father," the footman said, reclaiming Andrew's attention.

Andrew nodded and followed the man up to the first floor. The drawing room was as simple and elegant as the foyer. The blue damask furniture was elegant and above the fireplace was a painting of a horse. That was a little odd, since most people had paintings of family members in such a position of prominence, Andrew thought. He didn't have time to contemplate it further, as the most stunning young woman approached him.

Her rich, brown hair could almost be mistaken for a deep red and her brilliant blue eyes, while looking rather concerned at the moment, were as enticing as her lovely, petite figure. She paused a few steps away from him to curtsy.

"Lord Colburne, thank you so much for coming," she said. Her voice was soft and lyrical, with the slightest hint of an accent. It made Andrew think of the female nurse he'd worked with in Paris.

Recovering himself from staring at this beauty, he bowed. "Of course. I must say I was rather surprised to receive your note. I hadn't realized too many people even knew I had returned to London." He paused and gave a little laugh. "But I have thanked my father for talking about me to his friends. For once, his complaining has yielded something good."

She smiled. "Had he been complaining? What I'd heard was he was speaking of your excellent education and the time you spent in Paris. Is that right? *Êtes-vous récemment venu de Paris?*"

"Yes, I only arrived two days ago, in fact," he answered. "But you'll have to excuse me; while your French sounds almost like a native, mine is atrocious. I'm afraid I only speak the language when absolutely necessary." He shrugged apologetically. It had been awful when he'd been in Paris and had had to communicate in French. He'd suffered the frowns and pitiful laughter of the people there as they'd tried to make out what he'd been trying to say. Languages were not something that came naturally to him.

"Oh no, not at all. I lived in France for a few

years, but English is much easier for me as well," she said. She indicated they sit down.

"Thank you. What took you to France, if I may ask?" he asked.

"You may, but if you don't mind, I think I'll save our socializing for later. I'm most concerned about my father," she said, gently reminding him as to why he was there.

She had definitely put him in his place, no matter how sweetly. He felt like an idiot. "I do beg your pardon. Of course. Please tell me about him."

She gave a slight nod. "We were riding in a relay race this past Monday," she began.

"I'm sorry," Andrew interrupted. "Did you say 'we'?"

"Yes. We both race horses. We were at Empson Downs participating in a relay race organized by Lord Bunbury. I handed the baton off to my father to finish the race and then he... Well, he behaved as if he'd been shot in the shoulder. He dropped the reins and fell from his horse. I was certain someone had shot him, but when the surgeon examined him later at the inn, he said there were no bullet wounds."

"Which shoulder?" Andrew asked.

Miss Hemshawe's right hand, small and delicate, flew to her left shoulder. "Here. His left."

Andrew nodded. "And how has he been doing since then?"

"Well, he's got a broken leg and a few broken ribs, so it's hard for him to breathe, but considering the circumstances..." She paused. It seemed to be difficult for her to go on.

"You sound like you're very close to your father," Andrew pointed out, more for himself than her.

Tears welled in her eyes. She nodded. "He's all

I've had for the past nine years."

"I'm so sorry. Your mother…?"

"She's at our country estate. She refused to go to Europe with my father and me," she explained. "She stayed home with my younger brother."

"Oh!" He couldn't help being surprised, certain she was about to tell him her mother had died.

"Yes. So naturally, my father and I are very close," she said, finishing her answer.

"Naturally," Andrew responded. He would have loved to simply sit here and learn all about this fascinating, beautiful woman, but he was here to see her father and it sounded very much like he'd had a cardiac event. That in itself was also quite fascinating to Andrew, but he tempered his enthusiasm for her father's misfortune and simply stood. "Well then, perhaps you could show me to him, and I'll see what can be done to make him feel better."

"Thank you." The relief in her voice made him desperately hope there would indeed be something he could do for the man.

She gave a quick knock on a door down the hall before letting herself and Andrew into the room. "Papa, here's the doctor I told you would be coming."

The man lying in bed supported by a number of pillows was obviously Miss Hemshawe's father. A lock of rich brown hair was hanging over his forehead and would have been in his eyes were they open.

"Papa?" Miss Hemshawe said again quietly as she approached the bed. She reached out and pushed his hair out of the way as his eyelids fluttered open.

"Good afternoon, my lord," Andrew said quietly. He came forward and approached him from the other side of the large tester bed. "I'm Dr. Crowther, Lord Colburne." He really had to get used to simply saying Lord Colburne or Lord Dr. Colburne, he supposed. It was odd, though.

"Good afternoon." The man's voice was quiet, and he was clearly having problems breathing.

Andrew set his medical bag at the end of the bed and pulled out the wooden stethoscope he'd had made in Paris, based on the prototype created by his mentor.

"What is that?" Miss Hemshawe asked, staring at it as he moved back toward her father.

"It's a new device called a stethoscope. I've been working with the physician in Paris who invented it. It allows me to hear a patient's heart and lungs more efficiently than if I simply placed my ear to his chest."

"But it simply looks like a cylinder," she said suspiciously.

"Well, yes. The first one Dr. Laennec created was made of paper, but we quickly realized a wooden one would be more durable. Even now, Dr. Laennec is working at creating one that has more of a bell-shape at one end. We were experimenting with a variety of shapes when I was called back to London."

"How fascinating! And it allows you to hear inside of my father and thereby diagnose him?" she asked, staring at it.

"Indeed." Andrew carefully placed the six-inch wooden tube to Lord Rivers' chest, saying, "Hold steady if you would, my lord, and breathe normally." He then placed his own ear to the other end and listened. At the same time, he took hold of his lordship's wrist to feel his pulse. While his pulse was steady, Andrew could hear anomalies in the beating of his heart. When he withdrew, Lord Rivers looked up at him.

"Well?"

"Your heart seems to have suffered some sort of damage. I can only say that you've clearly suffered a cardiac event. *Angina pectoris*, if I'm not mistaken, but thankfully, it wasn't severe enough to kill you."

"Can anything be done?" Miss Hemshawe asked, beginning to wring her hands.

"Sadly, there isn't much. I have heard of a number of remedies for heart conditions, but nothing is known to work for certain. For now, I will recommend you drink willow bark tea. It should make your breathing slightly easier."

Lord Rivers nodded.

"But he doesn't have a fever," Miss Hemshawe pointed out. "The surgeon recommended bleeding," she added hesitantly.

Andrew winced. "That is what is recommended when a physician doesn't know what else to do. It makes patients feel as if something is being done and, well, I'm afraid even some doctors believe it does something helpful. I'm not one of them. If you wish your father to be bled, you'll need to find another doctor."

"Oh, no! In fact, quite the opposite. I *deliberately* didn't call the man the surgeon suggested, who *would* bleed him."

"Well, I'm very glad to hear that. It shows good sense on your part, Miss Hemshawe. While I don't have all the answers you want, I am absolutely certain that bleeding is not what is called for here. I have been working for the past four years with Dr. Laennec, and I intend to continue my studies into the heart and its function here in London. If you would allow me a little time, I have some other ideas I'd like to investigate further before recommending them to your father. The willow bark tea, I know, will make him more comfortable.”

“Sounds sensible to me,” Lord Rivers said on a breath.

“To me as well,” Miss Hemshawe said. “Thank you, my lord.”

Andrew nodded and put away his stethoscope, closing his case with a snap. “Please also refrain from any excitement, my lord.” He looked Miss Hemshawe in the eye to emphasize the importance of his words. Her blue eyes widened in concern as he said, “It could prove fatal. I strongly advise a calm and measured existence, at least for the foreseeable future.” He picked up his medical bag. “Thank you for your patience. I shall return in a few days to see how you’re coming along with the tea, if that would be all right?”

“Yes, of course,” Lord Rivers said. His eyes were drifting closed even as he spoke.

“Yes, rest, my lord. That will do you the most good for now.” He stepped away from the bed. Turning to Miss Hemshawe, he said quietly, “But don’t forget to give him the tea, at least two or three times a day.”

“I will. Thank you.”

Andrew was pleased to see some of the tension leave her face. Hopefully both she and her father would be feeling better soon.

# Chapter Five

About an hour later, after the maid had returned from the apothecary with the willow bark, the cook made a large pot of tea from it. Diana returned to her father's room with a cup of the bitter liquid on a tray, along with a small pot of honey to make it more palatable. She found her father staring out the window.

"Oh, I'm so glad you're awake," she said cheerfully as she came into the room.

He turned and smiled at her. "Is that...my tea?"

"Yes. And I've brought some honey for you as well. How much sweetening do you think you'll want?"

"A lot!" he said, giving her a wink. He did have a sweet tooth!

She dolloped in a good amount, gave it a stir, and then helped him to sit up a little.

He grimaced as he swallowed the first sip and then handed the cup back to her.

"More honey?" she asked.

He nodded and then asked, "What did you think...of the doctor?"

Diana gave a laugh. "I was going to ask you the

very same question."

"I asked first," he said, taking the cup back.

"He seemed to be very competent," Diana said, not mentioning what was at the forefront of her mind, which was that he'd made her heart race and her breath hitch just at the sound of his deep, calm voice.

Her father nodded. "Good-looking fellow. Young."

"Do you think he's too young? I could perhaps find someone—"

"No, I think young is...good," Lord Rivers said. "Up on the latest techniques," he clarified.

"Oh, yes. And willing to try new things. That's good, I believe," Diana said, deliberately letting the comment about the doctor's looks slip past as if she hadn't noticed. Goodness knows, *she* had most definitely noticed. He'd looked like an angel standing over her father's bed, with his pale blond hair and slender but muscular frame. If his eyes had been blue rather than green, she'd have wondered if he hadn't stepped straight from some religious painting—but to mention that to her father would have been courting disaster. Or, perhaps, courting the doctor.

"Don't mind trying something different," her father said, handing her back his empty cup. "And anyone is better than a leech."

~June 6~

"Diana, what a lovely surprise!" Lydia said the following afternoon as she joined Diana in her drawing room.

"I'm sorry to just drop in like this," Diana said.

"Oh no, don't be." Lydia indicated that they both sit. A maid came in with a tea tray, setting it on a side table. "Thank you, Sally, I'll pour," Lydia said, giving the girl a smile.

After being handed a cup of tea, Diana said, "I do hope you weren't offended by the ladies yesterday."

Lydia's already large eyes went wide.

"I'm certain not one thing they said was helpful—at least it wouldn't have been to me if I were afraid of childbirth," Diana continued.

Lydia gave a little laugh. "No, I have to admit, it wasn't helpful at all. I'm certain they meant well... It's just..."

"Knowing they all survived the ordeal doesn't have any bearing on whether you will or won't. And besides, just telling you they've had children doesn't alleviate your fear," Diana said.

Lydia reached out and put her hand on Diana's arm. "Thank you," she said emphatically. "You understand. I can't tell you how much that means to me. I wish with all my heart I could just let go of this fear, but...but..." She gave a helpless giggle.

"Well, just hearing their stories isn't going to do it, I'm certain. I wish I knew what would," Diana said, placing her hand on top of her friend's.

"So do I." Lydia sighed. She straightened up after a moment though and asked, "But tell me how your father is doing."

"Oh..." A little ache started in Diana's stomach.

"Oh dear, was the doctor Lady Blakemore recommended not good? Or did he not come?"

Just thinking about Lord Colburne turned her ache into a ball of tingles. "No, he did. He came yesterday and he's wonderful!" Diana quickly tempered her response. "I mean, he seems very knowledgeable and intelligent. He told my father to drink some willow bark tea while he explores some other options for him, and he didn't once suggest cupping him."

Lydia looked at Diana sideways for a moment before a smile slowly grew both in her eyes and on her lips. "I see. And tell me more of this Lord Colburne. Is he young? Old? Hunched with smelly breath?" She giggled.

Diana could feel herself growing warm with Lydia's teasing. "He's not old—perhaps in his mid or late twenties. Certainly not hunched and I don't think his breath smelled." She didn't mention that he'd smelled clean, like lemon and soap.

"Well, that's good."

"Best of all, my father liked him and actually agreed to drink the tea."

"And you're looking forward to him coming back to visit again?"

"He said he would, and that he'd recommend further treatment," Diana said, sidestepping the question. "However, I have to apologize to you now. I don't think I will be able to make your engagement party tomorrow night. I just wouldn't feel comfortable leaving my father alone for so long," she explained.

Lydia softened her teasing smile into one of understanding. "Of course. I don't blame you. I would feel the same way."

"Thank you. I feel bad, though. I would have liked to meet your father and his parents. I'm assuming they'll be there?"

"His father has passed, but his mother will be here. I'll convey to them your regrets," Lydia said.

"Yes, please do. And to Lord Welles as well," Diana said, standing. She'd already spent too much time sitting and chatting and was beginning to get a little anxious to get home to check on her father again. Hopefully he was asleep, but if not, she would sit with him and maybe read through the racing pages of the Morning Chronicle.

~June 7~

Diana had just seen her father settled down for a nap after a light mid-day repast the following day when the footman arrived in the drawing room to inform her a gentleman was requesting a moment of her time.

"It's not Lord Colburne, is it?" she asked.

"No, Miss, it is a Lord Swindon."

She'd never heard the name before. "Bring him up and send my maid in as well."

Her new maid, Susan, arrived a moment later, giving her a brief curtsy before taking a seat in the corner of the room, out of the way.

"Lord Swindon," the footman announced a few minutes later.

A tall man with sloping shoulders and a rather large, hawkish nose followed. He paused to bow to her as she curtsied to him.

"Thank you for seeing me, Miss Hemshawe. I am an acquaintance of your father's," Lord Swindon said as he took the seat she offered.

"Oh, I'm afraid he's not—"

"Yes, yes, I'm certain he's not up to visitors," the man said.

"Then you are aware of his accident?" she asked.

"I was present when it happened. In fact, I was observing that race quite closely, you see. Your father and I had a little wager riding on it." He pulled a slip of paper from a hidden pocket inside of his coat and handed it to her.

Diana looked at it, recognizing her father's distinctive scrawl immediately—and then nearly choked. "*Five thousand pounds*? My father wagered five thousand pounds we would win that race?"

"You see why I have come," he said with a slight smile gracing his overly wide lips.

"To forgive him this debt, I hope. Considering that he was unable to finish the race—"

"Is of no consequence," he said with a negligent wave of his hand as if he couldn't be bothered with her father's health. "He made the bet and lost. I am here to collect."

"But you can't possibly expect me to pay this outrageous amount! It's not his fault he didn't finish," Diana argued. She was feeling oddly both hot and cold at the same time and beginning to feel distinctly nauseated as well.

"He fell from his horse," the man pointed out.

"He had..." Diana searched her mind for the term used by the physician. "A cardiac event."

Lord Swindon frowned. "I'm not certain what that means. It doesn't sound very healthy."

"There is something wrong with his heart," she explained.

"Oh, well, how very unfortunate, indeed."

"Extraordinarily so."

"You have a physician attending him, I daresay?" Lord Swindon asked.

Diana nodded. "An excellent man, Lord Dr. Colburne. He's just come from Paris where—"

"Yes, yes, all very fascinating, I'm sure. However, what I am most concerned with is my money." He narrowed his eyes at her in expectation.

"But, my lord, you can't possibly expect—"

"But I do. Your esteemed father made a wager. I *expect* him to honor it, no matter what his health."

Diana opened and closed her mouth. Five thousand pounds! Where in the world would she get such a sum? She didn't even think her father had that much money at hand. Whatever in the world inspired him to wager it?

Well, *that* she knew—because he was certain they would win. They were a sure thing—except for the unforeseen circumstance of his heart giving out on him. But now... Diana sighed. She couldn't possibly go to her father with this problem. It would probably send his slowly recovering health plummeting again. The willow bark tea had been working miraculously at relieving him of his pain and making it easier for him to breathe, but he was still far from well. She didn't dare tell him about this.

"There is an option if the cash is not at hand," Lord Swindon said slowly.

Diana turned to look at him.

"I could forgive the debt in return for your hand in marriage." He quirked up one side of his lips and looked piercingly at her, as if he were unclothing her with his eyes.

Diana jumped to her feet, horrified. She reined in her response quickly, however. "Thank you, my lord, that is"—she swallowed the bile that had risen to the back of her throat—"very generous of you, however, I should be able to get a hold of this money. My father's solicitor will assist me."

"Really? Are you certain of that?"

No, she wasn't. Not at all, but she had no other choice because she definitely was not going to sell herself to this man for her father's debt. She simply pulled the corners of her lips up into what she hoped looked like a smile. "Thank you so much for coming by today, Lord Swindon. I will be in touch as soon as I have the money for you."

The man raised his eyebrows and then stood. "Of course. Within, shall we say, a week?"

"I would appreciate it if you could give me two or three. I might need to send to Europe for the funds from my father's bank there."

"We'll say two—and that, I believe, is exceedingly generous of me." He bowed slightly. "Good day, Miss Hemshawe."

She curtsied and opened the door for him. Before she could say anything, however, there seemed to be a bit of a commotion downstairs. There was the sound of thumping, as if something heavy was being set down on the floor in the foyer. Voices unfamiliar to Diana followed.

"Let me see you to the door," she said, curious as to what was going on.

There were two footmen Diana had never seen before standing at the bottom of the stair, each holding a small trunk and waiting for her to descend. Beyond them was a woman Diana hadn't seen in nine years... but who she remembered as if it were yesterday when they'd last met.

Fully conscious of the man following her, Diana hurried down, then indicated the front door to Lord Swindon without pausing to introduce him. It was horribly rude, she knew, but in a split-second decision she wanted him out and the other woman none the wiser as to who he was or why he'd been there.

He bowed to all briefly and then sailed out the door without another word, much to Diana's relief.

She then turned back toward the woman watching her. "Mother, what are you doing here?"

# Chapter Six

"Whatever do you mean? Why wouldn't I be here? I heard my husband had a horrific accident. Of course I'm here." Lady Rivers frowned at Diana.

"You heard?" Diana knew she sounded stupid. It must be the shock. She hadn't seen her mother since the day she and her father had left for the continent. Her father had begged Diana's mother to come with them, to just pack up their five-year-old son, her things, and come along for the excitement, for the challenge, for the fun.

Lady Rivers had scoffed and said no. She had responsibilities. If Lord Rivers wasn't going to see to *his*, the least she could do was stay and see to them. Diana's father had shrugged, saying there were solicitors for that, and he was leaving—with Diana. Lady Rivers and Diana's younger brother, Henry, had stayed.

But now her mother was here.

Lady Rivers didn't deign to answer Diana's question and instead asked, "How is he?"

Diana nodded. "Doing better. Please, come up." She paused, one foot on the first stair, to order tea before leading her mother up to the drawing room.

"Oh no," her mother interrupted, "no tea for me. I want to go straight to his lordship."

"Are you certain you don't want to refresh yourself first?" Diana asked.

"No, no. I'll do so after I see him," she said, seeming very impatient.

Diana had no choice but lead her mother directly to her father's room. As she expected, he was sleeping but awoke as soon as her mother rushed in crying, "Oh, Rivers!"

"Sophie?" Lord Rivers breathed. "Am I dreaming?"

Lady Rivers gave a little laugh. "No. It's really me. I'm here now. I'll take care of everything. You're going to be just fine."

*As if he weren't just fine under Diana's care?* Anger shot through her like a horse from a burning barn.

"Tell me," her mother said, taking her father's hand and cradling it to her breast. "Tell me what happened."

Lord Rivers struggled to sit up. Diana rushed over to help him, noticing that her mother didn't move an inch to do so.

"The doctor called it..." He turned to look to Diana for Lord Colburne's exact wording.

"A cardiac event," Diana supplied.

"Yes, yes, a cardiac event," her father repeated. "It was a sharp pain in my chest," he said. His breathing had become so much better now that he'd started taking the willow bark tea, Diana noticed. "I lost control of the horse—I was riding in a race."

"He has a broken leg and some broken ribs, but it is this heart condition which is truly worrying us," Diana added.

Her mother didn't even acknowledge she'd spoken. "Have you been bled? What did the doctor say we should do?"

"No, no. No bleeding," her father protested.

"But Rivers…"

"He's a young man, this physician, with new ideas." Lord Rivers paused and then added with a little smile, "he has this new-fangled device to listen to my chest."

Lady Rivers frowned. "I don't care about devices. How is he going to make you better if he doesn't bleed you?"

"With medicine," Diana said.

"Medicine?" Her mother finally looked up at her, frowning. "What sort of medicine?"

"Well, at the moment it's simply willow bark tea, but he said he was going to look into some other treatments as well," Diana said.

"No." Her mother didn't even pause to consider what she'd said. She didn't even think about for a moment. It was simply a "no."

"What do you mean? You don't even know what he's thinking of. You know nothing—" Diana started.

"Sophia, you must be exhausted. Did you just arrive?" her father interrupted.

"Yes, just now."

"Then go and rest for a bit. We'll discuss this when you've recovered from your journey," Diana's father said, playing peacemaker.

"I'll show you to your room," Diana offered.

Her mother let go of Lord Rivers' hand. "I know the way to my room," her mother informed her in a matter-of-fact tone. She turned back to her husband and brushed back the lock of hair that had fallen onto his forehead. "I'll return in an hour or so. You rest."

He nodded and slid a little lower on his pillows.

Diana started to follow her mother out of the room, when her father called her back.

He waited until the door clicked closed behind Lady Rivers before frowning up at her. "Why did you write to her? Tell her that I was hurt?"

Diana widened her eyes. "I didn't! I have no idea how she found out."

He pulled his eyebrows lower over his eyes. "Must have learned of it from one of her friends, then."

"You know I would *never* have informed her," Diana said.

He sighed. "Yes, actually, I *do* know that—which is why I was so surprised." He paused and then added, "You need to be patient with her, you know."

"In what way?"

"She hasn't seen you since you were eleven years old. She may still think of you as a child."

"Oh. Yes, I could tell." Diana couldn't help but frown.

Her father reached up and patted her cheek. "As I say, be patient."

~*~

After Diana had seen to her usual household tasks, making adjustments as necessary for her mother's presence, she returned to her father's room with a tea tray. Her mother was sitting with him.

"I've brought you your tea, Papa," Diana said, coming in. "And some for you as well, Mother."

"Thank you, Diana," her mother said. "I've already ordered tea." She indicated the tray on a small table that had been pulled up next to the bed.

"Oh, well, the tea for my father is his willow bark tea. His medicine," Diana explained.

She put her father's cup down on his bedside table and then moved a second chair next to the one her mother occupied.

"Diana, your mother has been asking about your marriage prospects," Lord Rivers said, accepting the cup of tea. "I've completely lost track of the day, but aren't you expected at a party on Friday?"

"Are you perhaps thinking of Miss Sheffield's engagement party?" Diana asked.

"Yes, yes, that's it."

"It is this evening actually, but today is Saturday, Papa, and I've already told Miss Sheffield I won't be attending," Diana explained.

"But you don't need to miss it, especially now your mother is here. I'm in capable hands," he said, nodding to his wife.

Her mother's eyes narrowed for a moment as she turned back toward Diana. "Tell me what you've done so far to find a husband. You are, what, eighteen now?"

"Nineteen," Diana said. "I'm attending some social events. Whenever my aunt or Audley can chaperone me. At times I've gone with Papa or with a friend."

"Don't you have a companion?" She looked from Diana to her father and back again.

"No," Diana answered.

"She's never needed one," her father said at the same time.

"What do you mean she hasn't needed one! Of course she does. She's a young woman alone! Are you going to tell me that she never went out when you were on the continent?" her mother asked, clearly shocked.

"Of course she did—with me," Lord Rivers answered.

"And I had a maid to accompany me when I went out without my father," Diana added.

Her mother frowned at them both. "Well, such behavior is not at all appropriate in London. She needs a companion who can accompany her to social events. I'm sorry I didn't bring clothes appropriate to attend social functions, but I came as quickly as I could and simply brought day dresses, certain that all I would be doing is staying here, looking after your father."

"That's quite all right," Diana said.

"We will hire a chaperone for you immediately. While you may feel you are well able to take care of yourself, you are not," her mother said disapprovingly. "You will wait until we have someone in hand before attending any more social events."

"I am frequently chaperoned by friends—" Diana started.

"Your friends are not old enough to chaperone you," her mother said, cutting her off.

Diana opened her mouth to contradict her mother but paused, knowing it would be rude. Luckily, her father jumped in.

"Actually, she is part of a very nice group of ladies of all ages called the Ladies' Wagering Whist Society, isn't that right, Diana?"

"Yes. The group includes Lady Blakemore, Lady Norman, and the Duchess of Kendell, along with a number of other ladies all older than me. They have all, at one time or another, chaperoned me at parties," Diana said.

"Lady Blakemore and the Duchess of Kendell?" her mother asked, her eyes going wide.

"Yes." Diana did her best not to gloat.

"Well, that is very good. You certainly couldn't do better than that, but we should still try to find a companion for you. It's not right to depend on such people. I'm sure they have much better things to do than chaperone a young girl."

"And I'm certain Diana will have no problems finding beaux if she were to *truly* try. Why, she was one of the most popular young ladies wherever we went," Lord Rivers said.

"Probably the only young lady," her mother said under her breath.

"There were always quite a few other women," Diana said.

"If you would actually try to be serious about this, Diana, and not so picky..." her father started.

"Papa, I'm going to be with the man I marry for the rest of my life. I think being picky is a good thing," Diana said.

"You're lucky your father is allowing you to choose your own husband. If it were up to me—"

"Mother—"

"Just try, Diana," her father said, interrupting her. "I'm probably not going to be around for much longer, and I want to know you'll be well cared for."

"You are not dying!" Diana protested.

"I am. I nearly did," he pointed out.

"You could have so easily," Lady Rivers said, taking hold of his hand and pulling it to her chest. "You've got to stop this racing, Rivers. You're too old for it now. Please—"

"Sophia, we'll discuss that later. Right now I just want Diana to be aware..." He removed his hand from his wife's grasp and turned back toward her. "Sweetheart, you no longer have all the time you might wish for. Please be more serious about this."

Diana bit down on the inside of her cheek. She didn't want to think about the possibility of her father dying. She'd relied on him, lived with him, traveled with him... he'd been her world for the past nine years. She nodded, however, knowing he was right.

"Lady Sorrell is hosting a soirée that I've promised to attend," Diana said quietly.

"Excellent. Be your charming self and I'm sure you'll have any number of gentlemen enthralled," her father said with an encouraging smile.

~June 9~

Sunday was the most difficult day for Diana. She alternated between wanting to tell her father about Lord Swindon's visit, but knowing the news of it might actually kill him, or thinking maybe she should tell her mother. This thought was quickly set aside, however.

Diana and her mother had never been close, but after not seeing each other for so long, their relationship was even more strained and awkward. Diana knew she needed to be patient as her mother came to terms with having an adult daughter, but it was taking much longer than Diana thought it should. Her mother was curt and condescending, treating Diana like a child more often than not, and when she did treat her like an adult, it was with the rude implication that Diana was more independent and knowledgeable than a girl her age should be.

It was her mother's own fault if she were, Diana thought. If her mother had come along to the continent, Diana wouldn't have had to learn to be independent. She wouldn't have had to take care of her father and his household from the age of thirteen, when they'd moved to Germany, and his housekeeper absolutely refused to leave her home country of France.

But none of that was material now. Diana was independent and knowledgeable, and being so, she would take care of this debt of her father's. With this determination firmly in her mind, she set out first thing on Monday morning for the office of her father's solicitor, Mr. Bennett.

Her presence caused a little stir, but the clerk was polite, and while he did ask her to wait for no less than twenty minutes, she was eventually shown into Mr. Bennett's office.

"Good morning, Miss Hemshawe," the tall, gangly man said, wringing his extraordinarily long fingers. "What a...a...surprise."

"Yes, I'm certain it is."

"Er...your father...?" He bent sideways to look behind her as if Lord Rivers would suddenly appear.

"Is not doing well, I'm afraid," she answered.

The man's eyes snapped back to her. "Oh! Er...yes. I think, I think I heard something about a...a tumble?"

"He had what the physician is calling a cardiac event," Diana explained.

The man's already large brown eyes seemed to bulge from his head. "What does that mean? Is he going to be all right?"

"I'm certain he is," she said with a great deal more certainty than she felt. "He is under excellent care."

"Oh, well, I am relieved to hear that." Suddenly

remembering his manners, he indicated the chair next to Diana. "Please, please, sit down."

She gave him a little smile as she did so. He sat in his own chair on his side of the desk but nearly missed it as he wasn't watching where he was lowering himself, and his chair had moved when he'd stood up.

"Er, oh, er, so how I can help you today?" he asked, once he'd gotten himself settled.

"I have been made aware of a wager my father made before riding in the race."

"Er, which he didn't finish?" the solicitor finished for her.

Diana pressed her lips together for a second before nodding. She took a deep breath. "A gentleman by the name of Lord Swindon came to me on Saturday and showed me a piece of paper on which my father had written out their wager—five thousand pounds to go to my father if he won, and he would pay the same amount to Lord Swindon should he lose."

"Five thousand!" The man jumped from his chair, sending it skittering backward where it slammed against the wall.

"Yes. My father didn't finish the race, but Lord Swindon counts that as a loss. He is demanding payment," Diana said, doing her best to contain her anger and frustration at Lord Swindon's callousness.

"Oh, er, yes. Yes, I imagine he would." Mr. Bennett retrieved his chair and sat back down.

"So, if you could just..."

"I'm so sorry, Miss Hemshawe, but your father..." He paused and pulled a ledger from the far corner of his desk. He opened it and flipped through a number of pages before settling on the one he was looking for. His fingers ran down a column of numbers even as he shook his head, frowning. "No, no." He looked up again. "Your father simply doesn't have that sort of money at hand."

"Might we be able to put it together from what he has here and from his bank in France?"

He looked down at the numbers on the page again, running his finger down another column of numbers. "No, he doesn't have it there either. Not even if we combined the two accounts... It's simply too large a sum." He gave her a small smile. "Five thousand pounds is an enormous amount of money. More than half of your father's entire fortune. He simply doesn't have it available to draw from. I'm so sorry."

Diana was beginning to feel nauseated. She swallowed hard. "But if, if he doesn't have it... What am I to do?"

The man shrugged his skinny shoulders. "Sell some jewelry?"

"But I don't have any jewelry," Diana said, fingering her only pair of good earrings, pearls her father had given her for her eighteenth birthday after he'd won a particularly grueling—and lucrative—race.

"Then, I'm afraid I don't know what to tell you. You will need to discuss this with your father."

"The doctor specifically told me he is not to be agitated."

Mr. Bennett closed the ledger. "I... I'm terribly sorry. There's nothing I can do."

Diana stood, trying to think about what could be done. She absolutely would not agree to marry Lord Swindon, that was certain. She had to find *some* way she could get money. If her mother hadn't brought any evening clothes, she certainly hadn't brought any jewelry—not that Diana even knew if she had any worth selling.

"Thank you, Mr. Bennett," she said.

"I... I'm so sorry..." he whispered as she left his office.

# Chapter Seven

Diana knew exactly what she needed to do as she walked out of Mr. Bennett's office.

Oh, no, not about this debt. She had absolutely *no* idea what she could do about that, but she knew what *she* had to do—what she always did when she needed to think. She needed to go for a ride.

It took her no more than fifteen minutes to change into her riding outfit, a split skirt with a matching military-style coat. She pulled on her gloves and left her hat at home. It would simply fly off as she was racing down the road, so there was no point in even attempting to keep it on. She was not going out for a gentle trot around the park. Oh no, not today.

She saddled her mare herself, much to the surprise of the English grooms at the stables where she and her father were stabling their horses.

"Are we going for a proper ride, Miss?" her own groom, Pierre, asked in his native French.

"Oui, Pierre, a proper ride," she responded in the same language. Poor man must be missing his home terribly, she thought. She turned back to him, as she tightened up the saddle. "How is your English coming along?" she asked in English.

He gave a very Gallic shrug. She took that to mean he hadn't been practicing much, but limiting his conversation to his friend and countryman, François, her father's groom and their coachman. She shook her head. "You need to practice."

"I am 'oping we return to France soon," he said slowly in English. "As we did when we go *en Allemagne.*"

She could only laugh at his wishful thinking. "I don't know, Pierre, if you remember, we were in Germany for nearly two years."

"But we go back to France, oui?" he asked hopefully.

"I do not know." She supposed it was a possibility. A coward's way out of her current predicament, certainly, she thought as she mounted her horse, but not really feasible considering her father's current state of health. She sighed as she led the way down the streets of Mayfair and toward the open road where she could allow her horse—and herself—free rein.

Half an hour later they were galloping down the road, headed nowhere in particular. Diana supposed she could—and very likely *should*—go to a pawn shop to see what she could get for her earrings. Honestly, she had no idea how much they were worth. Most likely not nearly enough, but it would be something. That, along with the pin money she'd saved, would at least buy her more time to figure out how she could get the rest of the money.

She was just wondering if her father had a safe in his study when three young bucks caught up and then passed her. They seemed to be having some sort of race. They were concentrating fiercely, pushing their horses to their limit, but they were nothing compared to Diana and her mare, Nike. Should she do anything or behave like an adult and not engage with them?

Her groom caught up with her. "Are you going to just let them pass you like that?" he challenged her.

Now she had no choice. Diana gave a little laugh and a shake of her head. With a whisper in Nike's ear, they took off chasing after the boys. As she gained on them, leaning forward over her horse's neck, she caught them glancing over at her, one by one.

They tried to spur their horses faster as she outpaced them, but truly it was a lost cause. As she passed the leader, she gave him a mock salute and continued on down the road. She'd also lost her groom.

At an intersection a little farther down the road, she slowed and turned around to meet back up with her groom. The young men caught up with her at about the same time as Pierre.

"Who are you?" one fellow asked.

"H-h-how did you p-p-pass us?" a second stammered.

Diana could only laugh. "Come to Epson Downs the next time there's an open race and you'll find out. Good day, gentlemen." She gave them a nod and headed back toward town.

She hoped she would have the opportunity to race at the Downs again, she thought with a constricting heart as she headed back into London. There were too many unknowns in her life just now. Too many things pending her father's recovery.

For a moment, she longed for the life she'd lost when she and her father had moved back to England, but it was pointless, she knew. There was no changing the past, only moving forward.

And forward just at the moment was toward a pawn shop.

The bell tinkled as she strode into the shop. This was not going to be a pleasant experience, and Diana wanted it over with as quickly as possible.

A greasy-looking, rotund man came from a back room and smiled at her, displaying browned teeth. "'Ow may I help ye, Miss?"

She removed her earrings and placed them into his pudgy hand. "How much will you give me for these?"

He pulled out a magnifying glass and inspected them closely for a minute. "In trouble are we?" he asked as he did so.

"That is none of your business," she said as gently as her growing anger and discomfort would allow.

He gave a little chuckle. "'Aven't seen too many young ladies, but plenty o' gen'lemen," he informed her.

"How much?"

"Give ya ten quid for 'em."

"What? That's robbery! They're worth at least fifty."

"That may be wat yer lover paid for 'em, but I'll give ye ten... Well, awright, fifteen 'cause yer so pretty. Give me a smile and I'll make it fifteen."

Diana narrowed her eyes at the man but managed to pull the edges of her lips up into something like a smile.

"Good enough," he shrugged. He went to his till and extracted the money from it. "Pleasure doin' business wit' ye," he said, giving her a little bow.

Diana simply took the money and left. She couldn't even bring herself to give the man a nod; her stomach was in such knots.

As she brushed down Nike at the stables, Diana finally allowed her mind to rest. There was nothing like a ride and then the mundane task of caring for her horse to clear her mind. She hadn't come to any revelations while riding, as she'd hoped, but she certainly felt better, more like herself, for having ridden.

Her father's illness had stifled her, and she was certain her mother would do so even further. She would take what opportunities she could and with that everything else would fall into place—it had to.

~*~

Diana wasn't sure she'd ever looked forward to attending a party as much as she was Lady Sorrell's soirée. It wasn't just seeing her friends, which was a wonderful thing to do, it was also a respite from tending to her father. It was an evening free of her mother, who seemed to be everywhere Diana wanted to be. It was a chance to think of something other than her father's debt, which hung over her head like a guillotine.

She wore her favorite new dress—one that had been designed just for her by Tina, Lady Norman's daughter, during the short time she'd worked professionally as a modiste. It was a beautiful soft cream color, which brought out the pink in Diana's cheeks while also accentuating her rich hair color.

She stopped in to say goodnight to her father before leaving. "Goodnight, Papa. Goodnight, Mother," she said, coming into her father's room.

"Let's see you," her father said, smiling from his bed.

She came forward and gave him a little twirl.

"I suppose that's from Paris and cost your father an absolute fortune," her mother said, looking at her critically.

Diana turned toward her mother, trying her best to keep her voice light and polite. "No, actually, it was made here in London by a friend who is absolutely brilliant at designing dresses and picking out just the right color to go with one's complexion."

"Harrumph," her mother said, sitting back in her chair and crossing her arms over her chest.

"I think you look stunning. You are going to have all the young gentlemen following you about like puppies," her father said, his eyes twinkling. His tea was still making him feel much better, but Diana had yet to see him even attempt to move from his bed, which meant he was still feeling too weak.

"Thank you, but I do hope you're wrong. That would be horribly embarrassing," Diana laughed. "However, I'm prepared to go with an open mind and will see if there isn't a gentleman or two who catches my eye."

"Good for you," Lord Rivers nodded approvingly.

"Just don't play the trollop," her mother warned.

"Sophie!" Even her father objected to that one.

"Well, we don't want gentlemen getting the wrong idea," Lady Rivers objected.

"I don't think anyone will think anything other than that I'm on the market for a proper husband," Diana said, frowning at her mother.

"That's neither here nor there. I've seen girls flirting, waving their fans about. Girls from good families who should know better, and you can be sure most of them were compromised in some way or another by the season's end," her mother warned.

"Well, I promise not to wave my fan about, in

that case." She curtsied and said her good-nights before her mother could say anything else offensive.

"Wait!" her mother called after her. "Who is chaperoning you?"

"Mrs. Aldridge, a friend of mine from the Ladies' Wagering Whist Society. Her carriage should be here any minute," Diana answered and then closed the door behind her before she could be detained any further.

She would much rather wait downstairs alone than have to deal with her mother for another minute. Luckily, she didn't have long to wait. Mrs. Aldridge was remarkably punctual.

~*~

The dinner before the soirée was lovely, and made Diana so grateful she'd been invited to that very first fashion party hosted by Lady Norman so soon after they'd arrived in London. From there had formed the Ladies' Wagering Whist Society, and suddenly Diana had had seven wonderful friends who all looked out for each other. Well, other than Mrs. Aldridge's relationship with the Duchess of Kendell. For some reason, those two just could not get along.

But now as she stood next to Mrs. Aldridge, watching the guests flow into Lady Sorrell's home, she felt so happy and comfortable. It was like being surrounded by family. If only her own mother were so warm and supportive.

"Miss Hemshawe," Lord Rosebury said, approaching her. He paused to bow to her and her companion. "Mrs. Aldridge, a pleasure as always," he said before turning a concerned expression on Diana. "Miss Hemshawe, how is your father? His tragic fall was all anyone could speak of for days at White's *and* Boodles!"

"Oh, dear. I hope the gentlemen didn't think less

of him for it. It was what the physician is calling a cardiac event," she explained.

"My word! No! I hadn't heard that," the man said, looking appropriately shocked.

"Yes, but thankfully he is under excellent care and already doing much better. Well, except for a broken leg and some cracked ribs," she said.

"You must be beside yourself with worry, and yet, here you are!" he said, indicating the room.

"My mother arrived a few days ago. She's looking after him while I enjoy an evening away," Diana explained.

"Oh, what good fortune!" He paused and smiled at her. "For us, that is."

Diana could only laugh at his flirting. "You are too kind, sir."

"Not at all. I shall spread the excellent news that Lord Rivers is on the mend." He bowed and sauntered away.

"Oh, goodness," Diana breathed.

Mrs. Aldridge gave a laugh. "He is quite the cad."

"Always looking for gossip, I'm afraid," Diana agreed.

"I know you can do better. Er, you are still looking, are you not?" Mrs. Aldridge asked.

"With more urgency than before, I'm afraid," Diana said. "My father is now frightened he's going to die before I become engaged. He told me I needed to find a husband as quickly as possible. It's quite ridiculous, of course; he survived the 'event', so surely he will survive at least for the foreseeable future." Unless he receives some sort of horrible shock, like being told he has to pay Lord Swindon five thousand pounds, she grimly thought to herself.

"Oh, dear. How difficult," Mrs. Aldridge tsked. "Well, lets see if we can't find you some pleasant gentlemen to flirt with." She craned her neck to look around the rapidly filling room.

"That would be fine except for one small problem, ma'am," Diana said. When her chaperone for the evening turned back to her, she said, "I don't know how to flirt."

Mrs. Aldridge burst out laughing. "Of course you do! You were just doing it with Lord Rosebury, were you not?"

"Was I? I was just speaking to him."

"That's all that it is."

"But I can't imagine that's enticing in any way, is it?"

"You don't need to be enticing, Miss Hemshawe, you need to be yourself. If the gentleman is intelligent, he will be attracted to you immediately," the lady said, giving Diana's cheek a little pat.

While it was a very sweet thing to say, Diana wasn't entirely certain it was accurate. Suddenly she felt like a filly at her very first race, skittish and anxious. What if she were herself and the gentleman wasn't "intelligent" as Mrs. Aldridge had said? In other words, what if he didn't find her interesting or attractive?

She looked around the now crowded rooms, wondering who she might speak to and put her mind at ease. Surely, if she spoke with a gentleman with whom she was already acquainted, she would feel more confident. That made her pause. Usually it was her father who made her feel confident and at ease, but he wasn't here with her. She missed him more than she thought she would.

"Miss Hemshawe, I am so glad to see you here this evening," a gentleman said. It was, in fact, exactly the sort of calm, reassuring voice she'd been wanting to hear.

She turned to see who it belonged to and found her father's physician approaching. "Oh, Lord Dr. Colburne, what a surprise!"

He winced. "I think for this evening just Lord Colburne should be more than enough. I'm not the doctor just now in this social setting." He gave her a warm smile that went perfectly with his lovely voice.

She laughed. "Of course. May I present my friend, Mrs. Aldridge?" she said, indicating her companion. "This is the physician who is attending my father, Lord Colburne," she explained.

"How very nice to meet you," Mrs. Aldridge said. "My, my, Miss Hemshawe didn't mention you were young and handsome."

Diana immediately felt herself flushing, although she couldn't imagine why. She had not, in fact, told any of the ladies that Lord Colburne was incredibly attractive. She wondered if she should try to flirt with him. Or perhaps she absolutely should not. He was, after all, in her father's employ as his doctor. Was it unethical to flirt with your father's physician? Diana had no idea.

*Just be yourself*, she reminded herself. *Just be yourself and then you won't be flirting.*

"How is your father doing? Much better, I expect, otherwise you wouldn't be here this evening," Lord Colburne asked.

"He is. The willow bark tea has done wonders for him. He's breathing easier and in a great deal less discomfort," Diana said, giving the doctor a warm smile. "Also, my mother is there watching over him."

Lord Colburne gave a nod. "Oh, she's come from the country?"

Diana was so surprised he remembered. "Yes, she arrived a few days ago."

"Well, I suppose since you're in England it's easier for her to be with him," he said.

"Much. And luckily the shock of seeing her didn't seem to disturb his heart."

"That's excellent," he said with a warm smile. "We never know what sort of shock it will take to bring on another episode—or perhaps none at all. The heart is a fickle organ."

"In more ways than one, I imagine," Diana said, giggling.

Lord Colburne burst out laughing. "Indeed, Miss Hemshawe, indeed."

# Chapter Eight

She was charming and beautiful. Her intelligence was unmatched by any other young English lady he'd ever met—not that he'd met very many. Living and working in Paris, he really hadn't had much time to socialize with anyone, let alone the very few English people who were there. But now he wondered if he'd missed something. Were all young ladies this clever?

He would have to do a study to find out, but right now he was more than happy to stand here and speak with this particular subject.

"So, what took you to Paris?" he asked.

Her smile grew as she was clearly reminded of happier times. "My father and I were in the racing circuit. We both own horses which are ridden by professional riders, and we ride in races ourselves."

"Ah, yes, that's right. You said your father was riding in a race when he had the pain in his chest," Andrew recalled.

"Yes. We were in a relay race at Epsom Downs— and would have won easily if my father hadn't suddenly taken ill." The thought seemed to worry her a great deal, he thought, watching her eyes lose their happy sparkle. He couldn't have that.

"Well, I'm sure he'll be better soon enough. Although, I don't know if the excitement of racing would be such a good idea after this," he said and then immediately kicked himself. He wanted to make her smile, not worry her further. Damn his overly honest tongue.

Miss Hemshawe sighed and nodded. "You only stayed in Paris?" she asked, changing the subject back to where it had begun, much to Andrew's relief. It was odd he cared so much whether Miss Hemshawe was happy or not. He'd never felt this way about a patient or a member of their family. But then, he had a feeling Miss Hemshawe and her father weren't going to be like any other he'd tended to before.

"Yes," he said, forcing his mind back to the conversation. "I was there to study with a particular doctor—"

"The one who invented that tube you used," she said.

He smiled, "The stethoscope. Exactly."

"Did you get a chance to travel elsewhere on the continent?"

"No, sadly. I didn't really have much time to do anything but work and study. When were you there, in Paris?"

She thought about it for a moment. "We moved to London in February, as soon as the crossing could be done without worry of winter storms. Before that we'd been in Lyon for about six months, Alsace-Lorraine for a time, Stuttgart, Frankfurt, and Dusseldorf for two years before that."

"My goodness! Do you speak German as well?"

"*Ja ein paar. Aber nicht sehr gut,*" she answered with a broad smile.

He could only laugh, amazed. "I have no idea what you just said."

"Yes, but it's not very good," Mrs. Aldridge translated for him.

He'd completely forgotten the woman was there! "Er, thank you," he said, giving her a smile and a nod.

"Do you speak German, Mrs. Aldridge?" Miss Hemshawe asked.

"Me? No! My parents did, though, and I remember some," the lady said. She turned to Miss Hemshawe. "But what were you doing traveling around Germany?"

"The same thing, racing horses. There are some wonderful race courses throughout the country."

"But you yourself didn't ride, did you?" Andrew asked. She said she and her father were riding in a relay, earlier, but she couldn't have actually meant *she* had been riding, could she?

"Of course! There are a number of women who race—enough, in fact, so that there are some ladies-only races. That doesn't stop me from riding against men, though, like I did last week in the relay."

"Oh my, that must be so exciting," Mrs. Aldridge said. "I've known that you race and have been meaning to come see you do so. Perhaps even place a bet or two," the lady giggled.

"Oh, yes, you should! It would be wonderful to have friends there. We could make a party of it," Miss Hemshawe said enthusiastically. "The next time there's a race at Epsom Downs, we could travel down together and make a day of it. Would you come, Lord Colburne?" she added shyly, smiling up at him.

If only for that smile, he would—except horses

terrified him. He stayed as far away from the animals as he possibly could. He wondered if she could hear the sudden pounding of his heart. It was certainly loud enough in his own ears. "No," he said apologetically. "I'm sure my work wouldn't allow for such amusements. I'm so sorry."

"Oh." She looked completely crestfallen, and Andrew felt like a cad. "Well, perhaps we can arrange something a little closer to London that wouldn't take an entire day, so you could attend."

He gave her a smile and tried his best to think of some excuse not to go. He'd rather not admit to his fear. "We'll see," he said noncommittally. "Now, I'm afraid you will have to excuse me." He bowed to the ladies and went off to speak to others. The mention of work had reminded him of why he was actually there at the party.

His mother had urged him to meet young ladies. His father had told him it was his duty, now that he was his heir, to marry. But Andrew had come in order to meet people and spread word of his services. He was a doctor in need of patients, and there was no better place to find them than at a society function.

He looked about and found exactly who he was looking for—a huddle of older ladies. There were a few younger ones—probably their daughters or granddaughters—standing with them, but it was the older ladies who he focused on. They and their elderly husbands were exactly the sort he needed to fill out his roster of patients.

~*~

Diana watched Lord Colburne head straight for a group of young ladies and their chaperones. Had she frightened him away by being too forward? Had it seemed as if she'd been bragging when telling him of her travels? He had asked, after all.

Mrs. Aldridge gave her arm a consoling pat. "What a very nice young man," she said. "And I'm sure there are many more. Perhaps even some who would be interested in going to the races," she added as an afterthought.

Diana could only sigh and follow the lady as she started through the crowded room.

~*~

Albert, Lord Rivers, waited until his dinner tray had been situated across his lap and Sophie's tray placed on a table next to his bed. The maid and the footmen left the room in silence.

Just as his wife had picked up her fork, he asked, "Is it money?"

Her hand paused just as she was in the act of spearing some vegetables on her plate. "Is what money?"

"Why you're here," he said.

She pierced some food onto her fork and then lifted it to her mouth. "Do you need some?" she asked just before taking her bite.

"No! I was wondering if you did," he said, reluctantly picking up his own fork. He hadn't had much of an appetite ever since his accident. It was probably the inactivity.

"If you remember, *I'm* the one looking after the estate," she said.

"I do. I haven't taken a look at the reports recently, though. Is everything going all right?"

"Yes, fine. We've earned about fifteen percent more than we did last year. It's the new livestock. I paid a visit to Lord—"

"Sophia, please," he interrupted her.

"Oh, right. Sorry. I forgot how much you hate talk of cattle and farming. It's what supports you and your family, but ask you to take the smallest interest in any of it... Well..."

"But that's what makes us such an excellent couple. You are interested in farming and do an excellent job taking care of all of that." He waved his meat-laden fork around in the air.

She paused and stared at him. "Do you actually believe I enjoy it?"

"Don't you?"

"No! I find it exceedingly boring. Gratifying, yes, but not interesting in the least. I do it because you don't and someone's got to."

"We have Mr. Smithson. Isn't it his job to take care of it?" he asked.

"Yes, of course it is, and he does excellent work, but someone must oversee him. If I didn't do it, he probably would have robbed you blind years ago," she pointed out.

"Really? Skimming off the top, is he?"

"Not with me watching!" Her eyes flashed dangerously.

Albert chuckled. His wife may be the most boring woman in England, but she was vicious when anything she considered hers was threatened. Sadly, that didn't extend to their daughter. Somehow Sophia and Diana had never gotten along, not since the child was able to say her first word—no!

"Well, then, if it's not money, what is it that brought you to London?" he asked again.

Strangely, Sophie looked a little hurt. She tilted her head just a touch as she looked at him, reminding him fiercely of her expression when he'd told her he was leaving for the continent for the first time. They'd been married all of two years, and Albert had been going stir crazy. He'd never been able to stay in one place for very long. Two years might as well have been an eternity.

"I came because you were hurt, Albert. I'm your wife. If you need me, I will be here," Sophie said quietly.

"What if I had needed you while on the continent?" he asked, putting his fork down and forgetting to even make a pretense of eating.

Her gaze dropped to her own plate as it sat on her lap. "You know I hate travel."

"Yes." It was amazing he hadn't discovered that until after they'd been married, but then, theirs had been a whirlwind of a relationship.

The moment her parents had caught wind of the fact he was remotely interested in their sweet little bluestocking of a daughter, they'd pushed and pushed until he finally gave in and proposed. His mother hadn't helped at all. In fact, she'd been quite in league with Lord and Lady Markham. Under so much pressure and, yes, he had to admit, a certain fascination with this woman who was his absolute antithesis, he'd agreed to marry sweet Sophie Markham after knowing her for only two weeks.

Within a year, it had all fallen apart. Two years after marrying her, he left to ride and race on the continent, leaving his young wife and baby daughter to deal with his estate and each other. It wasn't the kindest thing he'd ever done, but it had made being married so much more tolerable—for both of them.

"So..." he tried again to establish some sort of conversation. "How are things at Riverton? Aside from the excitement of the new livestock."

"Well. Everyone is flourishing. Last year five babies were born to the cottagers, only two out of wedlock. Mr. Smithson was the father of one of them," she added dryly.

Albert nodded and picked up his fork again. If Diana were here, she'd be scolding him for not eating.

"Missy Brown and Frances Wheaton were married a few months ago," she continued before putting another bite into her mouth.

Albert had no idea who these people were, but he nodded again as if the news was interesting. There was a prolonged silence, so he looked up from where he'd been shoving food around his plate. Sophie was staring at him. "What?"

"You aren't going to ask about your son?"

"Well, you've already told me he was doing well at Eton. Is there more?"

Her lips pinched together. "You don't care to know who his friends are? What he's studying? His interests?"

"Rather like you, isn't he? Interested in mathematics and the like?" he asked. He'd gotten reports from the school, the dean gushing on and on about what a brilliant student his son was, how he was certainly destined for great things considering his abilities with numbers. Albert hadn't seen the child since he was five. He didn't understand how he was supposed to be interested in a child he didn't know, despite the fact that he'd fathered the boy.

Sophia sighed. "Yes. He is very good in school. He has excellent grades and is even beginning to take an interest in the running of the estate despite his young age. All things in which you have absolutely no interest."

There really wasn't much Albert could say; they both knew the truth. "Does he ride, at least?"

"He does, but not like you and not like Diana did," she said. "Horses are transportation, nothing more."

"Well, then, I'm glad he's doing well in school."

# CHAPTER NINE

## ~June 11~

Diana found herself truly looking forward to the weekly meeting of the Ladies' Wagering Whist Society. Living in the same house with her mother was stressful. Diana was trying to run the household as she normally did, but kept finding her mother had given the staff her own contrary instructions. Diana just didn't want to deal with it.

Escaping for a few hours into Lady Norman's game room to lose herself in silly gossip and a good game of cards was just what the doctor ordered—or would have, had Lord Colburne known of her predicament, Diana thought with a little laugh.

Thinking of the doctor had Diana fretting over their last interaction at Lady Sorrell's soirée. She didn't know if she'd said something wrong, or if he was simply being polite and paying attention to the other young ladies present. She was trying to shake such thoughts out of her mind when Lady Norman's footman answered the door.

"Good afternoon, Miss Hemshawe," the man said. "The ladies are in the game room as always."

"Thank you," she said, coming into the house. She gave him a smile and then hopped up the stairs, eager to clear her mind of all of her many worries.

She was warmly greeted by a number of the other women who were already there taking tea before their game, as well as Mrs. Aldridge's sweet little Cavalier King Charles Spaniel, Duchess.

"Good afternoon, ladies," Diana said, coming into the room and pulling off her gloves. She bent down to scratch Duchess behind her floppy, silky black ears. The dog buried her head in Diana's skirts, her long fringed tail wagging furiously.

As soon as everyone had arrived, Lady Norman delicately suggested that the Duchess of Kendell join her, Diana, and Lady Moreton at one table while the other women took the other. It was a bit of a dance to see who played with whom as they switched every time they played. The only thing that always stayed the same was that Mrs. Aldridge and the duchess were never together at the same table. For some strange reason, the duchess simply could not stand Mrs. Aldridge's dog and was highly offended by her name. Diana was sure the duchess had a fine sense of humor, but she simply couldn't bring it to the fore when it came to the sweet little pup. It was a shame, but she took her animosity out on both the dog and her owner. Diana just thought the whole situation oddly funny, but managed to restrain herself from laughing when the dog tried so hard to get the duchess to pet her.

The dog was sitting in front of Her Grace, looking up at her with her big brown eyes, her tail sweeping the rug behind her, when Lady Norman indicated it was time to start their weekly game.

"As soon as Mrs. Aldridge removes this creature," the duchess said, not moving an inch more than to look down at the animal.

Lydia laughed and picked the dog up off the floor. "Come here, Duchess, let's go sit with your mama." She scratched the happy pup on her head as the dog snuggled in Lydia's arms. Diana couldn't help but reach over and give her back a scratch too.

"That is the most affectionate dog," Diana said with a little laugh.

"I know," Lydia agreed. She then said more quietly as the duchess strode toward the card table, "I just don't understand how the Duchess of Kendell can hate her so. How could anyone hate this adorable little face?"

Diana gave her friend's arm a squeeze. "It's good to see you happy too."

"Oh, I wish I were," Lydia whispered, tears springing to her eyes.

"Is everything all right?" Diana asked.

Lydia shook her head and said, "Not at the moment, but I'm certain..."

She clearly was a little overcome, so Diana said quickly, "You are with friends, Lydia. We can help you, no matter what it is, you know that."

Her friend nodded, giving Diana her best smile before taking the dog and sitting down with Lady Sorrell, Lady Blakemore, and Mrs. Aldridge.

Diana felt bad for her friend, but unless she knew what was bothering her, there was nothing she could do to help. The idea of helping Lydia with her problems made Diana's own worries fade into the background.

After the cards had been dealt and the women were well into their first hand, there seemed to be more talk than playing at the other table.

They could easily hear Lydia say in delight, "A whist party? What an absolutely brilliant idea!"

"What's that?" Lady Norman asked, turning around to look at the ladies of the other table. "Is there going to be a whist party?"

"Yes, to raise money to support the poor of the Rookeries. Lord Welles's people," Lady Sorrell said, turning around to speak to her.

"What a wonderful idea!" Lady Moreton agreed.

So *that's* what was bothering Lydia—money for the people of the Rookeries. Well, Diana could certainly understand how that could reduce her normally happy friend to tears. Diana felt the weight of her father's debt settle heavily on her shoulders.

"I would most definitely be interested in participating," the duchess said, contributing to the conversation, even though she usually frowned on people talking from one table to the other.

"Could we... Would you very much mind if we planned out how such a party would work and who we might invite?" Lydia asked, getting up, her own game of whist completely forgotten. "Lady Norman, do you have any paper I could use to make notes?"

"Of course!" the lady said, getting up and going to a small escritoire in the drawing room, which was attached to the game room.

"Oh, and I'd like a piece please. I think Lord Welles should be informed of our idea as well," Lady Sorrell said, turning back to Lydia.

"Do you think..." Lydia started.

"I believe he should be given the option to join us, don't you?" Lady Sorrell asked, with a sly smile on her lips.

"You see, your problem is solved, Miss Sheffield," Mrs. Aldridge said with a broad grin. "All you needed to do was share it with us and it is taken care of, easy as pie."

"You are all quite amazing," Lydia said, looking around the room gratefully.

"What was the problem?" Lady Norman asked,

coming back with paper, pens, and ink.

"There was a misunderstanding between Miss Sheffield and Lord Welles, but this party we're planning should take care of it. And...perhaps a whisper of an apology in his ear?" Mrs. Aldridge said, giving Lydia a significant look.

"Most definitely," Lydia agreed.

If only her own money problems could be solved so easily, Diana thought with a pang of jealousy. The idea that people would be willing to give away their winnings at cards to help others was incredible. She wished it could be so easy to get money for her father's debt.

Diana immediately chastised herself. It was clearly a sign of just how stressed and upset she was about this debt that she would even think of such a thing. She and her father were in no way in such dire straits as the people of the Rookeries. Her father had made an imprudent bet, but they still had a roof over their heads and food on the table, which was a lot more than many of the poor had.

But an idea was beginning to form in Diana's head nonetheless. It was the most obvious thought, and Diana couldn't believe she hadn't come up with it before. Naturally, the way to raise money to pay off her father's debt was to gamble—and win.

Her father's bet should have been a sure thing, and it would have been had he not become ill. But Diana was in perfect health. She could play whist for money and, with a little help, she could even place bets on horse races. She would have to be sure to only bet on races where she would be certain of the outcome—by racing herself—but she was certain that could be arranged too. And she knew the man to do it!

With her mind completely set at ease, Diana

threw herself into helping the other ladies plan their whist party fundraiser.

~*~

"Good afternoon, Lord Colburne," the Rivers' footman said upon opening the door to him.

"Good afternoon. I'm here to check on his lordship," Andrew said.

"Of course, my lord," he said, leading him up the stairs.

"Is Miss Hemshawe here?" Andrew asked. He still couldn't decide who he was looking forward to seeing more, his patient or his daughter. He hadn't spent one night without thinking of her since Lady Sorrell's soirée. But, of course, he was also curious as to how Lord Rivers was doing. Miss Hemshawe had said he was doing much better, which was gratifying.

"No, my lord. She is at her weekly meeting of the Ladies' Wagering Whist Society," the footman answered.

"Oh, yes, Lady Sorrell told me about that. She's a member too, I believe," Andrew commented, as much to himself as the footman.

The man reached Lord Rivers' room and knocked on the door. "Lord Colburne to see you, my lord," he said after being bid to enter.

Andrew came in, trying not to feel disappointed Miss Hemshawe wouldn't be there.

"I believe, my lord," the footman said, making Andrew pause for a moment, "that Miss Hemshawe will be returning soon. She's usually back by half past four."

"Thank you," Andrew said, slipping the man a coin from his pocket. That was very useful information, since it was nearly that time now. He approached his patient with more enthusiasm.

"Good afternoon, my lord." He paused upon noticing a lady standing next to Lord Rivers' bed.

"Ah, Colburne," Lord Rivers said. He sounded much stronger than the last time Andrew had seen him. "Come in. May I present Lady Rivers?"

Andrew bowed. So this was Miss Hemshawe's mother who had refused to leave her home to go to the continent with her daughter and husband. The woman nodded to him, her lips slightly pinched.

Andrew came to the end of the bed, setting his medical bag there. As he opened it and got out his stethoscope, he asked, "How are you feeling, my lord?"

"Better," the man said. "Much better than the last time you were here."

"Good! Lets take a listen," Andrew said. He placed one end of the wooden tube to his lordship's chest and his ear to the other. His heart sounded stronger and had a steadier rhythm. He put two fingers to the gentleman's neck and felt a steadier pulse there as well. "Yes, indeed, you sound much better. You've been taking the willow bark tea as I recommended."

"Yes, it's done wonders," Lord Rivers said enthusiastically.

"I want to know why you didn't cup him," Lady Rivers said.

Andrew stood up and faced her. "Because it was unnecessary, my lady. Bleeding him wouldn't have helped in this case."

"And how do you know that? How long have you been practicing medicine, Lord Colburne?" she asked.

"Four years, my lady. I have spent the past four year in Paris working with a renown physician who specializes in pulmonary and cardiac diseases including—"

"I don't care to know the details, my lord. I want to know my husband is getting the best care possible," she said, interrupting him.

"I assure you, my lady, he is," Andrew said.

"Honestly, Sophia, as you yourself can see, I am doing much better," Lord Rivers said.

"But how do we know you wouldn't be even more improved if you—"

"Were bled? No!" Lord Rivers said emphatically. He shuddered dramatically. "Can't stand leeches."

"But Rivers—" she started to argue.

"My lady, I am keeping his lordship under observation. If he needs to be bled, I will do so, but I don't believe it is what is best for him just now," Andrew said, lying through his teeth. He would never bleed a patient. He'd never seen it to have any positive effects.

"Would you really?" Lord Rivers asked, frowning at him.

"My lord, I believe what you may need is medicine, not cupping. I would like to observe you a little longer before I decide on the exact course," Andrew told him.

That seemed to satisfy the man.

"Now, how have you been eating?"

He got as much detail as he could about the man's habits, what went in and what came out. He then gave him a detailed examination—not because he needed to do so, but because he kept hoping Miss Hemshawe would join them. He'd nearly given up and just suggested Lord Rivers try getting up out of bed, despite his broken leg, when there was a soft knock at the door.

"Are you certain that's a good idea?" Lady Rivers argued as soon as Andrew had made the suggestion. She ignored the knock.

"Good afternoon—oh!" Miss Hemshawe came in and then stopped abruptly at seeing Andrew.

He turned and bowed to her, giving her his warmest smile. "Good afternoon, Miss Hemshawe."

"Well, you are finally back," her mother said.

"Hello, my sweet. You are just in time," Lord Rivers said.

"In time for what, Papa," Miss Hemshawe asked, coming farther into the room.

"The doctor wants me to get up," her father said with a little laugh.

Miss Hemshawe's eyes went wide. "Is that a good idea? I mean, you are his doctor but what about his heart and his leg?"

"I think it will do his heart good, and we'll do our best not to make it difficult on his leg," Andrew said. He moved to the other side of the bed so he could assist his patient.

Lord Rivers tossed the covers aside, revealing his legs, one bare and the other in its wrapped cast sticking out from his knee-length nightshirt.

"Ready, my lord?" Andrew asked.

Lord Rivers seemed to make up his mind. "I am." He sat up from his pillows and swung his legs over the side of the bed.

"Good, now try not to put any weight on your broken leg. Lean on me instead," Andrew said, taking him under the arm and preparing to support much of his weight. Luckily Lord Rivers wasn't a very heavy or large man. Andrew was taller, which gave him some leverage.

Lord Rivers stood, but immediately began to sway, forcing Andrew to fully support him.

"Rivers!" his wife screamed.

"It's all right, my lady," Andrew said quickly. "My lord?"

"My head is reeling," his lordship said, putting a hand to the side of his head.

"Yes, naturally, because you haven't been on your feet for so long."

"I feel as weak and shaky as a newborn colt," the man said, leaning all his weight on Andrew.

"An excellent image, Papa. Your legs will probably be just as wobbly until you rebuild your strength," Miss Hemshawe said, coming over and lending a hand. "You've been in bed for over a week."

"Precisely, Miss Hemshawe. With practice and exercise, your father will be able to get up and move about—in a limited manner," he added for Lady Rivers' benefit. "Are you ready to sit back down, my lord?" Andrew asked, beginning to feel his own arms tiring.

"Yes, yes," Lord Rivers said. Andrew lowered him back down as gently as he could and then swung his legs back onto the bed, taking extra care with his broken one.

"Well done, my lord," Andrew said. He felt his lordship's pulse once again and wasn't surprised to find it racing. "I think you should give that a try a few times a day until you can walk across the room—with help, of course, due to your leg."

"A few times a day? Are you trying to kill the man?" Lady Rivers protested.

# CHAPTER TEN

"My lady, I assure you, it will make him better. Stronger," Andrew told Lady Rivers with as much patience as he could muster.

The woman was clearly not convinced. Andrew was just as certain that no matter what he said, she wouldn't have faith he knew what he was doing—and he wasn't going to tell her how right she was! He was determined, however, to do more research. He was certain he remembered reading of some herbs that could make the heart stronger, and he wanted to find them and see if they wouldn't work for both Lord Rivers and Andrew's mother. Not that she'd let him examine her yet, but he was nearly certain it was her heart that was the problem, just like Lord Rivers.

Andrew packed his things back into his medical bag. Before leaving the room, though he caught Miss Hemshawe watching him. He gave her a smile. "It was very nice seeing you at Lady Sorrell's soirée the other night."

Her eyes shifted to look at her mother before she responded. "Yes, it was a lovely evening."

Andrew turned and bowed to Lord and Lady Rivers. "I shall return in a few days to see how you're doing. Do continue to take the willow bark tea as needed."

"I'll walk you to the door," Miss Hemshawe said.

"Thank you," Andrew nodded, and then paused so she could precede him through the door.

They started down the hallway. As they reached the stairs, she turned and said, "I do hope you weren't offended the other night."

"Offended? By what?" he asked.

"You seemed a little...uncertain about the fact that I ride in races," she said as she started down the stairs. Luckily, they were wide enough so they could walk next to each other as they descended.

"Oh no, I am sorry if I gave that impression. I admire the fact that you race. I'm certain I could never do anything so daring." There was the truth, he thought. He didn't need to mention he would never do anything as daring as even sit astride a horse, let alone ride one in a race. He hadn't had the nerve to ride since he was a child and had been repeatedly thrown from the animal his father had insisted he ride. After the fourth time, he'd had enough, and he hadn't ridden a horse since. He couldn't stand the animals.

"Really?" Miss Hemshawe asked, obviously relaxing toward him.

"Absolutely! I do hope we have the opportunity to talk more. Your travels on the continent sound fascinating. I am so sorry I didn't have the time to travel more while I was in France," he said.

"Oh, yes. I'd love to tell you more about them. Perhaps... Perhaps we'll see each other again, at another party?"

"Yes. I do hope so. As I mentioned, I don't have a great deal of spare time, but I will certainly do my best to attend what functions I can in the hopes of meeting you."

She ducked her head, flushing prettily. "I look forward to it, my lord. Thank you for coming."

~June 16~

Andrew was about to knock on his mother's door and try once again to convince her to allow him to examine her when he heard his father's voice from inside the room. The door was open a crack, and although Andrew hated eavesdropping, he couldn't help but hear his father's voice coming through clearly.

"Why? I just don't understand why it had to be Ian," his father was saying. "If we had to lose one of our sons, why couldn't it have been Andrew?"

"I know, Darby," his mother's voice was soft as she spoke from her bed. "Ian was...a model son. He was well-behaved...obedient."

"He did what a son is supposed to do—follow in his father's footsteps. Andrew does nothing of the sort, what with all of his medical nonsense. Ian was intelligent. He would have made a hell of an earl."

"Well, Andrew is...just as smart as Ian was.... Perhaps more so," his mother said, defending him.

"Brains! As if that counts for anything. No, Marietta, I don't need my son to have brains, I need him to have drive. To know where to stand on the issues in Parliament. To know how to run my estates. To—"

Andrew had heard enough. He slipped away.

The footman in the foyer stood as Andrew took the last step from the stairs. Words Andrew had never thought to utter dropped from his lips. "I need a drink."

"There are decanters of port and whiskey in his lordship's study," the footman offered.

"Thank you." Andrew turned and headed in that

direction.

He'd just poured himself a good-sized drink when his father came into the room. Lord Darby stopped just on the threshold. "What do you think you're doing?"

Andrew didn't answer but instead lifted his glass to his father and downed the contents. He nearly choked as the liquid burned its way down his esophagus, but he swallowed and cleared his throat instead.

"I'm going out to drink," his father informed him and turned to go.

"Where?" Andrew asked, stopping him.

"Powell's, not that it's any of your business," Lord Darby answered.

Andrew frowned. He'd never heard of Powell's. "Is it new?"

"It's been there for about five years."

"May I join you?" Andrew asked. Maybe this was just the opportunity he needed to try to get to know his father—and, more importantly, have Lord Darby get to know him. Perhaps if his father actually knew him better, he wouldn't feel so bitter and angry. Maybe he could help him through his grief. Maybe...

"No." His father turned away and started out the door.

"Father," Andrew said. He put down his glass. "I know almost no one here and belong to no clubs. If I am to be your heir and a member of society, don't you think we should remedy that?"

The earl paused as he thought about it. He slowly nodded. "Very well. You may come along and I'll introduce you to Wickford—he's the owner of the establishment. I'm certain with my backing, he'll grant you membership."

"Thank you." Finally, he was getting somewhere with his father.

Twenty minutes later, they were admitted into the exclusive gentleman's club.

"Where might I find Lord Wickford? I have someone here who wishes to join the club," Lord Darby said to the footman at the door. Andrew pinched his lips together at how his father distanced himself from his own son. He could only hope things would get better with time—and perhaps a drink or two.

"I'll fetch him for you, my lord," the footman said. He disappeared into a room on the left. The low hum of men's voices came from there and, even more loudly, from a room to the right.

"That's the gaming room," his father said, indicating the room on the right. "The other is the reading room."

He might have said more, but the footman returned with a dark-skinned man dressed all in black. His white shirt and cravat stood out against the darkness of his coat. His waistcoat was also black, and once the man was standing directly in front of him, Andrew noticed it was covered with intricate black embroidery. It was a very elegant look—Andrew's valet would most certainly approve—and it made Andrew wonder if he *shouldn't* go to a tailor after all.

Andrew had seen people of African descent any number of times, but this man was not as dark. He almost could have passed for an Englishman who'd been out in the sun but for his black-lashed golden eyes. Only his lips were thicker than one normally saw in a gentleman, but it was those lips that broadened into a smile as the man approached.

"Lord Darby, what a pleasure to see you here

this evening," the gentleman said.

"Ah, Wickford. I'd like you to meet my son, Andrew...er, Colburne now, I suppose," Lord Darby said reluctantly.

Andrew put out his hand. "How do you do?"

"Very well. My condolences on your loss," Wickford said, shaking his hand.

"Thank—" Andrew started.

"More like his gain," Andrew's father scoffed.

Andrew's head snapped to him. "I beg your pardon, my lord. I consider my brother's loss to be nothing of the sort."

"He's interested in membership. Can you see to it?" Lord Darby asked, ignoring Andrew and walking away.

They both watched him disappear into the gaming room, and then Andrew turned back to Lord Wickford. "I beg your pardon, my lord. He is still grieving, as you might expect."

"Of course. That is very kind and understanding of you," Wickford said. "Please, come in. I have a feeling you're in need of a drink."

He led the way into the reading room, motioning to a footman. The man nodded, understanding Lord Wickford's unspoken request immediately.

They sat down in comfortable wingback chairs on either side of a small, round table. "Powell's, as you see, is an exclusive gentleman's club. We have a gaming room, where your father went, and this reading room where we ask gentlemen to keep their voices down, although conversation is most definitely not frowned upon."

Andrew nodded. "And is, er, Mr. Powell here?"

Lord Wickford chuckled. "You're looking at

him."

"Oh!"

The footman came back before Andrew could make more of a fool of himself than he had already. Two small glasses were placed on the table and then filled with a deep, rich amber fluid.

"This is the specialty of the house—rum from my estate in the West Indies," Lord Wickford said, picking up a glass.

Andrew followed suit. "Thank you." He took a sip. He'd never had rum before. It was a full-bodied liquor—not quite sweet as he expected, knowing it was made from sugar cane, but smooth with a very pleasant taste. "This is delicious."

"Thank you. I assure you, it is some of the finest to be had in the British Isles."

"I believe you," Andrew said, taking another sip.

Lord Wickford laughed again. "So, tell me, my lord, how is it that I've not seen you around town until now? Your brother used to come here frequently, and I met him at society parties as well, but you've been elsewhere?"

"Yes. I've been working and studying in Paris. I'm a physician," Andrew explained. Briefly, he told his host about his work, now knowing to keep his explanations short and simple. The previous evening at Lady Sorrell's soirée, he'd forgotten himself at one point and had droned on about his work to another man until the fellow's eyes had glazed over and he quickly excused himself.

Wickford was most kind. He nodded and smiled and when Andrew finished, asked, "And do you plan on setting up a practice here in London?"

"Yes, as a matter of fact I am. I have one patient already, Lord Rivers, and I'm looking for more."

"I see. So you are only interested in tending to peers?" the man asked, narrowing his eyes a bit.

"No! Not at all," Andrew said. "In fact, some of the most gratifying work I engaged in in Paris was when we went out into the poorer areas of the city to tend to the people there. We saw people with every sort of ailment, from cholera to broken limbs. It was quite a learning experience, absolutely fascinating."

"Excellent! I'm very glad to hear it. I've done some work in the Rookeries, and I know others who do as well. I'm afraid the need for a medical professional there is, well, rather desperate," Wickford said.

"I will be more than happy—"

"Good evening," a tall, blond man said, walking up to them.

"Good evening," Wickford said, standing up. "You know, I don't believe I've ever seen you in the reading room before, Welles. Normally you prefer the gaming room." He smiled at the fellow. "Is there something you needed from me?"

"I'm sorry to be so obvious, but yes. Might we have a word? It won't take above a few minutes," the man said with a friendly smile.

"Of course. Not a problem. You'll excuse me?" Lord Wickford said to Andrew. Andrew nodded and then watched as the two walked over toward the wall just behind him so they could speak privately.

A few minutes later, they both returned. Andrew stood as they approached.

"Lord Colburne, I'd like you to meet Lord Welles. He's looking for someone to help with a lady of the Rookeries. Considering what we were just speaking of..."

"I would be more than happy to help. I'm a

physician. What's the issue?" Andrew asked, shaking the hand Lord Welles proffered.

~June 17~

Lord Audley looked from behind his desk in his study as Diana let herself into the room.

"I can hardly believe it. The esteemed rake Lord Audley doing actual work?" she asked as she came in.

He stood and bowed. "It is lovely to see you too, cousin. Please come in. Shall I order some tea for you?" He came around the large mahogany table and headed straight for the sideboard, where a few decanters and glasses were laid out.

"Oh no, thank you. Actually, I might have some of that," she said, nodding toward the glass he was pouring for himself.

He laughed. "I don't think you'd want port. I have a very fine Madeira, however."

"Perfect." She sat down on the sofa near the fireplace.

He handed her a glass. "And to what do I owe this lovely surprise?"

"Two things, actually." She paused to take a sip of her drink. "I'm sure you've seen my mother?"

"Yes, indeed. She's come to visit with mine a few times in the past week."

"You don't happen to know how she came to learn of my father's accident?" She raised an eyebrow, a trick that had always unnerved her cousin since he couldn't do it.

He suddenly found his drink very interesting. "Well, you know how these things happen. Word gets around."

"Yes, especially when one tells one's mother and she writes to her sister, perhaps?"

He cleared his throat. "Er, yes, something like that, I imagine."

"You owe me," Diana said baldly.

He winced. "I know. I'm sorry. I should have realized..."

"Yes, you should have."

"It's just that she hasn't left the estate in, well, at least ten years! How was I to know she would come running to London?"

Diana sighed. "I grant you, I was shocked she did so, as well."

"Is it difficult?"

"Well, it's deuced awkward, I can tell you that. I give instructions to the staff only to find she's already instructed them otherwise. They don't know who to listen to—me, who they've been taking directions from for the past three months, or her," Diana complained.

Audley frowned at her. "Oh yes, that would be awkward. What are you going to do?"

"I don't know. I haven't gotten up the nerve to confront her about it yet. I imagine I'm going to have to do so sooner or later, though. We can't go on like this for too much longer."

He just nodded as he took a seat across from her. "And, er, what was the other thing you wished to discuss with me?"

"Ah. I want you to arrange for a race—at Epsom Downs, if possible," she said, turning her mind to the much more important matter which was constantly weighing on her mind.

"A race? A horse race?"

"Is there any other sort run at the Downs?" she asked, tilting her head inquisitively.

He gave a little laugh. "No. But, er, why?"

"I want to race," she answered.

# Chapter Eleven

Audley nodded. He of all people, would understand Diana's desire to race. Even though he wasn't as passionate about actually being out on the course as she was, he loved the races themselves as much as she.

"The relay organized by Lord Bunbury seemed to be very well received. I imagine there are a number of people who would like to see—and have an opportunity to gamble on—another race. Which is the other thing I want you to do."

"What's that?"

"I want you to place a bet for me on that race you'll be arranging." She was being more bold and brazen than she'd ever been in her life, but then she'd never owed five thousand pounds to anyone before. Luckily, her cousin loved her and would forgive her for this. And eventually, if she ever told him the truth of it, which she had absolutely no desire to do, he would completely understand.

For now he simply frowned at her. "Let me see if I am understanding you correctly. You want me to arrange a race for you to ride in and then you want me to place a bet on you, for you. Is that right?"

"Yes. I plan on winning this race, naturally."

"Naturally," he said, continuing to think about this. "May I ask why?"

Diana was afraid he would do so. She gave a little shrug. "As I say, the relay was very popular. I also miss racing much more than I expected."

"And the bet?"

"Why shouldn't I earn a little money for my time and effort?" she asked, giving him her best carefree smile. She really hoped he was convinced.

He thought about it for a moment as Diana finished her drink a little too quickly. She was probably going to feel dizzy when she stood up.

"I'm not going to offer to refill that for you," he said, a little smile playing on his lips.

She laughed. "No, you shouldn't."

"Is this important to you?" he asked finally.

"Yes. If it weren't I wouldn't have asked," she answered truthfully.

He gave a nod. "That's what I figured. Why do I have the feeling something else is going on?"

Diana widened her eyes, trying to look innocent. "I have no idea. I've explained to you what I want and why. Why do you think there's more to it than that?"

"Because I know you. You've never asked me to do such a thing before."

"I haven't had to. If I wanted to race, my father always arranged it. Since he can't just now, I'm relying on you. Should I not?" she asked, knowing it would prick at him.

"No! Of course you should. What else are cousins for?" He paused and then added, "And your father knows about this?"

"I don't want to worry him with such things. It would make him feel bad because he wouldn't be able to attend," she said.

Audley nodded again. "All right, Diana. I'll arrange this for you. How much do you want to bet?"

Relief flooded her and she gave her cousin a broad smile. "You won't regret this."

"No, I don't think I will, actually. I heard Bunbury made a nice little bundle on that relay race, despite the fact that your father didn't finish."

~June 20~

Diana was so relieved when she woke up to bright sunshine. It hadn't rained in days, so she was certain they were due for a thorough soaking. But happily, it wasn't going to come today.

Today, she was going to Lady Hartfell's garden party.

She supposed she should be thinking about her friends—would Lydia be there? Lady Sorrell or any of the other members of the Whist Society? But strangely, all she could wonder was whether Lord Colburne would be attending. She wondered if he had the time to attend such a frivolous function. She wondered whether he had the inclination to do so.

He seemed to be a rather serious gentleman. She'd love more than anything to see him laugh and relax and enjoy himself. Perhaps, if he did attend the party that afternoon, she'd be able to get him to do so. With these lovely thoughts in mind, she dressed with care in one of her prettiest frocks.

There was just one bit of unpleasantness she had to take care of today before the party. Diana reached into the back of her wardrobe and pulled out her old reticule in which she'd hidden all of her money.

She'd dropped the money she'd gotten from pawning her earrings into it without first even seeing how much was already there. So now she dumped it all out onto her bed and counted. It nearly totaled a hundred pounds. It was a good amount for a young lady to have, but it was merely a drop in the bucket compared to how much she needed to collect to pay off her father's debt.

The one place where she hadn't yet looked for money was her father's safe. She hadn't figured out how to ask her father about it—yet. She probably should have done so before she'd asked her cousin to arrange the race for her, but now as she stood with her reticule in her hand, she knew just how to broach the subject with her father.

"Good morning, Papa," she said, coming into his room after checking to make sure he was awake.

"Good morning, my sweet," he said, before taking a bite of his breakfast.

"I am so glad to see you eating properly again," Diana said, coming up to his bed. She was relieved her mother wasn't there. She would have had to wait until later if she had been.

"Actually, getting up and trying to move about has revived my appetite," he said. "Although, apparently, that doctor told the housekeeper the first time he was here that I should be fed mainly vegetables. Can you imagine? I feel like an ill-used thoroughbred."

Diana laughed. "Well, ill-used or not, like any thoroughbred you need to be back on your feet and healthy again. Maybe the vegetables will get you racing again."

He sighed dramatically. "Maybe."

She held up her reticule. "I was thinking, Papa, that it might be wise for me to keep this in your safe."

He cocked his head to one side. "Your reticule? Why?"

She giggled. "It's my money. I've saved my pin money and some winnings I've earned, and I realized it should be kept someplace safer than hidden in the back of my cupboard."

"Oh! Yes, indeed. Very clever, my girl." He told her how to find the hidden key to the safe in his study and how to work it.

After he did so, she gave him a kiss on his scratchy, unshaven cheek and headed down to explore the contents of his safe. She prayed it would contain some money, although she didn't dare hope it would be the five thousand pounds she needed.

Sadly, she'd been right. It didn't have the amount she needed, but it did have five hundred, which, added to her own riches, moved her a good step closer to her total. There wasn't any jewelry there, which was the other thing she had hoped she might find. Not that she could have pawned it even if there had been. Any jewelry would belong to her mother, and only she could give Diana permission to touch it.

Diana left her reticule in the safe then sat at the desk to write out what she had and keep a tally of how much she still needed. It was a paltry amount that she sat and stared at for a good five minutes. She hid the paper under a stack of her father's correspondence and then went off to find some breakfast for herself.

~June 21~

"The day just couldn't be more perfect," Lady Hartfell gushed, looking around at all of the people who'd come to her party.

"I couldn't agree more, my lady," Lord Rosebury said, giving her a bow. "This is definitely going to be one of the prime parties of the season."

The older lady positively giggled. "I know!"

Diana could only laugh and move on to see who else was present. She turned to see Lydia and her faux-fiancé, Lord Welles, come out the French doors from the house. They must have just arrived. She waved to them and they immediately changed direction and headed her way.

"Diana! I'm so glad to see you here," Lydia said, reaching out a hand.

Diana took it and then cocked her head a little. "You are positively glowing, what's happened?"

Lydia giggled. "John and I have decided to *truly* get married," she whispered, leaning closer but still not letting go of his arm.

Diana opened her mouth in surprise, but then gave her friend and Lord Welles a big smile. "So no calling it off at the end of the season? I am *so* happy for you. That's wonderful!"

"Thank you. I have to say that while it was a great deal of work getting her to say yes to a real engagement, it's going to absolutely be worth it," Lord Welles said, smiling down at his fiancée.

"What's the big news?" Mrs. Aldridge asked, coming up to them with Duchess in her arms.

"Lydia and Lord Welles have decided to truly marry," Diana said, reaching out and giving the dog a scratch behind her ears.

"Oh, how wonderful! I am happy for you both," the lady said, giving them a smile. She turned to Diana. "Well now, Miss Hemshawe, it is your turn."

Lydia burst out laughing. "Oh yes, Diana, we must find someone for you!"

Diana could only smile and shake her head. "My father would be very happy if you did, but I don't know if it's possible."

"I am certain of it," Mrs. Aldridge said. "There

are so many eligible gentlemen here today. Come, let's go for a walk." She put her dog down, allowing her to scamper around their feet as they slowly ambled across the lawn, their arms linked together.

"Oh my," the lady said, looking off to her right. "Just look at the prowess on display there," she said with a giggle.

Diana turned and looked to see what her friend was looking at. At the far end of Lady Hartfell's garden were three gentlemen standing next to each other, each with a bow and arrow in their hands.

"It looks like they're competing," Diana said. A tingle of excitement went through her. She did love competitions.

"Yes, it does. Come, let's watch." She scooped up her pup again to be sure the dog didn't get in anyone's way and then walked with determination to the archery.

*Thwunk! Thunk!* Two of the arrows hit the target a good twenty feet away. The third flew over the wall and off into a neighbor's yard.

"Goodness, I hope no one could be hurt by a misaimed arrow!" Diana exclaimed.

"No, no," Mr. Hershawn said, turning toward her. He had been one of the archers whose arrow hit the target. "The neighbors are here, apparently, and have been warned.

"That's good." Diana smiled at the gentleman. "How did you do, sir?"

"Not too bad," he admitted, puffing out his chest a little.

"At least he hit the target," Lord Featherington said, coming forward. His had been the arrow that had gone over the wall.

"Yes, and I believe you owe me twenty-five

guineas for that," Mr. Hershawn said.

Lord Featherington nodded. "I'll pay you later."

Diana widened her eyes. "You are betting on who can hit the target?" she asked. That tingle of excitement flowed faster through her.

"It's more fun that way," Mr. Hershawn said.

"How about if *I* challenge you, Mr. Hershawn," Diana said, sashaying forward. "Would you dare make a bet against a lady?"

"Miss Hemshawe!" Mrs. Aldridge said, clearly shocked.

Diana turned around. "Is it wrong to challenge a gentleman?"

"Not at all," Lord Featherington said. "I would certain take that bet."

"For twenty-five guineas?" she asked.

"Absolutely." Lord Featherington held out his hand to her and they shook on it.

"I'd make the same bet, but I'd feel bad bankrupting such a beautiful young lady," Mr. Hershawn said.

"I've got the money to pay you both and would be more than happy to accept yours, Mr. Hershawn," Diana said.

"You've got a deal, then."

Lord Featherington handed her his bow. With a flourish of his hand, he indicated the stand of arrows.

Diana weighed the weapon in her hand. Not too heavy. She'd shot with one of this weight before. She turned her back to Mr. Hershawn as she nocked an arrow into place and then looked back at him over her shoulder. "Are you ready?"

"Ladies first," he said with a broad smile.

"On the count of three," Mrs. Aldridge said, taking command of the situation. She counted off, "One...two...three!"

Diana aimed at "one," steadied herself and pulled back the string at "two," and let her arrow fly at "three."

*Thwunk!*

A perfect bullseye!

*Thunk!*

Mr. Hershawn's arrow landed to the left of hers nearly to the edge of the target a second later.

Lord Featherington burst into applause. "Oh, well done! Well done, Miss Hemshawe!"

Diana laughed and curtsied after turning around to face her challenger. "Well done, sir, but now I believe you owe me some money."

Mr. Hershawn nodded. "Perhaps it was just beginner's luck."

"Would you care to try again?" Diana asked sweetly.

"I'll take you up on that, Miss Hemshawe," Lord Rosebury said, coming forward. He turned to the lady accompanying him. "Miss Pensley, would you care to try as well?"

"Oh, no! I don't know how to shoot," the taller blonde lady on his arm said with a giggle.

"You'd probably do very well," Diana said. "Shall I show you how?"

"Thank you, Miss Hemshawe, but I don't think my mother would approve," the girl said.

"Probably wise," Diana agreed, but then turned back to Lord Rosebury. "Well then, my lord? Was that a challenge? We've been wagering twenty-five guineas."

"I'll make it fifty," his lordship said, coming forward to take the bow Mr. Hershawn was holding out to him.

"Well, since I just won that amount from these two gentlemen, it's a bet!" Diana said with a laugh. She turned back to pick up another arrow, noticing a footman had stepped in and removed the other two from the target. "Mrs. Aldridge, would you do the honors once more?"

"Happy to," the lady said. She waited for Lord Rosebury to ready his bow and arrow and then counted off.

Diana aimed once more then let her arrow fly on three.

"Bullseye again!" Lord Featherington shouted as soon as their arrows had struck.

"No! No, it's not it's just below the mark," Lord Rosebury said, leaning forward to see the target better.

"It's close," Diana pointed out.

"It's closer than yours," Lord Featherington said with a laugh. Lord Rosebury's arrow had lodged in the target a few inches below Diana's, just barely within the center-most ring.

"I concede, Miss Hemshawe! Clearly you have a great deal of experience shooting," he said good-naturedly.

She shrugged and gave a little laugh. "The Marquis de Poire taught me when I was a girl."

"I was going challenge you, Miss Hemshawe," Lord Egerton said with a laugh approaching them, "but after that display, I think I'll pass."

The other gentlemen standing around laughed and agreed, so Diana put the bow down and returned to Mrs. Aldridge's side.

"That was very well done, Miss Hemshawe," the lady said as they walked away.

"I do hope the gentlemen remember to pay me what they wagered," Diana said, thinking aloud. Another hundred guineas was going to be a very welcome addition to her collection for her father's debt... and would allow her to make an even larger bet at the race Audley was arranging for her.

# Chapter Twelve

Lady Buton was lounging on a divan when Andrew was shown into her bedchamber. Her eyes were closed and she had one arm thrown over her forehead in a dramatic pose.

"Lord Colburne to see you, my lady," the maid said, after clearing her throat.

Lady Buton's eyelashes fluttered open. "Oh, Lord Colburne," she sighed. "I'm so glad you could come." Her words were followed by a loud belch. "Excuse me! I've been doing that for the past two days. Ugh!"

Andrew gave her a little smile and came over and placed his medical bag on the chair next to her. "I'm so sorry you're feeling under the weather, my lady. I promise I'll do everything I can to get you back up on your feet." He peered at the lady's dainty little feet, which seemed to be crammed into shoes too small for her, flesh overflowing the sides. In fact, the lady's entire person seemed to be rather generous.

She released some gas from her nether regions. Her cheeks flushed. "It's coming from everywhere," she complained.

He knelt down on the floor next to her and put

his fingers to her neck to feel her pulse. It seemed normal. "If you'll pardon me, my lady, I'd like to feel your abdomen."

"Of course," she said, her watery brown eyes widening at him.

He felt her stomach, which seemed to be distended with gas—his prodding causing her to belch once again. Her lower abdomen was the same, but he didn't feel anything out of the ordinary.

"Do you think you'll need to cup me?" she asked with a slightly tremulous voice.

"Oh, no," he answered quickly, continuing to examine her abdomen. "How have you been eating?"

"Quite well until yesterday," she answered. "What do you mean you won't bleed me?"

"I mean it's unnecessary," he answered. "What did you eat for dinner the night before last?"

She rattled off five to seven dishes all sounding extremely rich.

"It sounds like you have a lot of meat and rich sauces, is that right?"

"Well yes, I suppose so," she said hesitantly.

"Hmm-humm. I will recommend you have nothing but a light broth for the next two days. Oh, and mint tea. That will make you feel better."

He got to his feet.

"But you... You aren't going to give me any laudanum? Or bleed me?" She sat up. "What kind of physician are you?"

He smiled at her. "A good one."

She opened her mouth and then shut it again.

"And I would recommend you lighten your diet. Eat less meat, more vegetables, and not so many dishes in cream sauce. It will be easier on your system," he said, picking up his medical case.

"But that sounds awful!"

"Would you rather be bloated and uncomfortable?"

"No," she hedged.

"Well then, follow my recommendations and you'll be feeling better in no time." He bowed to her. "Good day, my lady."

"Wait! Where are you rushing off to, doctor?" the woman asked.

He smiled at her and gave a little laugh. "I had thought to attend Lady Hartfell's garden party. What do you think?"

A large grin covered her face and her eyes lit up. "Oh, that I could go! It's an excellent idea. Lady Hartfell *does* throw the most wonderful parties. Oh, the food! Tea cakes and sandwiches with bacon." She rolled her eyes in ecstasy.

"None of that for you, now. I told you, vegetables and broth—"

"Yes, consommé." She shuddered visibly.

"And don't forget the mint tea. That will relieve your symptoms right away."

"Very well, off to your party you go."

He started out of the room.

"Eat a piece of cake for me," she called after him.

Andrew could only laugh, although a piece of cake sounded like a fine idea—for him, not Lady Buton.

~*~

Andrew's eyes immediately started searching for Diana among the people in Lady Hartfell's overcrowded garden. There were so many ladies, however, finding one auburn-haired beauty wasn't going to be easy.

"Lord Colburne!" a man called out to him.

Andrew turned and saw Lord Welles coming toward him with a pretty, blonde young lady on his arm, who he recognized immediately. "How do you do," Andrew said, holding out his hand to Welles. "I have to say I'm surprised to see you both here today. Er, it's Lydia, right? I'm afraid we weren't properly introduced last night at Mrs. Small's."

The young woman laughed, but before she could say anything, Lord Welles said, "Lord Colburne, may I introduce you to my fiancée, Lydia Sheffield?"

Andrew bowed. "Miss Sheffield, an honor. And congratulations, I didn't realize you were engaged," he said to them both.

Miss Sheffield curtsied. "It's a rather recent state of affairs, and I believe we have you to thank for it," she said, her eyes twinkling.

Andrew almost took a step back in his surprise. "I'm sorry? How is that?"

Welles laughed. "Lydia was having some problems accepting my proposal because she lost her mother to childbirth when she was young."

"Ah," Andrew said, trying to piece things together. "Your mother died giving birth to a sibling of yours?"

"Yes, they both died," Miss Sheffield said, slowly losing her smile.

"I am so sorry, that is very difficult," Andrew said.

"Yes, and because of that, she wasn't certain she wanted to take the risk..." Welles began.

"Oh, I see! Of course. Naturally!" Andrew said, understanding immediately the young lady's fear of childbirth. He then connected more dots. "But last night, what you witnessed changed your mind?"

"Yes," she said, her smile growing once more. "Seeing Mary so happy and healthy afterwards—she was positively glowing."

"Yes, she was, wasn't she?" Andrew agreed. "Life, childbirth... They're miracles, really. And yes, sometimes the miracle goes awry, but happily, more often than not, it happens just the way it's supposed to."

"It was incredible," Welles agreed. "But I didn't have a chance to properly thank you for being there. It was incredible timing."

Andrew scoffed. "Indeed! But really, it was my pleasure. There is nothing more incredible than assisting a new life into the world." His gaze wandered a moment, and he caught sight of Miss Hemshawe speaking with a few ladies. He recognized one as her chaperone from Lady Sorrell's party and Lady Sorrell herself, but he didn't know the others. "Oh, I beg your pardon, but I see some friends. If you will excuse me." He bowed and headed straight for Miss Hemshawe before she could disappear into the crowd.

Coming up behind Lady Sorrell, he could hear Miss Hemshawe speaking. "It's truly quite remarkable, he puts a wooden tube to my father's chest and can listen to his heart with it! He's made some excellent recommendations, so now, after only a little over a week, my father is getting back on his feet."

"And he didn't bleed him?" an older lady asked skeptically.

"No, my lady," Andrew said, joining them. "I don't believe in bleeding patients." He turned to Miss Hemshawe. "Good afternoon. I do beg your pardon for interrupting."

"Oh! Not at all." Was it his imagination or did her eyes light up the sight of him? Probably wishful thinking.

"How lovely to see you here, Lord Colburne. You don't have any patients you need to be visiting this afternoon?" Mrs. Aldridge asked.

"I have just come from one and, happily, the rest of my afternoon is free," he said.

"Well, that is good news. From the way you were talking at Lady Sorrell's soirée, it sounded as if you rarely had the opportunity to be social during the day," the lady said with a lift of her eyebrows.

He supposed he deserved that one. He gave her a small bow. "It does happen that my days are filled with consultations, madam. Happily, not all the time."

"It's such a shame you weren't here just a little earlier, my lord. You missed Miss Hemshawe's amazing display of talent," Lady Sorrell said, turning a smile toward the young lady.

Miss Hemshawe flushed prettily.

"Really? I'm so sorry. Did you sing, Miss Hemshawe? Or play an instrument?" he asked, looking around for some hidden musical instruments.

"No, no," Mrs. Aldridge said with a chuckle. "Nothing so tame and ordinary. She shot an arrow, hitting the target dead-on twice in a row!"

"Some gentlemen were shooting at the far end of the garden. They very kindly allowed me a try," Miss Hemshawe said quietly.

"Ha! She wagered with them both and won a tidy sum! What was it, twenty-five from each Lord Featherington and Mr. Hershawn and another fifty from Lord Rosebury?"

"You have an excellent memory, Mrs. Aldridge," Miss Hemshawe said, turning a deeper shade.

"How very nice!" Andrew said with a laugh. "Well, remind me never to challenge you. I don't think I could afford it."

She gave her head a little shake, smiling broadly.

"Would you care to promenade, Miss Hemshawe? Perhaps you can show me where you attained your riches," he said, offering her his arm.

"Of course," she said, putting her hand on his forearm. He immediately straightened his back and felt like the luckiest man in London.

He did his best to hide his grin, as he bowed to the ladies and led Miss Hemshawe off for a walk about the garden.

It was easier conceived of than done, it was so crowded, but they squeezed through knots of people standing around talking and drinking glasses of wine and lemonade. "So now the world knows your great secret," he said teasingly.

She turned widened eyes to him, her beautiful lips losing their smile.

"That you can shoot a bow," he clarified quickly, but wondering what other secrets she might have. Clearly, she'd been thinking of something else when she'd turned to him.

"Oh, yes." She forced out a polite little giggle.

"There isn't anything else—"

"No! No, I, er…" She laughed again. "That's what I was wondering—what you could possibly be referring to."

"Of course." Why did he not believe her? Perhaps because her eyes had been filled with both guilt and a touch of terror for a split second when she'd turned them toward him? He was certain he hadn't imagined it. "I doubt anyone will be so stupid as to arm you again—unless you go to a hunting party, of course."

She gave a little laugh. "I tried that once. In Germany, we went hunting with some people we'd met at the races." Her eyes lit up with true happiness as she remembered. "They said I was aptly named, as I sat astride my horse with a bow in my hand."

Andrew laughed. "My goodness, yes! I can easily picture that."

She lost her smile a little. "Unfortunately, I was successful that day too. I managed to shoot a deer."

"Why do you not look happy about the fact?"

"Shooting one arrow into an animal that size does not kill it right away. It suffered," she said quietly. "Our host had to come and shoot it dead with his gun to put it out of its misery."

Andrew took in a deep breath. "I am sorry."

"No, it's all right. Sometimes it's not such a good thing to be an excellent shot."

"But when you're shooting at a stationary target for a wager, I imagine it's much more pleasant," he said, trying to lighten things.

"Yes," she said, turning her smile toward him once again. Why did that make him feel so good? It just warmed him from head to toe and made him...happy.

~*~

"Mary, just where do you think you are going with that stack of linen?" Albert could hear his wife's voice just outside his room.

"It's Missy, my lady. I'm going to the servants' quarters to change the sheets on the maids' beds," another voice responded.

"And who said you could do that?" Sophia asked sharply.

There was silence for a moment, then the girl said, "Miss Hemshawe, my lady. She told us to change the sheets the first and third week of the month, every month. This is the first chance I've had this week to do so, my lady."

"Well, you turn right around and put those back where you found them. You may change the sheets on the servants' beds once a month at the end of the month," Sophia said.

Another moment of silence passed before the girl said, "Yes, my lady."

Her footsteps echoed away, and Sophia came into the room.

"A little household trouble?" he asked as she sat in the chair next to his by the window.

"No. Why do you say that?" she asked, pulling some knitting from the bag she'd brought in with her.

"I overheard you speaking with Missy in the hall."

"Oh, that." She shook her head. "Naturally, Diana has no idea how to run a household. Telling the servants they can change their sheets twice a month! It's a waste of time!"

"Diana has been running my household since she was twelve years old. I think she knows what she's doing by now."

"Has she, now? And who taught her how to do so?" his wife asked, looking up from her knitting.

"Madame Bernard, our housekeeper in Paris," he answered.

"Well," Sophia huffed, "perhaps that's how they do it in France, but it's not how we do it here in

England."

"No household has their servants change their sheets more than once a month?"

"Well, I don't know about anyone else, but it's how my mother did things. It's what I was taught."

"But you never taught Diana, so she's had to learn how other people do things."

"Don't I know it! I'm having to go about the house countering her orders left and right! It's quite a nuisance, I can tell you."

There was silence for a moment as Albert struggled with a gentle way of saying what was burning in the pit of his stomach. No, there just didn't seem to be a nice way of putting this. "Why don't you like my daughter?"

"I beg your pardon?" Sophia's knitting dropped down into her lap.

"You heard me."

"*Your* daughter? She's my daughter too."

# Chapter Thirteen

"Yes, but you don't act like it," Albert said. "You are not kind to her. I've overheard the two of you speaking, and I have to say I've been extremely proud of her for not yelling, being rude, or giving you a good shaking, which is something I've been tempted to do on her behalf."

Sophia's mouth dropped open.

"You go around the house contradicting her orders instead of showing her the way you believe things should be done. You criticize her to her face and in front of the servants. That is not kind, Sophia. That is not the way a mother treats her daughter."

She didn't say a word. In truth, what could she say? He was right and she knew it.

Finally she said, "You took her away when she was only eleven years old..."

"Yes, and she had to learn how to run a household and become a young woman without a mother's guidance. Frankly, the way you two would fight and carry on *before* I took her away was one reason why I did so. You two have *never* gotten along." He frowned at her.

She sighed. "No. No, we haven't. She's... She's very much your daughter. Horse-mad and always running around. She never sits still for very long—she can't! What sort of young lady is that?"

He smiled. "One who is her father's daughter."

"Precisely!"

"But have you ever tried to speak to her? To tell her not just that she must sit still, but why? Have you ever given her a reason to do so? Or a way to do so that wouldn't be too taxing on her?

"We married too quickly, Sophia," he continued, leaning forward and taking her hand. "We weren't really compatible, but we didn't realize it at the time. Yes, Diana is just like me, but you can't blame her for that, and you can't take out your dissatisfaction with me on her."

"I'm not dissatisfied with you," she said, pulling her hand away.

"You clearly are," he said, taking hers again.

"No. It's just... As you said, we're very different people."

"Yes, but that doesn't mean we can't get along. And it doesn't mean you can't get along with Diana. Be patient with her and try to understand her," he said.

"I don't even know her," Sophia said with a sigh.

"No, you don't, but that doesn't mean you can't."

"I suppose we could try to have dinner together," Sophia offered.

He frowned. "You haven't been eating together?"

"No, I've been eating here with you most nights, when I don't I take a tray in my room. Honestly, I don't know what she does—the same, I imagine."

"Sophia..." he said, caressing the back of her hand. "Share a meal. Break bread. Talk with her."

She sighed and nodded. "Very well. You are right, my lord. I should do so."

~June 22~

Diana couldn't take it. Not anymore. Her mother had just gone too far.

She stormed into her father's room, not knowing if her mother would be in there or not. Diana was rather hoping she would be, so they could have this out once and for all.

"Where is she?" Diana asked, by way of greeting.

"Good morning, Diana," her father said from the chair near the window where he was spending a good part of his time now.

"Good morning, Papa. Where is my mother?" Diana asked again.

"I believe she's gone to visit her sister, why?"

"Because she has gone too far, too far!" Diana began to pace, her anger not allowing her to stand still.

"My goodness! What has she done?"

"What? She's made complete chaos of my orderly household, that's what she's done!"

"Oh, really, don't you think you are exaggerating just—"

"Papa, she has the cook tearing her hair out because she cannot find partridge at this season—really! Partridge in the spring! There is no footman at the door because they're all in the butler's room counting silver. The maids are going through the good china for some reason rather than airing out carpets, and she has disallowed them from changing their sheets, which has both George and his sister, Georgina, sneezing and wheezing. They need to have their sheets changed regularly or else they can't breathe properly." Diana paused to take a breath.

"And, finally…"

"There's more?" her father asked.

"Yes! She had Missy inform me—*inform me*, not ask, not request, but inform me—that I am expected at dinner in the dining room this evening!"

"Well, that one was my idea," her father admitted.

"What? Why?"

"Because you two have hardly spoken since she arrived. And when you have, it hasn't exactly been civil," he pointed out.

"How can you possibly expect me to be civil to a woman I haven't seen in nine years, who just comes into my house and starts countering my orders and behaving as if…"

"As if she were the mistress of the house?" her father finished for her.

"Well, yes!"

"Because she is, perhaps?"

Diana clenched and unclenched her fists.

"Diana, she is your mother. She *is* the mistress of the house. Just because you aren't used to her being a part of our household doesn't mean she doesn't have every right to be here and try to run things," her father said, clearly trying to keep his own temper at bay.

"But she is ruining—"

"That's enough! She is ruining nothing. You have to get used to her being here. You have to step aside and let her run the house as she sees fit," he said, interrupting her.

Diana clenched her teeth together to keep herself from saying something inappropriate.

"If there are some things of which she is not

aware, like the consequences of the sheets not being changed, then you need to inform her. Don't simply go behind her back, and don't get angry. Speak to her! She's a perfectly reasonable woman—although I have to agree on the partridge. They aren't in season. I have no idea what she was thinking."

"I told the cook to use chicken instead."

"Ah, clever. See, that wasn't too difficult," her father said, giving her a smile.

"But it was irresponsible of Mother to make the demand and then leave so the cook had no authority to make the change."

Her father sighed. "Diana, I asked your mother to have dinner with you so the two of you could talk. You need to get to know each other. We've been away for so long, and you have gone from a child to an adult in that time. She needs to see that. Please, just try to calm yourself and show her what a responsible, well-behaved young lady you've become."

Diana took a deep breath and then gave her father a nod. "You're right, Papa. We don't know each other, and she does need to understand I'm no longer a child. Very well. I will do my best to be kind and charming this evening. And I will explain to her about the sheets."

"There's my girl."

~*~

Andrew knocked at the door with peeling paint on one of the smaller streets of St. Giles. The last time he'd been greeted by a woman screaming in pain. Luckily, the door hadn't been locked, and he'd run straight in and been in time to aid Mrs. Small just as she'd been about to give birth.

This time, a window above him opened up and Mary's head popped out. "What d'ya want?" she asked.

"It's Dr. Colburne," Andrew called up to her. "Come to check on how you and the baby are doing." He decided to use this combination of his hereditary title and his professional one. It just seemed to make more sense to him.

"Oh, doctor! Come on up!" Mary called down.

Andrew found that, like before, the door was unlocked. He went in, immediately striding up the stairs to Mary's flat.

"Is it safe keeping your door open like that?" he asked, after being let in through the door at the top of the stairs.

"I keep this door locked most times. It's easier than havin' to run myself down all those stairs and back up again every time someone comes," Mary said. She held the baby in her arms and seemed to have been feeding her. Her dress was hanging off one shoulder and her corset untied.

"I hope I'm not coming at an inopportune time," he said.

"Oh, no. Not at all," Mary said. She stopped to pick up some clothing off the floor and shoved aside some dirty dishes sitting on the table before seating herself on one of the two chairs. She indicated for Andrew to take the other.

"Thank you. I just wanted to see how you and the little one were doing."

"Oh, we're just fine, thank ye."

"I have to admit, I'm surprised to see you up and about," he admitted. He'd only attended to a couple births before, but none of those women had been up out of bed earlier than a week or even two. Of course, they weren't of the same class as Mrs. Small, who clearly didn't have the luxury of lying abed. She seemed to have no one to care for her or her baby but herself.

"That's wonderful. Have you had any bleeding?" he asked.

"Nothing more than normal after havin' a baby. Ugh, with my first I bled like a stuck pig for over a week!" She gave a laugh.

"I didn't think this was your first child," Andrew said, smiling at her.

"No, no. This is the third. The other two are at the Dorothy School. I'm hopin' I'll be able to bring 'em home soon. We'll see if I can get back my old job or not. If'n I can, I'll bring 'em home to look after this one while I go back to work."

"How old are they?"

"The oldest is six. The younger three."

Andrew frowned. "And you would leave an infant with a six-year-old?"

"He took care of the younger from the time he was only four. He's good with babies."

Andrew opened his mouth but found he had nothing to say. He was completely dumb-founded. Instead, he turned his attention to the infant. While she was still in her mother's arms, he gave her a quick examination and then said, "She seems to be very happy and healthy."

"Thank ye. It's good to hear it." The baby started rooting for her mother's breast and making mewling noises. Mary laughed and exposed her breast for the baby to latch onto.

Andrew could only stare for a moment at the miracle that was woman. An idea struck him, however, as he watched the baby suckle. "Do you have enough to eat, Mrs. Small? Are you eating healthy food? Lots of vegetables? Plenty of meat?"

She shrugged her shoulder. "I's got a friend who's bringin' over what she can. I haven't the funds to go to the market meself."

"That's what I was afraid of. I believe Lord Welles mentioned a grocer nearby where you can purchase food on credit. Perhaps there is a butcher and baker like that as well?"

Mary laughed. "Oh yes, we all knows about Lord Welcome an' how he pays off the bills for some folk." She shook her head. "He's a good man."

Andrew smiled. "Yes, he is." He stood up, slipping some coins out of his pocket and under a plate sitting on the table. "Well, I will leave you to feed the baby. All seems to be well with both of you."

"Thank ye for stoppin' by, Doctor," Mary said. "Ye'll excuse me fer not seein' ye to the door."

"Absolutely." He gave her a nod and left, carefully closing the door behind him.

As he walked past his mother's room after returning home, he could hear his parents talking inside. This time, instead of pausing to eavesdrop, he knocked and then entered the room after being bidden to do so.

"Good afternoon, Father, Mother," he said, bowing to them. His father was sitting in a chair by his mother's bedside, so Andrew walked up to the other side of the bed.

"And where have you been? Out seeing patients?" his father asked with a scowl.

"As a matter of fact, I have. I assisted in a birth the other night and went today to check on the mother and babe," Andrew said.

"You helped a woman give birth?" his father asked, sitting back in his chair.

"I did," Andrew said with a nod. "It's the most miraculous thing you can imagine. And today I had the honor of seeing the baby, pink and healthy, nursing at her mother's breast." He turned to his own mother. "Women are incredible and I just wanted to thank you for bringing me into the world, Mother. I just wish…" He paused for a moment, a little overcome with emotion. He swallowed and then continued, "I just wish you would allow me to examine you and help make you better, because I most sincerely don't want to lose you. Especially if it's within my power to keep you on this earth a little while longer."

Lady Darby's eyes grew shiny with unshed tears for a moment before she blinked them away. "Your gratitude is appreciated…even if it was twenty-six years…ago that I did that. And I…will think about…your offer…and let you know." It pained him to listen to her attempt to breathe.

Andrew bowed. "That's all I can hope for, I suppose. Thank you." He nodded once more to his father and left them to their discussion.

# Chapter Fourteen

### ~June 22~

Lady Rivers looked curiously at the piece of chicken the footman, George, had served to her. Before she could say anything, however, Diana said, "I believe you had ordered the cook to make partridge for this evening, Mother."

"Yes, that's right. But this looks like chicken," Lady Rivers said, poking at the offending poultry.

"It is. Partridge is only in season in the winter, so I told the cook to make this instead."

Her mother raised her eyes and frowned. "And who gave you the right—"

"First of all, you were out of the house and Cook was pulling out her hair because she didn't know what to do," Diana said a little more sharply than perhaps she should have. "Secondly, I have run my father's household for the past eight years. I believe that gives me every right to fix a problem that *you* created by not thinking about what might or might not be available in the market."

"I was under the impression that almost everything was available here in London," her mother said with a sniff while cutting into her food.

"Nearly everything is, but not even London

butchers can produce a bird that isn't in season." Diana took a long drink of her wine. This dinner was already worse than she'd imagined it would be. How could her mother think... No, she promised her father she would keep an open mind, be pleasant and charming.

"Your father told me you were taught to manage the household by his French housekeeper?" her mother asked.

"Yes. Madame Bernard was wonderful. So patient and really quite good at explaining how things were done. And of course, since she had been running Papa's household for so many years, she could easily teach by example," Diana said, cutting into her own meat. "It was such a shame when she refused to accompany us to Germany. We sorely missed her there."

"But you managed," her mother said, with a hint of grudging respect in her voice.

"We did. It wasn't easy at first, since none of us really spoke German, but Papa had a few friends and they were able to get us a maid and a footman who spoke both English and German. After that everything just fell into place."

"It's just incredible to me that you were able to... That you *wanted* to be there and to deal with it all."

Diana couldn't help but laugh at the confusion mixed with curiosity in her mother's voice and in her expression. "It was exciting, a challenge."

"I would have hated it," Lady Rivers admitted.

"It was just as well you didn't come, in that case. It really takes someone willing to put up with some discomfort and confusion," Diana said before popping a bite of chicken into her mouth.

"You are clearly a stronger person than I," her mother said with a shake of her head.

"I don't know... I think we all have our own strengths. I wouldn't have been able to stay home, knowing Papa was out there somewhere in the world having new experiences, riding and racing his horses, meeting new people, and all of the excitement that comes with traveling."

"Speaking of riding..." her mother started. She paused to take a drink of her wine as if to fortify herself to broach the subject.

Diana waited, feeling her stomach begin to clench. She was certain her mother was not going to say anything she would like.

"While I understand it is very important to you—"

"I could not live without it, honestly, Mother," Diana interjected.

"You and your father," Lady Rivers said on a sigh, with another shake of her head. "However, you must think of how you're going to attract a husband with...with that."

"There are a good number of men who are also interested in horses and racing. In fact, I think it gives me an advantage over many other young ladies of society," Diana said.

For the first time that evening, her mother actually smiled. "You may not be wrong, but you should still be careful."

"Oh, I am! I have seen men's eyes glaze over when I begin to talk about horses and racing," Diana said with a little laugh. "And I've learned to keep my comments short and shallow."

"Excellent! I am very happy to hear that." She looked at her daughter, her eyes softening a touch. "Perhaps you do have some of me in you, after all. You are very intelligent."

Diana laughed. "Are you saying my father isn't?"

Lady Rivers' lips twitched as she tried to hide her smile. "He is a wonderful man—fun and full of life. I'm not entirely certain how intelligent he is, though. I wouldn't admit this to anyone but you, but he isn't always very good at understanding the way his estate is run."

"Or money?" Diana asked, realizing this was probably how her father had managed to wager money he didn't have.

Her mother didn't answer her directly. She just lowered her eyes and took another bite of her dinner, leaving Diana to infer that managing finances wasn't one of her father's strengths.

Diana toyed with her wine glass a moment, wondering for the first time if she should tell her mother about her father's debt. Clearly, she *did* have a good understanding of money and perhaps even knew more about the family's finances than Lord Rivers did. But what if she wanted to tell her father? If she did that, it was possible the shock of what he'd inadvertently done would kill him. Lord Colburne had specifically said he should not be overtaxed.

No, it was safer to keep the problem to herself. She was managing it. Didn't Audley inform her just that afternoon that he'd arranged for a ladies-only race to be run at Epsom Downs in just a few days?

That would be her chance to win a good deal of money. Yes indeed, this problem was going to be solved in no time. There was no need to disturb either of her parents with it.

~June 23~

The following day, Diana was sitting in her father's study reading when she heard male voices in the foyer. She got up to see who was there and was pleased to see Lord Colburne retrieving his hat from

George.

"Good afternoon, my lord," she said, coming out of the study. "Have you been to see my father?"

"Oh, Miss Hemshawe," he said, turning his smiling face to her. "Yes. Yes, I have. Just a quick visit to ensure he's doing well."

"I think his progress has been nothing short of remarkable," she offered.

"I'm so glad you think so. I may have something that will speed his recovery even more, but... Well, we'll see. I want him to be a little stronger before we try anything new."

She nodded. "I was wondering," she started, not even allowing her mind to think a moment before continuing, "would you be interested in attending a race tomorrow?"

"A race? You mean a horse race?" he asked.

"Yes."

He shifted his gaze away for a moment as if he were thinking about it, but then said sadly, "No, I'm sorry. I don't quite know how to tell you this, but..."

"You have patients to see?" she asked, wondering if he always used that excuse.

His mouth opened for a moment, but then he said, "I might. I don't know as yet. But I'm afraid I need to be honest with you. I simply don't like horses very much."

That stopped Diana. "What do you mean, you don't like horses? How is that possible?"

He shrugged and gave her an apologetic smile. "I was thrown—repeatedly—from a horse my father insisted I ride when I was young, and I developed a bit of a fear of them, I'm afraid."

"But that's terrible!"

"He thought it would make a man of me. Instead, it simply instilled a fear and certainty that, while the beasts are necessary for transportation, I truly want to have no further interaction with them. I haven't ridden a horse since."

"How old were you when this happened?" she asked,

"Seven."

"Oh, dear!" Her heart went out to the little boy so wrongfully treated.

"Yes. I know you love them and riding and so on, but I just... Well, they terrify me," he admitted.

"I admire that you are able to admit that, my lord," Diana said.

He nodded. "Thank you. I have to say, I don't confess my fear to most people, so, er, if you could keep it to yourself, I would appreciate it." The twinkle returned to his beautiful green eyes.

"Of course," she laughed. "It is such a shame, though."

"About my fear?"

"Well, that you wouldn't want to attend the race. I'm going to be riding," she said.

"Really?" Oddly, he did seem to be rethinking it.

"Yes. It's a ladies-only race."

"I see. Do you know if there's going to be a doctor present—just in case of accidents?" he asked, lifting one side of his lips into a little smile.

Diana widened her eyes. "I don't believe there will be. I certainly wish there had been one when my father fell."

"So do I, but if there isn't..."

"Might you...?"

"I think it's important, when dealing with large,

dangerous animals going at top speeds that a doctor be on the premises."

She widened her smile. "And might you be available for such a role?"

"I might."

She clasped her hands together, excitement growing in her breast. "The race will be held at Epsom Downs in the early afternoon."

He nodded and gave her a smile that warmed her through and through. "I will see you there."

"Oh, and will we see you tonight at the whist party?" she asked quickly before he left.

He paused. "Whist party? I'm afraid I haven't heard of it."

"What? You weren't sent an invitation? How could we have missed you? I sincerely apologize! But you must come! Please don't say you don't play whist," she said, pleading with him with her eyes.

Happily, he was well and truly caught. He gave a laugh. "I haven't played in years, but thank you, I would love to come to your whist party."

She clapped her hands. "Oh, thank you! It's actually a fundraiser for the poor of the rookeries. We will charge five guineas to get in and then ask everyone to donate twenty-five percent of their winnings."

His smile grew brighter at her explanation, warming her and knowing for certain that this was a man she wanted to spend more time with. "In that case, there is absolutely no question that I will be there. I can't promise I'll win anything, but I'll do my best."

"Excellent! It will be held at Lady Norman's home. I'll see you there at nine."

~*~

Andrew showed up to the ladies' whist party and was greeted warmly by Mrs. Aldridge—for once without her little dog—and, surprisingly, Miss Sheffield.

"Good evening, Lord Colburne. We're so glad you could make it!" Mrs. Aldridge said, accepting his entrance fee and dropping it into an already rather full-looking reticule dangling from her wrist.

"Good evening, Madam," he said, bowing to her. He turned to Miss Sheffield. "I'm surprised to see you at the door as well, Miss Sheffield. I admit I thought I'd be greeted by Lady Norman."

"This party is hosted equally by all of the ladies of the Wagering Whist Society," Miss Sheffield said after she'd curtsied to him and he'd bowed in response.

"Ah, that makes sense. And you are a member as well?" he asked.

"Yes, indeed," the young lady said with a giggle.

Someone bumped into Andrew's back, and he realized he was holding up a considerable line of people all waiting to come in. "I do beg your pardon," he said to the gentleman behind him. "I'll look forward to speaking more later. Ladies," he said with another nod, before moving off to enter the house properly and see if he could find Miss Hemshawe.

She wasn't difficult to locate, being surrounded by a number of gentlemen who were all talking excitedly. "You should have seen the elegance with which she shot!" one man was saying.

"There was no hesitation, no wavering at all," another agreed.

"Oh, Lord Colburne," Miss Hemshawe said, noticing him standing behind one of the men. Her words had the other stepping aside to make room for him.

"Good evening Miss Hemshawe. Gentlemen," he gave everyone a nod.

"Lord Colburne, are you acquainted with Mr. Hershawn, Lord Rosebury, and Lord Wrexford?" Miss Hemshawe asked.

"No. I'm pleased to meet you," he said, shaking each man's hand.

"I believe I've seen you at Powell's, haven't I?" Mr. Hershawn asked.

"Quite likely. I just joined," Andrew said.

"Only just?" Lord Wrexford asked.

"It's all the rage. Has been for about two years now. What took you so long to join?" Lord Rosebury asked.

"Lord Colburne has only just returned to England. He has been studying and working in Paris for the past few years, isn't that right, my lord?" Miss Hemshawe said. If he wasn't mistaken, a quiet pride was shining from her eyes, making Andrew feel rather wonderful.

He gave her a warm smile. "That's right. I've only just arrived in town after a rather prolonged absence."

"Well, you did right by joining Powell's right away," Hershawn said.

"Perhaps you gentlemen could continue your conversation over a game of whist?" Miss Hemshawe asked, delicately reminding them as to why they were there.

"Yes, of course, of course!" Lord Wrexley said, clapping and rubbing his hands together in anticipation. "Shall we partner, Colburne? Are you any good?"

Andrew laughed. "I haven't played in years, but I wasn't too bad, if I say so myself."

"Well then, lets give it a go," Wrexley said. "Can always change partners later, right?"

Miss Hemshawe showed them to an open table where there were cards and markers laid out. She called over a footman, who provided the men with glasses of port to make the evening all the more enjoyable.

Andrew was sorry to see her move off to assist others, but supposed she had her duty to attend to. He was there to play cards, after all, not to flirt with the most lovely girl present. He bent his mind to the game at hand.

At the end of the hand, he was shocked to see the number of tricks he'd taken piled up next to his elbow.

"Well, it looks like you lucked out, Wrexley, and picked the right partner," Lord Rosebury said with a laugh as he counted out markers so they could tally their tricks after the rubber was done.

"I'd actually forgotten how much I enjoyed playing," Andrew admitted. "And the fact that this is all for a good cause makes it even more fun."

Mr. Hershawn gave a little laugh. "Wait 'til you play at Powell's. You'll enjoy it even more knowing you'll be able to keep all that you win."

Andrew gave a little shrug but didn't see the point in arguing with the man. He was here to raise money for the people of the rookeries and hopefully spend a little more time with Miss Hemshawe. That was all.

~June 24~

Diana felt like a novice. Butterflies were dancing in her stomach, and she had problems sitting still nearly the entire journey to Epsom Downs. Her groom had brought Nike down the day before so she could be well rested for the race. Diana wasn't sure which was making her more nervous—the fact Lord Colburne was coming to watch her or that she *had* to win in order to build up her funds and pay off her father's debt. Both were extremely nerve-racking.

As she rode in a slow warm-up around the track, she could feel her nerves beginning to affect Nike. The horse pranced and sidled sideways. Diana straightened her back, loosened her hold on the reins, and took a few calming breaths.

And then she spied Lord Colburne standing at the rails.

Nike snorted her displeasure at Diana's tension and gave a little kick to her stride.

"Yes, yes, you're right," Diana said, stroking her hand down the horse's neck. "I'm sorry. I will calm myself and focus."

She headed toward Audley, giving Lord Colburne a little smile and a nod. She hoped he would forgive her for not greeting him properly, but she couldn't. She just couldn't. Not now. Not when she needed to keep her composure and her concentration on the race.

"Is all set?" she asked her cousin.

He gave a nod. "See you in the winner's box afterward."

She smiled and turned Nike around to join the other horses at the starting line.

The ribbon was dropped and Nike took off like the thoroughbred she was. Now that nervous energy would come in handy—but no, it was too much, Diana realized right away. Her nervousness was throwing Nike off her stride. They just couldn't get into a smooth rhythm as usual.

# Chapter Fifteen

$\mathcal{C}$*ome on, come on,* Diana thought to herself. She pushed herself and Nike awkwardly around the first lap. They were nearly at the tail of the pack.

"Move, move, move!" She could hear Audley's shouts. "Go, Miss Hemshawe, go!" another voice called out. It was Lord Colburne. She was sure of it. He was cheering her on, standing at the rails, wanting her to win. She caught a glimpse of him as she sped past. His hat was askew and he was leaning out calling for her to win. How could she disappoint him?

No, she couldn't. She just couldn't.

Diana lowered her body over Nike's neck and focused her mind and energy on winning this race. Her horse immediately felt the difference in her focus. She lengthened and smoothed out her stride. The other riders fell back as Diana and Nike overtook the field, passing the rider who had been in the lead, just a short two strides before the final flag.

Breathing hard, Diana swung around and headed toward Audley. He wasn't happy, Diana could see it in his face, but then he got called away to deal with other matters. Diana breathed easier at her reprieve and redirected Nike toward Lord Colburne.

He took a step back, away from the rail as she approached. Recalling his fear, she dismounted and motioned for her groom to take her horse. Only once Nike was on her way for a celebratory rub down, did Diana head toward Lord Colburne once again.

The smile with which he greeted her made it all worth it.

~June 25~

"Finally I get to pop in on you when *you're* not expecting it," Diana's cousin said, joining her in the Rivers' breakfast room the following day.

Diana laughed as she put down her teacup and stood up to greet Audley. "Good morning, cousin. You are always welcome in my home. Would you care for something to eat?"

"Thank you, yes! I'm starving."

"Are you not fed at home?" she asked, retaking her seat.

"There might have been something, but I've got a busy day ahead so I didn't take the time to sit. I will happily join you, however," he said, accepting the plate the footman was holding out to him. He helped himself to food from the sideboard, loading up his plate with eggs, ham, and potatoes.

The footman placed a pot of coffee on the table, and Diana pushed the teapot closer to him as well.

He gave her a smile and reached for the coffee. "So, that was quite a performance yesterday," he began, picking up his fork.

Diana could only shake her head. "It was my fault, I'm afraid. I was nervous."

"You? Nervous? At a race?"

Diana ducked her head shyly. "Lord Colburne was there. Have you met him?"

Audley's eyebrows reached for his hairline. "No,

I haven't. Who is this?"

"He's Papa's physician and Lord Darby's new heir. His eldest son died a few months ago in a hunting accident, I believe," Diana said. She'd never heard the details of how the previous Lord Colburne had died, except for bits and pieces of gossip she'd picked up.

"Your father's physician is a peer?" Audley asked, unsurprisingly confused by this.

"Yes. I think he never expected to become the heir, so he went to medical school and began a career as a physician. He's quite dedicated to being a doctor, and he's continued seeing patients. My father is one of them."

"How fascinating. And he was there yesterday, at the race?" Audley asked before shoveling a large forkful of food into his mouth.

"Yes. He said he wanted to be there in case of any accidents."

"And obviously, to see you," Audley added around a mouthful of food.

Diana took a slice of toast and buttered it, saying nothing.

"I see," her cousin said meaningfully. He gave her a sly smile. "So you were nervous about him being there, watching you. And that's all?"

Diana looked up from her toast and widened her eyes innocently. "Yes, that's all. What else would there be?"

"Oh, I don't know... Perhaps the real reason you asked me to arrange the race in the first place?" he asked, before taking another healthy bite.

"I told you, I wanted to race. I love racing," she said, carefully spreading marmalade on her now well-buttered toast.

"And you wanted me to place bets for you—for quite a bit of money," he said. He turned and reached into his coat pocket pulling out a small purse. It hit the table with a satisfying clink.

"Why shouldn't I? My father always did so," she said, trying not to sound defensive but failing.

"Diana."

She took a bite of her toast and looked at her cousin.

"There's something you're not telling me," he said, holding a full fork but not eating.

She simply shook her head, her mouth full, making it impossible to speak—thankfully.

Audley put the fork down and leaned across the table toward her. The fact that he'd stopped eating told her how concerned he was. "You can tell me, Cousin. You know you can tell me anything."

Diana had a hard time swallowing her toast. She took a sip of tea to help it down. "There's nothing, Audley," she finally managed to say.

"You know, you're a terrible liar." He sat straight and picked up his fork again.

"I am not! And I'm not lying to you." She *was* a terrible liar—especially to Audley. They'd been close for years. He'd stayed with Diana and her father during his summer holidays for four years in a row when he was in school, and they'd become fast friends, telling each other everything and maintaining a regular correspondence even when he wasn't with her.

"Why don't you want to trust me with whatever is bothering you?" he asked, looking concerned.

"Because there's nothing," she insisted again. It would be so easy to just let Audley take care of this. He would, too. He probably had the money and could just pay off the debt, but she couldn't do that to him. She couldn't be so beholden, and although she'd always confided to him all of her silly adolescent dreams with impunity, she honestly didn't know if he'd be able to *not* tell her parents about this. He might feel it was his duty to do so, and she couldn't have that.

No, it was best she do this on her own—yes, with Audley's unknowing help, but still, on her own.

"Now, you said you had a very busy day," she said, trying to change the topic.

"Are you kicking me out?" he asked with a little smile before cleaning his plate with his toast and popping that into his mouth.

"No, of course not! I was just wondering what you were so busy doing," she said, smiling sweetly at him before taking another bite of her toast. This one went down much more easily.

~*~

Andrew was sitting in his parents' drawing room, once more going through the various journals he'd been reading, trying to find a cure for Lord Rivers. There didn't seem to be any definitive consensus on what medicines would work best for a heart condition. Why couldn't there simply be one answer that had been proven to work? It would make things so much easier, Andrew thought.

He had a stack of publications and letters he'd written and received, trying to learn all he could. He'd been to see a number of physicians who'd been known to both successfully and unsuccessfully treat people—for surely one could learn as much from both instances. So far he had two possible solutions, but which one he should try first, he just didn't know. And he most certainly didn't want to risk harming his patient, either.

"Excuse me, my lord," a woman said, coming into the room. Andrew recognized his mother's dresser.

"Yes?"

"Her ladyship wishes to see you," the woman said, indicating he should follow her.

He did so, coming into his mother's bedroom a moment later. "Yes, Mother," he said, coming up to her bedside.

She frowned up at him. "I've decided...to allow you...to examine me."

Andrew laughed. "You don't look happy about this."

"Well, I'm not," she admitted. "But I'm not ready...to die." She paused and looked down at her hands, folded neatly in her lap. "For a little...after your brother...I thought I was." She looked up at him, her eyes shining with tears. "But you convinced...me. Maybe it's better...that I stay...and help you get...settled."

Andrew sat down on the edge of the bed and placed his hand on hers. He noticed they were cold, despite the warmth of the room. "Mother, it would be a great loss if you were to die. To me, to Father, and to all of society. Thank you for letting me help you." He placed a hand on her cheek. It felt warm, but not feverish. So it was only her hands that were cold.

She nodded.

He patted her hands again. "I'll just go and get my stethoscope. I need to listen to your chest. I'll be back in a moment."

He got up and retrieved his medical bag from his room as quickly as he could, not wanting to risk her changing her mind. When he returned, he sat back down and touched her shoulder. She was incredibly tense.

"Just lay back and relax. This isn't going to hurt one bit. I'm just going to listen," he said.

She gave another nod and relaxed a little against her pillows.

He placed one end of his stethoscope against her chest and listened. Moving it slightly to the left and then below her breast, he could easily hear the congestion in her lungs. Her heart beat was too rapid and weak. He put two fingers to her neck to feel her pulse to confirm what he was hearing, but could barely feel a thing.

This *wasn't* good.

He sat back. "You have dropsy. I've been doing some research for another patient who has *angina pectoris*. They are both diseases affecting the heart. My other patient, Lord Rivers, has been doing much better after drinking willow bark tea, but I've sent a letter to a physician in Edinburgh who's been doing extensive research into heart conditions and testing different medicines for their treatment. As soon as I hear back from him, I'll know what our next move should be. In the meantime, I'll have your maid prepare you some tea. I'm hoping it will make you feel more comfortable."

"But you don't know?"

"There hasn't been enough research done, sadly. But from all I've read and from those physicians I've spoken to, the willow bark tea will help, and there are some other possible herbs we can try."

Her breathing was labored, so she simply nodded.

"Don't worry, Mother, you're in good hands. I'm going to do everything I can to get you back up on your feet again." He leaned forward and gave her a kiss on her cheek. "I'll send the maid in with the tea and then you should get some sleep."

~June 26~

Andrew had never been more impatient to receive a letter than he was in the following days. Although Lord Rivers was able to get up out of bed, his heart was still working too hard, and its pace was unsteady. His mother's breathing remained labored, although the tea had eased her symptoms somewhat.

Finally, a few days later he received the answer he'd been waiting for. A physician in Edinburgh had been working with different herbs, testing them out on heart patients and seeing what worked. Andrew had heard of his research from another physician he'd spoken to at his medical school. There was only one problem. Even though the man in Edinburgh knew these herbs worked to ease symptoms, he didn't know many details as yet, since his research was still in its infancy.

There were two concoctions the man was working with—a decoction of hawthorn berries and another of foxglove. He sent directions on using both, but they each contained a good many cautions. Both, when used inappropriately, had caused patients to die.

Andrew sat back, thinking this through. How could he make the decision to dose his mother and Lord Rivers with these herbs when he could kill them just as easily as he could be curing them? On the other hand, if he did nothing, they would both die for certain.

~*~

Andrew was greeted later that afternoon by Lord Rivers. His wife, as usual, sat in a chair next to him.

After listening to his heart and feeling its rapid pounding, Andrew stood back and took in a deep breath. "I've heard back from a physician who has been doing some research on heart conditions. He recommends one of two herbs, hawthorn berries or foxglove. They both will work to ease your symptoms and get your heart functioning properly again," he started.

"But?" Lord Rivers asked.

"But they come with risks, and there hasn't been enough research done as yet to know precisely which one you should take nor how much," Andrew finished.

"I say you bleed him, get the bad humors out of his system, and be done with it. No more of this ridiculous talk of herbs and medicines," Lady Rivers said.

His lordship frowned at his wife. "You would have me submit myself to something we are nearly certain *doesn't* work instead of trying something that might?"

"We don't know that bleeding doesn't work! It's been used for centuries," his wife argued.

"And people have been dying from it for just as long," Andrew pointed out.

"People have been dying of what?" a voice asked from the doorway. Miss Hemshawe came into the room. "Good afternoon, Lord Colburne. Mother, Papa. What are you discussing?"

"How was your card game, my dear?" Lord Rivers asked, smiling at his daughter.

She gave a little laugh. "It was fine. We learned that over five thousand pounds was earned the other night at our whist party. But you seemed to be having a very important discussion that I've interrupted."

"That's excellent! I'm very happy to hear it."

"Very impressive," Lord Rivers agreed.

"We were discussing treatments for your father," Lord Colburne said, addressing the second part of Miss Hemshawe's statement.

# Chapter Sixteen

"His lordship wants to give your father some herbs. We don't know whether they will work or not, and he is completely dismissing my idea of cupping him," Lady Rivers informed her daughter.

"I didn't think cupping would do anything positive," Miss Hemshawe said, coming up next to her father's bed.

"It won't," Andrew concurred.

"And what are the herbs?" she asked.

"Either hawthorn berries or foxglove," Andrew answered.

"And they are known to work?" she asked.

"There is research being done on them. They have been used in the past and have, at times, been found to work," he answered honestly.

"At times!" Lady Rivers nearly shouted.

"My lady, as I explained, the research is still being done, but yes, they have been known to work—more often than not."

"If the odds are in our favor, Papa should try them," Miss Hemshawe said.

"You speak of this as if it were a horse race," her mother snapped.

"But what she's saying makes sense," Lord Rivers said.

"Oh, so now you are listening to her too?" Lady Rivers said, turning on her husband. "First the servants and now you!" She threw her hands up into the air. "Well, I might as just go home, shall I? Clearly no one thinks they should be listening to me."

"Sophia, you're being ridiculous." Lord Rivers turned to Andrew. "I say we go with these medicines."

"But you could be killed!" his wife protested.

"And I could die if I don't try," he argued back.

"I think it would be best if our discussion was done in a calm manner," Andrew reminded them both. "Overly exciting his lordship would certainly cause more harm."

Lady Rivers clamped her mouth shut and sat back in her chair, folding her arms across her chest.

"Papa?" Miss Hemshawe asked, looking to her father.

"We try the herbs," he said, clearly having come to a firm decision.

"Very well." Andrew gave him a short bow and packed up his medical case.

"I'll walk you to the door, my lord," Miss Hemshawe said quietly. She avoided looking at her mother.

A few minutes later, they were walking to the stairs. "I'm sorry about my mother," Miss Hemshawe said quietly.

"It's perfectly all right. I understand her reluctance. It's not an easy decision to be made," he said, preceding her down the stairs.

"No, I'm sure it's not. But you feel confident one

of these herbs will truly help my father?"

"Yes, I am. If I wasn't, I wouldn't have suggested it."

"Then that's all I need to know," she said, looking at him. Even standing on the second stair from the bottom, with him on the floor, she still barely saw eye to eye with him. She was such a delicate, petite woman. His protective nature roared within him. Miss Hemshawe's stature and fragile beauty practically demanded nurturing, and he wanted nothing more than to be the one to care for her.

Yet he still couldn't believe how strong she'd looked; with what ease she had controlled the enormous beast that was her horse at the races earlier in the week. He was completely in awe and admiration of her strength and courage. He was so much larger and stronger than she was, and yet he was terrified of the animal she had controlled as if it were her second nature.

"My lord?" she asked, clearly trying not to laugh.

She had said something and he'd completely missed it, standing there staring at her, imagining her on horseback.

"I'm so sorry, Miss Hemshawe, my mind was elsewhere for a moment."

"I could tell." She laughed. "I asked if you knew where to find the herbs you need."

"Oh! Er, no, as a matter of fact, I don't. Might you?"

"I think I know where we could find some foxglove. Would you like to go searching for them tomorrow?"

He gave her a bright smile. "I would like that very much."

~June 27~

"Oooh, what a lovely phaeton," Diana said, after greeting the horse pulling the vehicle and allowing the tiger, who'd jumped down from the back, to help her up.

"Would you care to take the ribbons? I imagine you're a much better hand at driving one of these than I am," Lord Colburne said, offering her the reins.

Excitement jumped within her. "May I? That is very kind of you, my lord."

"More prudent than kind, I'm sure," he said with a laugh.

"Then what made you purchase such a beautiful equipage if you don't feel comfortable driving it?" she asked, taking the ribbons from him and starting off down the road.

"I didn't. It was my brother's. I've borrowed it, assuming it was better that it be used than just sitting taking up space at the stables. I don't even want to think about what my father would say if he found out," he added under his breath.

"Oh dear. Do you think he'll be unhappy?"

"He's still mourning my brother's passing."

"I am sorry. It must be very difficult for your parents to have lost a son."

"Not just any son," he said, "the favorite."

"Oh, I can't believe—"

"They have made that fact abundantly clear to me my entire life," he said. Oddly, he didn't sound very hurt, it was merely a fact.

"Oh."

"Sadly, my relationship with my father seems to be similar to the one you have with your mother."

Diana could only nod and commiserate, completely understanding. "Parents can be so difficult."

"Indeed. But honestly, I don't want this outing to be a sad one. Let's change the topic to something more pleasant, shall we? For example, where *are* you taking me?"

Diana laughed as she deftly maneuvered around a slow moving dray cart laden with vegetables. "To the Kew Gardens. I'm certain they'll have foxglove growing there. I don't know about hawthorn, but we can look."

"What an excellent idea! And they don't mind if you pick the flowers?"

She gave a little shrug. "I believe there are areas where no one will notice." She gave him a little smile and a wink.

He burst out laughing. "Well then, off we go to Kew!"

Diana parked the phaeton and left it in the good hands of the tiger as she and Lord Colburne took to the paths of the gardens. It couldn't have been a more perfect day. The sun was shining and temperature was warm, but not overly so. It was an easy walk as the walkways were well maintained.

"Have you been here before?" Lord Colburne asked as Diana opened the parasol her maid had insisted she bring along.

"Only once when we first arrived," she admitted. "My father and I were looking for places where we could ride."

"But there are a great many places to ride," his lordship said. "The most popular, of course, is Rotten Row in Hyde Park."

Diana laughed. "Yes, the park is fine if you want

your horse to walk at a slow pace and greet people. But we were looking for someplace where we could really *ride*.”

“Oh, I see. You mean gallop and race,” he said, finally understanding what she meant.

“Yes. We need to keep our horses in good form and well exercised.”

“Naturally, that makes sense. So, did you find some place?”

“A friend of my father’s has an estate not too far where we can go, but too frequently it is merely the main roads that we take to.”

“I can’t imagine that Kew would be a good place either,” he said, looking up at the old trees, which surrounded the path.

Diana laughed. “No. We ruled this out quickly.”

“Well, let’s see if it can’t be useful for something. Would you be willing to leave the path and venture farther into the woods?”

“Absolutely!” With a slight lift of her skirts, she stepped over the low fence. The area was covered with tall grass and bluebells and dotted with moss-covered trees. It was all so green and lush, Diana just paused to take in a deep breath of the fresh, clean air—so very different from the city she was now used to with its scents of horses and too many people.

“I’m afraid I’m woefully ignorant when it comes to flowers and where they might grow,” Lord Colburne admitted.

“I can’t say I’m much better, but I do have some slight idea as to where I remember seeing some foxglove growing,” Diana answered. She paused to look around and then headed in the direction of the sun to the west.

“I can’t tell you how very glad I am to hear that,”

he said with a laugh.

The ground began to slope downward and a lovely little valley revealed itself to them filled with fern and tall spikes of beautiful bell-shaped flowers in purples and pinks.

"Those, my lord—if I'm not mistaken—are foxglove," Diana said, pointing ahead of them.

"My goodness! Yes, they are! They look just like the pictures I have seen." He started down the hill and Diana followed, but with an odd misstep, she suddenly found herself sliding and then falling.

Strong hands caught her before she could hit the ground. "Miss Hemshawe! Are you all right?"

"Yes, yes. Thank you. The ground is more slippery than I anticipated," she said. He hadn't immediately removed his arm from around her waist, and it felt very nice there.

"Perhaps, er, perhaps I should assist you moving forward," he said, holding her close to his side. He seemed reluctant, but he let go of her and instead took her hand in his.

"I would greatly appreciate that," Diana said, oddly finding herself a little out of breath.

They continued forward, his hand engulfing hers. It gave her a feeling of warmth and care she didn't think she ever wanted to let go of.

~*~

They returned to Miss Hemshawe's home nearly an hour and a half later, after picking the flowers they needed and enjoying a lovely, slow walk back to the phaeton. Andrew could hardly remember a more pleasant day.

He felt as if the feeling of her body pressed against his—even for just that fleeting moment—would be burned into his memory forever. It had felt so good. She was small but soft, curving in all the right places. He'd been sorry to let go of her, but then they had to continue on and pick the flowers.

He carried in half the bouquet they'd collected, just a few stalks, but each filled with a number of pretty purple flowers. He kept the other half for his mother.

"You've returned," Lady Rivers greeted them as soon as they'd walked in the door. She was just coming down the stairs.

"Yes, and we were successful in finding the foxglove," Miss Hemshawe said.

Andrew presented Lady Rivers with the bouquet.

"How very pretty. They look like they should be put into a vase, not cooked up to make some medicine."

Andrew gave her a smile. "It's very important that the decoction be done just right, my lady, and only a very small amount be given to his lordship," Andrew said. He proceeded to point out to her that only the stem and leaves should be used in preparing the medicine and explained just how much of what was to be used and the dosage as well, all of which had been explained to him in the letter he'd received from Edinburgh. He was halfway through his explanation when he realized the lady's eyes had shifted to her daughter.

Miss Hemshawe seemed to be deep in conversation with a maid, but they were speaking too quietly to hear what they were saying. It was obvious Lady Rivers was doing her best to overhear them.

"Lady Rivers, are you listening to me?" Andrew asked, becoming slightly annoyed. He was giving her vital information. The life of her husband relied on her understanding what he was telling her.

"Yes, of course I am—the leaves and stem should be crushed and then steeped in freshly boiled water. Go on," she said.

"No, no, not the stem. Only the leaves," Andrew said. This wasn't good. "My lady, may I write these instructions down for you? It's vitally important they are followed precisely."

"Yes, of course," she said, her eyes still firmly focused on her daughter.

"My lady?"

She turned toward him with a start.

"I'll send the instructions to you later," he said, finally giving up.

"Excellent." She gave him a sharp nod as Miss Hemshawe rejoined them.

"Do you understand how to make this medicine for Papa?" she asked her mother.

"Of course I do," her mother snapped. "It's not difficult."

Andrew bit his tongue and said nothing.

Miss Hemshawe took a step back at her mother's attack. She wisely chose not to address it, but instead turned to Andrew and placed a kind smile on her lips. "Thank you so much, Lord Colburne, for your help today. I truly enjoyed the excursion."

"As did I, Miss Hemshawe, and I couldn't have done it without you. Thank you for your assistance," he said, desperately wishing they didn't have an audience. If her mother hadn't been there, he would have taken her hand in his once again and placed a kiss onto the back of it. Truly, what he wanted to do was to place a kiss onto her beautiful lips, but that was out of the question—at least at present. Perhaps someday…

"Thank you, my lord," Lady Rivers' voice cut into his thoughts. It was a clear dismissal so he bowed and left.

~*~

Diana watched the door close behind Lord Colburne and felt a strange loss, as if he'd left her forever, which was completely ridiculous. She was sure she'd see him again before too long. She gave her head a shake and then turned to go up to her room. She found her mother blocking her way, however.

"What were you speaking with that maid about?" Lady Rivers demanded.

Diana frowned. "We were discussing the changing of the sheets on the staff's beds."

"I have already seen to that," her mother informed her.

"Yes, you told her not to change those sheets more than once a month, but both George and his sister, Georgiana, suffer from congestion and breathing problems if their sheets aren't changed more often than that. I've been meaning to speak to you about it."

"Why was I not informed of their malady? If they are sick—"

"They're not sick. They breathe perfectly well when their sheets are changed more often, that's all," Diana explained, trying to maintain her patience.

"Then I should have been informed. I am the mistress in this house, Diana, and while I know you've been accustomed to running things, you will please remember that while I am here, I am in charge." With that, her mother turned on her heel and went back up the stairs.

Inwardly, Diana fumed. She was well aware of

the fact the butler was standing just a few feet away at the door, however, so kept her feelings to herself and escaped into her father's study.

# Chapter Seventeen

Albert was sitting in his favorite chair by the window, recovering from the move from his bed. He was still too weak to make even such a short journey on his own and without having his heart pounding uncomfortably afterward.

"That girl just can't stop!" Sophia said, coming into the room. She paused when she didn't see him in his bed but then quickly changed direction when she found him in his chair.

"Can't stop what, my dear?" he asked, trying his best to keep his voice even and not sound overly winded.

"She just can't stop trying to run this household! I've told her it is my responsibility, but she just can't let go," his wife said, sitting in the chair opposite.

"Well, she's not used to having someone else running the house. It's not surprising."

"But I've told her—"

"Sophia, she's been running my household since she was twelve years old!"

"I know. You told me so, but that doesn't mean she needs to continue to do so when I'm here."

Albert could only sigh and wonder if his wife and daughter would ever make amends.

"Rivers, did you have that girl educated?"

Albert looked up. "What do you mean? Did I send her to a school? No."

"Did she have a governess or tutors?"

"She had tutors for a while, but when we moved to Germany, I didn't engage one. Couldn't find one who spoke English, and neither of us knew enough German," he explained.

"But did she learn the pianoforte? How to dance? Paint? Any of the arts that make a young lady eligible to be married?"

"She's excellent at running a household," he pointed out.

"Yes, I understand that, but what about general knowledge? What about—"

"She knows how to dance. I did hire a dancing instructor for her. And she educated herself in everything else. Quite an avid reader, that one." He gave a little laugh. "Takes after you in that way."

"Does she?" Sophia asked, finally showing some interest in her daughter.

"Indeed! Anytime she could find a book in English, you can be sure she bought a copy, no matter what the subject. And when some friends of ours were moving and wanting to leave behind much of their library, she snapped it up. I wanted to leave it all behind when we came here, but she insisted on bringing a number of crates of books back. Her favorites, I suppose."

"How fascinating. Do you know where she's kept them? I'd be very interested to see what she's been reading."

Albert shrugged. "They're all in my study. There's nearly a whole wall of them. It was actually a good thing she brought them back—she filled in a couple of empty bookcases that were there when we moved in. Although I'm not quite sure why they were empty to begin with..."

"Because I had some books removed and brought to Riverton after I cleaned out the library there," Sophia admitted.

"Did you really?"

She nodded. "There were a number of extremely outdated books on agriculture and the raising of sheep." She waved a hand. "I had them all removed along with some others that were too old to be of any use and had books brought from here to fill in the shelves."

"You didn't throw the old books away!" Albert protested. He wasn't much of a reader, but even he knew enough not to throw away books.

"No, no. I gave them to a local school for boys. They were quite pleased to have them."

"Oh, that's all right, then."

"But I do believe I'll take a look at Diana's books and see what she's brought back and what she's taught herself."

"I think that would be a fine idea. Give you two something to talk about, rather than just arguing over the household," he said, raising his eyebrows at her.

~June 28~

Andrew spent twenty minutes in the kitchen of the Darby residence with the cook, watching him make the decoction he'd just explained to Lady Rivers. Well, at first it was just the cook, then a maid joined her. A few minutes later, a footman stood and watched as well. By the time Andrew was simply standing there slowly stirring the pot and waiting for the water to boil down, he had five people standing around watching him.

"It's extremely important not to allow it to remain overly thin," he informed the assembled group.

They scattered.

He gave a laugh as he watched them disappear to wherever they were supposed to have been.

"What is it you're making, my lord?" the cook finally asked.

"It is medicine for my mother," he answered.

"Ah." She gave an understanding nod and then went off to finish preparing dinner.

After allowing the resulting liquid to cool slightly, Andrew kept it in a small pitcher and brought it up to his own room, along with a small wine glass. He poured just a very small amount into the glass and then left the pitcher on his dressing table with a note saying, "Danger! Poison! Do not touch!"

He took the glass to his mother.

"Good afternoon, Mother," he said, entering her room after a brief knock.

"Andrew," she said, smiling at him.

"I've brought you some medicine I believe will make you feel much better."

"Excellent!"

"What is that?" his father asked, coming into the room. "Good afternoon, my dear," he said, coming over to the bed.

"It's a medicine, I believe—"

"Yes, yes, heard that part, but what is it?" his father asked, interrupting.

"A decoction of foxglove," Andrew answered. "It has been known to help heart patients."

His father frowned. "And you're certain it's your

mother's heart that is the culprit here and not pneumonia or some other respiratory ailment?"

"Absolutely certain. She has dropsy," Andrew answered.

His father *humphed* unconvinced. "And what does this medicine do?"

"It's a diuretic. It makes it easier for the heart to pump, evens out the rhythm, and will also clear her lungs of the congestion there."

"All with a tiny bit of liquid from foxgloves?" his mother asked.

"Yes." Andrew came forward and handed the glass to his mother.

"You're certain?" his father asked again.

"Father, this is the best known cure, but like everything in medicine, it's not guaranteed to work," Andrew said, trying to keep his patience. First Lady Rivers and now his own father was questioning his methods, and he didn't like it. Why couldn't they just let him do his job?

"Well, let's hope it does." His father's tone held a note of warning. He turned to look at his wife, watched her drink it down and then stayed, staring at her as if there would be an immediate reaction.

"It will take some time to work," Andrew said. "Possibly even a few days."

"Days?" his mother asked.

"I'm afraid so. But let's give it a try. If nothing changes within the next three days, I'll give you another dose," Andrew said.

"Well, while we're waiting for that to work," his father began, "I'd like to have a word with you downstairs." He didn't wait for Andrew's consent, but instead simply headed out the door, certain his son would follow.

He did.

His father went straight to the decanter of port sitting on a side table. Andrew was rather happy with that choice. He could certainly use a drink himself.

His father handed him a glass of the golden liquid.

After they each drank, his father said, "I want you to come with me to my tailor's tomorrow."

Now, that was unexpected. "My valet will be beside himself with joy. But may I ask why?" Andrew had to ask.

"Because you can't go to Parliament dressed that way," his father said, indicating the wool breeches and boots Andrew had chosen to wear for his outing to the park.

"I was dressed for a walk through the woods today, firstly," Andrew said. "And secondly," he continued, "when do you believe I would attend Parliament?"

"You'll go with me, naturally, to observe and meet people. And speaking of meeting people, I've put your name in for membership at White's. You can't find a better place than that to meet the sort of gentlemen you should be meeting."

"I've been meeting a number of people already."

"I don't know who or where," his father said, dismissing him, "but you need to make proper connections, build alliances; it's all part of governing, of being a member of Parliament."

"I beg your pardon, Father, but I have no intention of taking my seat in Parliament. I'm busy enough as it is." Andrew downed the last of his port in one go, relishing the burn of the alcohol through his system.

"Yes, you will. I have been patient with this

doctoring nonsense, but it's time you took up your responsibilities. Not only do you now have a title, but someday you'll have mine as well. You need connections, coalitions, and"—he pointed a finger at him—"a membership at White's. All of which requires a better wardrobe than the one you presently own.

"You'll also need to attend proper society functions so you can meet the right sort of girl. You should consider marrying. You need a black suit with knee breeches to be admitted into Almack's. I'm sure we can get you vouchers even this late in the season."

With his father's clearer explanation, Andrew immediately saw what it was his father was doing, but he wasn't going to have any part of it. He put on his best bedside voice, the one he used with patients who, in all likelihood, weren't going to make it. "Father, I am not Ian. I understand that you miss him. That you wish I were the dutiful son he was. That you want me to step into his shoes and follow in your footsteps. But I'm not him and I can't do that. I'm very sorry. It's not who *I* am."

"Don't you dare take that tone with me!" his father raged, suddenly losing his temper. He turned and slammed his glass down on the table in between them. "You will do as I say, is that understood, boy?"

Andrew took a deep breath. He was not going to engage with his father. It would be so easy to scream right back at him, but he wasn't going to do it. He stood there for just a moment, counting to ten slowly, then he said, "I am *not* a boy and I am *not* my brother. You are going to have to learn to accept me for who I am. I will not be accompanying you to Parliament, and I have no need to make connections. Although, I have to admit, being a member of White's might help in getting me more patients. I thank you for putting my name up. And as for meeting eligible young ladies, I think I'm doing just fine on my own, thank you. No vouchers for Almack's are required."

Before his father could respond, Andrew turned and started out the door. He didn't quite get there before his father exploded once again. "You can just forget this medical nonsense. You are going to be a marquis with a seat in Parliament that you are going to fill. You will have estates you will need to look after. You need a wife who can handle—"

"I need a wife who can handle the irregular schedule a physician maintains," Andrew said, spinning around and confronting his father. "I will manage the estates with the help of stewards, just as you've always done, and I will *not* be taking a seat in Parliament. That is final. And if I feel the need for more clothes, I know where Bond Street is, thank you."

He left the room quickly and then the house. He needed a walk. He did not like arguments. He did not like shouting. But more than either of those things, he did not like being told how he was going to live his own life.

~June 28~

The following morning Diana woke up with a bit of a headache. She knew just what it was—it was this damned debt! She had fallen asleep thinking about it the previous evening and had tossed and turned for hours trying to think of a way to win more money.

She had *wanted* to be thinking of Lord Colburne and the absolutely wonderful day they'd had together. He was, without a doubt, the most fascinating, handsome, and caring man she'd ever met—and she'd met a good number of men, many more than the average girl her age.

But there was something about Lord Colburne...

She couldn't put her finger on it, but it just made her insides go to mush. She really enjoyed being with him. But this debt was going to kill her before she ever had a chance to further that relationship, she was sure of it!

She could hardly eat anything that morning, but managed to swallow a few pieces of dry toast before heading to her father's study to go over her accounts once more. Maybe if she could ride in another race... But that would mean asking Audley to arrange it, and he was already overly suspicious of her motives for the first one. She just didn't know.

"Good morning." A voice stopped Diana as she headed for her father's desk. She looked up and found her mother standing in the far corner of the room, a book open in her hand.

"Good morning, Mother," Diana responded. What was she doing here? Diana changed direction to join her. "What is that you're reading?"

"I was just looking through the books you brought back from Europe. It's quite a fascinating collection." She showed Diana the book she had in her hand. "I don't know German, but I'm assuming this is a book on household management?"

"Yes." Diana was surprised. She never expected her mother to go through her books.

"And you've got another one in French, as well as two in English," her mother pointed out.

"I felt it best to get as much information on the subject as I could. It was quite interesting comparing the different ways of doing things in each country," Diana said.

"Are there a great many differences?"

Diana nodded, "Surprisingly, there are."

"Well, I would love to hear all about it," her

mother said, replacing the book on the shelf. "And I see you've got quite a fondness for history as well," she pointed out, looking over the books on another shelf.

# Chapter Eighteen

Diana was momentarily stunned into silence. Her mother wanted to hear about what Diana had learned on the continent? Her mother was interested in her life? It was so unexpected, but Diana managed to pull herself together and responded to her. "Er, yes. I tried to learn all I could about the history of the countries we visited."

Her mother nodded. "I asked your father, and he said he didn't engage a tutor for you in Germany."

"No, we couldn't find one who spoke English well enough. I had a governess for some time in France, but I quickly learned all she knew and didn't see the point of keeping her on when all she was doing was reading my own books aloud to me."

"Oh dear, no, that doesn't sound very efficient. But why didn't you keep her on to chaperone you?" her mother asked.

Diana shrugged. "I had a maid for that."

"It's not quite the same thing," Lady Rivers pointed out.

"No. I do understand the difference, but really it wasn't necessary to have both. I was perfectly fine with just Claudette."

Her mother nodded her understanding. "But

she is not still with you?"

"She was French, and wanted to stay in France when we moved to Germany."

"So you got another in Germany?"

"Yes, although… I never found anyone who was interested in staying for very long. I can't imagine it was very interesting to just sit off in a corner of a room filled with people speaking in a language you can't understand." Diana studied her hands clasped in front her. "And to have a mistress who couldn't communicate with you either—well, it was frustrating for everyone involved."

"So who chaperoned you?"

"I did usually have a maid, or when I didn't, one of the other wives would play the role as needed." She gave her mother a little smile. "It was fine. The rules there weren't so strict as they are here."

Her mother frowned at her, which Diana found annoying. It wasn't her fault she couldn't find a maid who either spoke English or was patient enough with her own very bad German.

"But that means you were alone," her mother said.

Diana stopped. That wasn't at all what she'd thought her mother was thinking.

"You had no companionship at all?" Lady Rivers persisted.

"I had Papa," Diana said.

Her mother made a face. "Your father is fine for a man, when he's around, but a young lady needs the company of other young ladies, or at the very worst, an older lady to guide her and answer her questions or…well, just to talk to."

"There were ladies there, as I said," Diana said, turning to study the books on the shelf. She didn't really see them, though. Her mind was filled with memories of those days when she'd tried so hard to find a companion or anyone, really, who she could talk to.

Her mother was right, though, her father hadn't really had the time or the inclination to sit and talk with a silly teenage girl. Most of the other ladies they knew were more concerned with their own lives, and the lives of everyone in their set, to speak with Diana or explain things to her. No, more often than not, it was Diana who would be sitting off to one side listening as conversation flowed around her.

She felt a gentle touch one her arm. "I'm so sorry I wasn't there for you, Diana."

Her mother's sympathy was almost more than she could take—especially considering all of the horrible things she'd been thinking of her mother lately, all the animosity that existed between them. Now, suddenly, her mother was being...well, motherly.

Diana blinked rapidly as the books in front of her blurred for a moment. She gave a shrug and pulled her lips up into a smile as she turned back toward her mother. "It's all right. I was fine on my own. Really."

Lady Rivers tilted her head a little. "I don't believe that for a moment. You're just like your father—bold and outgoing. It must have been extremely hard for you."

Diana could only shrug. It *had* been hard. Very hard. But she'd survived. She'd grown and learned, despite the fact she had no close female companionship. "We all have to live with the decisions we make. I did, and survived just fine."

Immediately, Diana could see she'd said the wrong thing. Her mother pulled her hand back and her eyes filled with hurt.

Diana didn't know what to do. She hadn't meant to hurt her mother. She hadn't meant to accuse her mother of anything, just to say that she'd had to live with the consequences of her own decisions.

"I... I've got errands I need to run. Please excuse me," Diana said, giving her mother a quick curtsy. She needed to escape, that was what she had to do. She needed a ride.

~June 30~

Lady Norman arrived at nine o'clock sharp to pick up Diana on her way to Lady Middleton's ball.

"Thank you so much for agreeing to chaperone me this evening, my lady," Diana said after she'd climbed into the carriage.

"Oh, it's entirely my pleasure," Lady Norman said. "I can't tell you how lovely it was to meet your mother after all these years." She gave a laugh. "We got to know each very well at a house party when we were both young and on the lookout for husbands. Well, *I* was on the lookout for a husband, Sophia was coerced into attending."

"Really? I don't believe I've heard this story," Diana said, fascinated to hear a little of her mother's history.

"Oh, yes! We were the only two young ladies at a Christmas party held at the home of the Viscount Terras. My parents brought me there in the hopes I would find a young man before I made my official debut—I didn't. And your mother was there because her parents simply could not convince her to *have* a season, and they were trying to convince her she would enjoy society."

"And did it work? Did my mother have a season after that?"

"Oh, no! Not because she didn't want one, but

because she didn't *need* one. It was there she met your father, and I can tell you, he had eyes only for Sophia. I don't think he even knew I was there." She burst out laughing again.

"Oh, I'm so sorry! That must have been awkward," Diana said with an embarrassed little laugh.

"No, no, not at all. I was very happy for your mother. She was the quietest thing. So shy. I was happy a gentleman had noticed her at all—and to be honest, I think she and her parents felt the same way. I have to say, I wasn't surprised when I saw the announcement of their engagement in the papers only a week after the party ended. Ah! Here we are."

The door to the carriage swung open, and a footman wearing brilliant blue and gold livery stood waiting to help them alight. Diana waited for the older lady to precede her and then got down and followed her into the ball.

Not ten minutes after they had entered, Mr. Hershawn and Lord Rosebury were at her side making their bows and arguing as to which one would be the first to lead her out onto the dance floor.

Diana couldn't help but laugh. Her friend and Lady Norman's daughter, Tina Ayres, and Lord Ayres joined them, coming around the two bickering gentlemen.

"Good evening, Miss Hemshawe," Miss Ayres said. She looked at the two men and asked, "What are they going on about?"

"They're trying to decide which one of them will be leading me out first. Have you ever seen anything more ridiculous?" Diana asked with a laugh.

Miss Ayres giggled. "No, I can't say I have, and I have seen a good many silly things since I joined society."

Diana was still impressed with how quickly Miss Ayres had acclimated from being a seamstress in a small village, to being a modiste in London, to being the accepted daughter of the Earl of Ayres and a member of society. It had been a head-spinning turnabout, but Miss Ayres had handled it all with grace and good humor.

"It will be I, Miss Hemshawe," Mr. Hershawn said finally, turning toward them. "Oh, Miss Ayres! How absolutely wonderful to see you this evening. When did you magically appear?"

Miss Ayres burst out laughing. "Just a moment ago. My father and I just clapped our hands and, *poof*! Here we are."

"You know, I almost believe you," Lord Rosebury said as he bowed to her. "Ah, and Lord Ayres is there," the gentleman said, after looking around for a moment for the aforementioned father.

Lord Ayres was already deep in conversation with Lady Norman and had taken a few steps away so they could talk privately. The two of them were engaged to marry, which Diana thought was the most adorable thing ever. Only the ladies of the Wagering Whist Society knew they were Miss Ayres' natural parents. Because they had never been married, they could never admit publicly to the fact, but now finally after twenty years, they could be together as they'd always wanted.

"Well, since you have decided that Mr. Hershawn shall be the one to accompany me onto the dance floor, that leaves you available to escort Miss Ayres," Diana told Lord Rosebury.

"I *am* learning to dance," Miss Ayres admitted, "but I'm not yet quite comfortable enough to display my skills in public. However if you wouldn't mind a promenade about the room, my lord, that would be very pleasant."

His eyes grew wide, and he looked around very conspicuously. "I would be honored, but would only dare do so with the duke's permission." He was, of course, referring to Miss Ayres' fiancé, the Duke of Warwick.

"Oh, he and Lady Margaret haven't yet arrived. It would be lovely if you would walk about with me until then," Miss Ayres said with a smile.

A broad smile grew on the gentleman's face. He bowed low saying, "It would be my great honor."

Mr. Hemshawe led Diana out onto the floor, and Lord Rosebury and Miss Ayres set out on their walk.

The dance had just finished when Lord Rosebury was right at Diana's side again, begging her to join him in the next dance. She couldn't say no. Lydia had arrived and permitted Mr. Hershawn to lead her out onto the floor as well.

The four of them were right next to each other, which allowed for a lot of laughter, teasing, and chatting all through the dance. Diana hadn't had so much fun at ball...well, ever! There was definitely much to be said for having good friends.

"Oh, my!" Diana said, fanning herself after the dance.

"Are you warm, Miss Hemshawe?" Lord Rosebury asked.

"Yes. Would you mind if we stepped outside for a few minutes to get some fresh air?" she asked.

"I would be very happy to do so, but first let me fetch you a glass of lemonade."

He went off to do that, and Diana went out into the garden to get some much-needed air, certain he would return momentarily.

~*~

Diana was happy to slowly wander the garden paths while she waited for Lord Rosebury to return with her lemonade. It was a lovely garden, filled with the wonderful, heady scent of the many rose bushes, which lined the walkway.

She was admiring a bush full of beautiful white blooms when a man's voice sounded much closer than she expected.

"Well, well, Miss Hemshawe. What a surprise to see you here this evening," Lord Swindon said from just behind her. He was so close, she wondered if he could be standing on the hem of her dress.

She had nowhere to go. She couldn't move forward because the rose bush with its thorny branches was right there. She couldn't move back, for she would step directly into Lord Swindon's person. She attempted to move to her right, but he stepped right along with her.

"Good evening, my lord," she said, turning around to face him. To do so without brushing her chest against his, she had to take a small step back. Immediately, she could feel the branches of the bush pressing against her knees.

"Why are you not at home tending to your ill father?" he asked, not moving an inch away from her. "Might I surmise that he is feeling better?" His breath was heavy with the stench of alcohol.

"My mother is with him," Diana replied, resisting the urge to turn her face away. "And yes, he is doing better, but still the doctor has cautioned us all not to worry him overly much as that might cause his heart to fail altogether."

"Oh, dear, I am so very sorry to hear that. In that case, may I assume you are still taking charge of that little problem of his?"

"Yes. Yes, I am," she admitted.

"Excellent. I am very happy to hear that. You do realize it's been two weeks. We did say you would have my money within that time period, did you not?"

Diana swallowed hard. "We, we did. Well, I asked for three, but you insisted on two, and I'm afraid I truly am going to need another."

"May I suggest you now reconsider my exceedingly generous offer?" he asked, leaning even closer. "We can have this thing settled tonight." His breath reeked and it was all Diana could do not to shove him away.

"No! Er, I mean—"

"I believe the lady isn't interested in any offer you have put forward, sir," said a new voice approaching from the direction of the house.

Much to Diana's relief, Lord Swindon took a step back to face the newcomer. She turned as Lord Colburne joined them and couldn't help the sigh of relief that escaped her.

He gave her a smile and a small bow. "Good evening, Miss Hemshawe. I do hope I'm not interrupting anything?"

"No, no, not at all. In fact, I'm *very* pleased to see you, my lord." She paused and realized that Lord Swindon was staring at her with a frown so fierce it gave her chills. "Er, Lord Swindon, may I present Lord Colburne?" She wasn't about to tell either one how she knew the other, so she just left it at that.

"My lord," Lord Colburne said, giving the other man a nod.

"Colburne? I heard you'd died," Swindon said bluntly.

Lord Colburne just stood there for a moment

blinking, perhaps unable to believe the man's rude comment. "You are thinking of my brother." He offered his arm to Diana. "Miss Hemshawe, may I escort you back into the house?"

"Yes, thank you." She gave Lord Swindon a nod and then walked off with Lord Colburne, not even daring to turn around and look back.

As soon as they were a few feet away, she whispered, "Thank you."

"You are trembling. I'm not surprised," he said just as quietly.

"He, he caught me off guard," she admitted.

# Chapter Nineteen

"And what were you doing out here on your own, anyway?" Lord Colburne asked as he slowly walked Diana back to the ballroom.

"Waiting for Lord Rosebury to fetch me a glass of lemonade," she said. She hated the fact that his voice was colder than usual.

"Lord Rosebury? I saw him talking with some woman wearing a dress cut so low she was in danger of an indecent display."

Diana couldn't help but laugh at his description, but said, "Oh dear, yes, that does sound like something the gentleman would do. I imagine with a display like that, he forgot all about me."

"I'm very sorry," he said with sincere sympathy in his voice.

"Oh, no, it's perfectly fine. I have no interest in the gentleman, but I did want a glass of lemonade. And then, of course, it would have deterred Lord Swindon had I been accompanied as Lord Rosebury had promised."

"Well, come, and we will fetch your refreshment together," Lord Colburne said, giving her hand a pat as it rested on his arm.

Once again, Lord Colburne had the incredible

ability to make Diana feel warm and cared for. She gave a silent sigh of relief.

~*~

If he could have, Andrew would have hauled off Lord Rosebury and given him a sound thrashing. He'd left an innocent, vulnerable young lady outside in the garden alone while he'd stood ogling some woman's bosom. Sadly, Andrew could do nothing but see to it that Diana was taken care of in the way she deserved.

He saw her thirst quenched and then when the next quadrille began, invited her to dance. "If you wouldn't mind taking the chance, I would be honored if you'd dance with me—and I promise to do my best not to step on your toes."

Miss Hemshawe gave a laugh. "Well, at least I know if you break any you can tend to them afterward."

He burst out laughing. "Yes, absolutely. It's a promise!"

He led her onto the floor, admitting, "It's been a rather long time since I've danced."

"You've been too busy with your work?"

"Yes. I was invited to a few parties in Paris, but I was usually too tired to attend," he said.

"I understand. It must be exhausting..." She continued speaking, but he couldn't listen to her and to the man calling the dance at the same time, and Andrew decided it would be better if he knew what he were doing and then apologize to Miss Hemshawe later.

The music began and Andrew did his best to remember the steps, concentrating on not stepping on any toes and taking Miss Hemshawe's hand to spin her about at the right time. He kept a close eye on the man next to him and followed along with what he was doing. Miss Hemshawe quickly caught on to the fact that he was concentrating and stopped talking.

After they had progressed a few places ahead in the line, she finally said, "You're doing very well, my lord."

Her smile was so sweet and encouraging, Andrew nearly lost his place in the dance. He grinned back at her like an idiot. "Thank you. I'm sorry for having to concentrate so," he admitted.

"No, that's fine. I understand. I think I would have been lost too if I hadn't danced in a number of years."

"I never attended many parties where there was dancing when I was in school," he admitted before returning his attention to the movements of the dance.

"You concentrated on your studies," she said, passing him to take the hand of the man next to him.

"Yes," he said, taking another lady's hand. He turned her about and then managed to end up in the correct position across from Miss Hemshawe once again. He was just about to step forward to take her hand when someone tapped him on the shoulder. He stopped and turned around but was quickly given a little push to move out of the way of the other dancers, who were continuing the complicated steps of the dance. Luckily he and Miss Hemshawe were the very last couple. While it would disturb the dancing of the couple next to them, the rest of the dancers wouldn't even notice

He stepped away.

"Lord Colburne?" the footman asked.

"Yes."

"You're needed. There's been an emergency in the card room."

"Oh! Er, wait." He turned to see where Miss Hemshawe was, but she'd just arrived at his elbow. "My sincere apologies—" he started.

"No, that's perfectly all right. It sounds as if a physician is needed, is that right?" she asked the footman.

"Yes, Miss. Immediately. It's Lord Bradmore. He's collapsed."

"Oh dear!" Miss Hemshawe said. She turned to Andrew. "You go on. I'll find my chaperone."

"Thank you for understanding," he said, before rushing off in the footman's wake. He owed that girl a huge bouquet of flowers, he thought as he went. Maybe a box of sweets as well. She was truly wonderful and understanding—not to mention beautiful and well... His mind started to drift into the future, but he quickly recalled it, reminding himself he had a patient to attend to.

Lord Bradmore was a larger man and currently sprawled on the floor of the card room surrounded by at least five or six other gentlemen.

"Excuse me, excuse me," Andrew said, pushing a man aside. He suddenly realized the fellow was his father. They made eye contact for a moment before Andrew refocused on the man on the floor. "Please, give him some room to breathe," Andrew told the other men.

"There's the rub," one of the men said. "He's not breathing."

Andrew knelt next to Lord Bradmore and put his hand above his mouth and nose. No, he was not breathing. Andrew gave a sharp strike to the man's chest then held his hand over his mouth and nose again. Nothing. He pressed a good deal of his weight on the man's chest and then released it. He did so again, and again at the pace he thought his heart should be beating. He'd read of physicians in the Netherlands doing this with some success to revive who'd drowned.

After a few minutes, the fellow began coughing and took in a deep breath. Andrew stopped and placed two fingers against his neck to feel his pulse. It was weak, but it was there.

"What..." Lord Bradmore croaked, opening his eyes.

"It's all right, my lord. I'm a physician. You're going to be all right, now," Andrew told him.

A round of applause started and quickly spread throughout the room. Andrew looked up, shocked. He'd completely forgotten he had an audience. He held up his hand. "Please, thank you, but we need to get Lord Bradmore home and cared for."

"Lady Bradmore is here," someone said from the doorway. A woman came rushing into the room. "Bradmore? Brad... Oh my God, Bradmore! What's happened to him?"

"He's had a coronary event, but I'd like to get him home and see to him," Andrew said.

"And who are you?" she asked, staring at him.

"He's a talented physician and my son," Lord Darby said, stepping forward. "And he just saved your husband's life."

"Oh," the woman said, turning to look at Andrew's father and then back at him. "Well, then..." She turned and motioned to some footmen behind her. "Help Lord Bradmore to his feet and fetch our coach," she commanded.

"Where do you live? I'll just run home and fetch my medical bag and then join you," Andrew said, standing.

"I'll take you in my carriage. I know where to

go," his father said, stepping forward.

Andrew nodded. They paused to watch as the footman got Lord Bradmore to his feet and then followed them out of the house. After they had gotten into his father's carriage, Andrew turned to him. "Why were you there, at the ball?"

"Can I not attend a ball?" his father asked, sitting back.

"You can, it's just odd for you to do so, considering my mother's health," Andrew answered.

"Well, if truth be told, I was there to see that you danced with the right sorts of girls," his father admitted.

"You were there to spy on me?" Andrew couldn't believe the nerve of his father.

"I was not spying. I was...overseeing."

"Father, I have told you this once already, and I'm going to tell you just once more, stay out of my personal life. Do not tell me what I should and shouldn't do, or who I should spend my time with. It is none of your business."

"It most definitely is my business! You're my son and my heir!"

"And an adult who can make his own decisions," Andrew informed him.

"So, who *was* that girl you were dancing with?" his father asked, looking out the window.

"Miss Hemshawe. The daughter of Baron Rivers. And how do you know I was dancing, weren't you in the card room?"

"I was, when Bradmore collapsed. But before that I was in the ballroom watching you. You were in the garden for some time with the young lady, I noticed."

"Nothing untoward happened, I assure you." At

least not on my part, he added silently to himself. It was none of his father's business what had occurred in the garden, and he didn't want word to get out of Miss Hemshawe's unfortunate incident, just in case someone took it into their head to insist on a marriage of convenience between her and Lord Swindon. They had been alone together, but only he knew it had been unwanted.

No, truly, Andrew couldn't think of anything worse than that getting out.

~July 1~

Diana almost hadn't heard about the race being held at Epsom Downs in time to enter. Luckily, she'd run into an acquaintance she'd known in France who mentioned it to her. She'd sent off three notes immediately—one to the organizer of the race, entering her name into the race; one to Audley telling him to place a bet for her to win; and finally, one to Lord Colburne asking him if he was interested in attending once more.

She heard back the same day from each gentleman. The organizer confirmed she was entered to race, Audley confirmed he'd place her bet for her, and Lord Colburne said he'd see her there. Everything was falling into place beautifully.

The day of the race was wonderfully clear, and Diana looked forward to another easy win. With this, she would be very close to having all the money she needed to satisfy Lord Swindon and get rid of him from her life once and for all. She could hardly wait.

She was just on her way out of the breakfast room that morning when she met her mother coming in to break her own fast.

"Ah, Diana," her mother said, stopping her. "Do you have plans for today?"

"Yes, as a matter of fact, I'm going to be

participating in a race at Epsom Downs," she said.

"Really?" Her mother seemed to think about this for a moment and then said, "Would you mind if I came along? I've never seen you race."

What was with her mother, Diana wondered. First she was concerned with Diana being alone when she'd been in Germany, and now she wanted to come with her to a race? If Diana didn't know better, she'd think her mother actually cared. Could she want to have a real relationship with her?

Diana didn't know, but she decided this could only be a good thing. She had to be an adult about this and put aside her feelings of animosity. It wasn't easy, but it was the smart thing to do.

Diana quickly drew her lips up into a smile and said, "Of course, I would love for you to come! I was planning on leaving about noon; the race begins at three, and it takes about an hour or so to get there. Would that be convenient for you?"

"Perfect." Her mother gave a nod and started into the breakfast room. "Oh, how do you go—do you ride or take the carriage?"

"The carriage. My horse went down yesterday with the groom."

"Excellent, I'll meet you at twelve, then." Her mother gave her a happy smile and went to eat.

This was certainly going to be an interesting day, Diana though as she went off to have a chat with her father. She should definitely tell him of this nice turn of events and the positive changes in her relationship with her mother. She was certain he'd be happy to hear it, if sad that he wouldn't be able to come along to the race.

~*~

Diana leaned over Nike's neck later that day, urging the thoroughbred to go faster. This time, she hadn't seen Lord Colburne before the start of the race. In fact, she hadn't seen him at all today. Perhaps he hadn't been able to come after all. It was disappointing, but perhaps he'd had a medical emergency he'd needed to take care of. It was a shame, she'd been prepared not to allow his presence to rile her at all this time.

The race was mixed men and women, but it was an odd assortment of people. There were people she'd known from the continent, including her friend who'd told her about the race, who were experienced riders like herself. There were others who seemed to be looking at this like a lark—just a fun way to pass an afternoon.

She quickly passed all of the horses and was in a comfortable lead when a chestnut came from behind her, flying and flailing like he'd been spooked. Occasionally, the horse bucked as if it were trying to get its rider from his back, but then once again would put on a burst of speed. It was the strangest thing Diana had ever seen. She kept as much of a distance as she could between herself and the other horse without losing her place. They crossed the finish line with Diana in second.

She dismounted and handed her horse off to her groom, while still keeping a sharp eye on the other horse. It finally succeeded in throwing his rider. As soon as its back was free, it started bucking and kicking up its forelegs as if it were possessed.

Some people started shouting; others just kept their distance. No one could get close enough to the horse to calm him down.

Eventually, after five minutes or more of this erratic behavior, the animal ran out of steam. But to Diana's horror, instead of just settling down and walking it off, the animal completely collapsed to the ground.

She watched as a couple of young men approached the animal warily. It was still blowing and foaming at the mouth. One of the men started to stroke the horse's neck, encouraging it to calm down.

"What did you give him?" she overheard one of the young men say to the one who was stroking the horse.

"Just what you told me. You didn't say he'd go crazy. If I lose my horse because of you—"

"You drugged the horse?" asked another man, who looked to be older and more in charge.

"Rhiner told me it would just give him a little more energy," the horse's owner said.

The older man looked at the one named Rhiner and then back to the man on the ground. "You disgust me. Both of you. You've been disqualified," he informed the fellow still petting his horse.

# Chapter Twenty

The man in charge turned away from the two young men and looked about for a moment. He then shouted loudly to be sure everyone heard him, "Minotaur and his rider forfeit the race. The winner is Nike!" He turned toward Diana and gave her a firm nod.

Her mouth dropped open for a second, but she caught herself and gave the man a small curtsy of thanks.

The regular mumble of voices following a race grew louder as the new winner was announced. Wagers were collected and cursing could be heard as those who'd bet on Minotaur had to pay up.

Diana turned and saw her cousin Audley concluding an exchange of money with another man. She walked up to his side just as the other man bowed and walked off in the other direction.

"Well, that was exciting," she said, by way of greeting.

He turned. "Yes! I heard the other horse was drugged."

"Yes. I overheard the owner talking with a friend of his. I sincerely hope the horse will be all right. It would be too sad if he had to be put down because of his owner's stupidity."

"I couldn't agree more." He looked down at the purse in his hand, seeming to weigh it. "This is yours, but I'm not going give it to you until you tell me why you need it—and I want the truth, Diana." He stared straight and meaningfully into her eyes, waiting for an answer.

She looked down at the purse. It probably contained enough to bring her tally up to three thousand pounds. She was nearly there. One more bet and she would have all she needed to get Lord Swindon out of her life for good.

She looked up at her cousin. "Fine. You keep it. You'll need it for my next wager anyway." And with that she turned and walked away, ignoring the fact that he kept calling after her. She knew he wouldn't stop pestering her until she told him the truth. The easiest thing was to simply walk away.

She needed to find her mother, anyway.

~*~

Andrew arrived just after the start of the race. He'd had to check in on Lord Bradmore before he could take the time off. Happily, his patient was resting comfortably. As soon as he figured out the correct dosage of foxglove and how long it took to take effect, he would feel more comfortable prescribing it to Lord Bradmore and any other heart patients he had.

He was watching his mother closely, but so far there'd been very little change in her condition. The only thing slightly encouraging was her report that she'd had to urinate more frequently. He hoped this meant it was working.

As he approached the rails, he saw a familiar face watching the race avidly.

"Lady Rivers, what a surprise to see you here," he said, squeezing between two men who were also watching.

"Oh, Lord Colburne, what are you doing here?" she asked.

"Miss Hemshawe invited me," he said.

"Really?" She seemed to find this extremely interesting, and Andrew almost wished he'd made up some other excuse.

"Er, yes. How is she doing?" he asked, turning back to the race.

"Oh, quite well, I believe. Look, there she is," Lady Rivers pointed to the unmistakable rider in blue. There only seemed to be two women riding in the race, along with six men.

"What is that other horse doing, do you suppose?" Lady Rivers asked, as Miss Hemshawe was overtaken by another horse that seemed to be running wild.

"I don't know." Andrew watched curiously as the other horse tried to buck and run at the same time. It managed to keep the lead mainly because it seemed as if Miss Hemshawe was doing the safe thing of keeping her distance.

He and Lady Rivers watched the end of the race in silence, fascinated by the crazy antics of the first horse. Once the race was won and the winning horse finally rid itself of its rider, things got very disturbing. No one seemed to be able to control the enormous beast as it jumped and kicked in every direction.

"Oh, please, Lord Colburne, take me away from here. This is too frightening," Lady Rivers said, pulling on his sleeve.

"Of course, my lady. I have to agree with you. I'm not a fan of horses to begin with, but that one—"

"It's disturbed and dangerous. Please, let's go."

She worked her way through the crowd. Andrew followed.

When they'd gotten well away from the track, she finally paused. "Which is your carriage?" she looked around.

"It's over there, but how did you arrive, my lady? Might someone be looking for you afterwards?"

"Oh, yes, you are right. I came down with Diana, naturally. Oh, wait, there's her groom. Smart fellow, taking her horse away from all the excitement." She rushed over to a man leading Miss Hemshawe's horse away.

"You there," she called out to the groom. "You are Diana Hemshawe's groom, are you not?"

"Oui, madam," he said in a strong French accent. He stopped and bowed to her.

"I am her mother, Lady Rivers. Could you please inform her that Lord Colburne is going to take me home?"

"If I see 'er, my lady, I will do so."

"Very good." She gave him a nod then turned back to Andrew. "She'll be informed."

"Very well. Please, come this way," Andrew said, holding out his arm for her.

She took it, but it was clear she was still upset over seeing the wild horse. "I'm sure everything will calm down soon, my lady."

"I'm afraid I'm not very fond of horses," she admitted as he handed her up into his phaeton.

"May I admit a secret to you?" he asked, getting up behind her.

She turned and looked at him, her eyes still a little wide and nervous.

"Neither am I," he said, giving her a wink and

starting them off toward London.

She managed a smile. "Don't let my daughter hear you say that. You would quickly find yourself in her bad graces."

"I actually have already told her so, and she has been kind enough to overlook this little flaw of mine," he admitted.

"Really? Now *that* is something," she said with a little laugh.

She was calming down. That was good.

Andrew felt it was a fine time to change the subject, so he asked, "Have you given Lord Rivers a dose of the foxglove yet?"

The lady looked down and fiddled with her gloved fingers. "No, I'm afraid I haven't." She looked back up at him. "You're certain it will make him better?"

"I just gave a dose of it to my own mother, my lady. I am that confident in it," he told her.

"Really? Has she heart problems as well?"

"She has dropsy, which, yes, is also a heart condition. Slightly different from Lord Rivers' but related."

"And the same medicine will work on them both?"

"Well, if the foxglove doesn't work with Lord Rivers, I do have another herb we can try, but I believe it will—once you give it to him," he said meaningfully.

She sighed. "Yes, I don't suppose it wouldn't work at all if I don't."

He gave a little laugh. "No, it won't."

They passed the rest of the journey back to London in good accord, talking about inconsequential things.

~*~

That evening Andrew had just settled back in his room to do something he hadn't done in too long—read a novel. After his long day of driving to and from Epsom Downs, he just wanted to relax.

The vision of Miss Hemshawe being offered a purse full of money was still haunting him, but he was determined to put it out of his mind. He didn't know who the man she'd been speaking to was, and it was none of his concern.

He might have thought the purse was her prize for winning the race, but he didn't remember whether she'd been given one after the last race she'd won. She'd also refused the money, which was very strange.

It had looked like she and the man knew each other, and Andrew remembered seeing him with her at the last race she'd run, but then they'd seem to have been on good terms. This time he had clearly said something to upset Miss Hemshawe. If Andrew hadn't been showing Lady Rivers to his phaeton at the time, he would have intervened.

But no, it was none of his business. Miss Hemshawe's personal business was just that, her personal business, and he had no right to stick his nose in where it didn't belong. But oh, how he wished it did belong there. If he had his way, he would make all of Miss Hemshawe's business his business, and all of her his.

The thought put a smile to his lips. With that happy thought in mind, he sat back with his novel, opening the book and thinking that a glass of brandy would make this moment even better.

He'd just read the first sentence when there was a knock on his door. He nearly groaned aloud. He withheld it, however, and instead called out for the person to enter.

A footman walked in and said, "Your father wishes to speak with you, my lord."

"You don't think he can be put off until tomorrow, do you?" He paused, knowing it was an unfair question to ask of the fellow who was simply following orders. "No, no, don't answer that. Very well, I'm coming."

Andrew got up and the footman turned to leave. "What sort of mood is he in?" Andrew asked the man's departing back.

The footman paused and thought about it for a moment before turning around to say, "He seems to be in a pensive mood, my lord."

"Not angry? Not determined?"

"No, definitely neither of those."

Andrew nodded. "All right. Maybe this won't be as bad as the last time he called me down to his study to have a word." He gave the man a pat on the back as he passed him and went out to see what his father was feeling pensive about.

"Ah, Colburne!" his father greeted him as he walked into the room.

Andrew stopped. That was the very first time his father had ever called him by his new title. Until now, it had always been his given name. "Good evening, Father. I was told you wanted to have a word."

"Yes, yes. Brandy?" Lord Darby asked, taking his glass to the side table to refill it.

"I would love one, thank you." Andrew came forward and took the glass that was soon proffered to him.

"I've been thinking," his father said as he poured

out a glass for himself. "While I would like you to take your new responsibilities more seriously, I think I'm beginning to understand your devotion to your occupation."

"Really?" Andrew asked skeptically.

"Yes." His father took a hearty sip from his glass. "I watched you tend to Lord Bradmore the other night and it was... Well, it was impressive. You took a man who had collapsed and was no longer breathing—honestly, for a moment we all thought he was dead—and you got him breathing and well enough to walk out of the room on his own. That's a bloody miracle in my book." He raised his glass to Andrew in salute.

Andrew nodded, raising his glass as well. "Thank you. That actually means a lot to me." Just his father acknowledging the fact that what Andrew did was meaningful meant a lot.

"Now, that doesn't mean I'm completely letting you off the hook," his father continued.

Andrew could only laugh. "No, of course not."

"I still want you to spend at least one evening a week at White's, building relationships with the other men there. They are the most influential people in this country—or, in the case of the younger ones—will be. You need to know them and be friends with them, so when your time comes, you will be able to build coalitions and—"

"Father, I told you I'm not going to take my seat in Parliament," Andrew said, interrupting him.

"That's what you say now, but you never know. You might want to someday, and knowing the right people won't hurt." His father paused and then added, "And you might find some new patients there. I can tell you there are a lot more like Bradmore—just ready to fall dead of dropsy or whatever."

Andrew laughed. "That I believe!" It was clear his father was making an effort here, so Andrew thought it only fair he did the same. "Very well, I will be happy to join you at White's some evenings. And I will take more interest in what is happening in Parliament, even if I don't choose to participate." He paused and then added. "Perhaps, after Mother is feeling better in another month or so, we can all go up to Darby, and you can show me what's what at the estate—farming or cattle or whatever else. Goodness, I don't even know," he realized suddenly.

It was his father's turn to laugh. "Sheep, son, sheep and mining."

"Mining? Really?"

Lord Darby settled down in a chair by the empty fireplace and nodded. He picked up a book by his side. "I thought I'd read this book by Robert Southey, *Madoc*. Have you read it? It's apparently quite popular."

# Chapter Twenty-One

Diana was sitting and reading the following morning when her mother joined her in the drawing room.

"Where are the flowers you and Lord Colburne picked?" her mother asked, coming into the room.

"They're there on the side table," Diana said. The flowers had been sitting in water for the past few days and Diana had wondered if her mother was going to use them to prepare the medicine for her father before they died.

"Oh, good." Lady Rivers picked up the vase and started out of the room.

"Are you going to make the medicine?" Diana asked.

"Yes. I promised Lord Colburne that I would."

"Should I come with you and help?"

"You don't need to bother. Lord Colburne sent me the instructions," her mother said and continued out of the room.

"It isn't a bother," Diana said, putting down her book and jumping up to follow her mother into her bedchamber.

Lady Rivers shuffled through a drawer in her

dressing table for a moment while Diana waited. She then moved to the other drawer before standing up and putting a hand to her mouth.

"Is everything all right?" Diana asked.

"What? Oh yes, yes. Er, I seem to have misplaced his instructions." She gave Diana a little smile. "It's all right. I remember them well enough."

"Are you certain?"

"Yes, of course." She headed down the stairs to the kitchen with Diana following in her wake.

She watched as the water was dumped out, and her mother started to sort through the flowers. "Such a shame to destroy the pretty blooms," she said as she began to pluck off the leaves.

Diana took another stem and began to do the same.

After tearing off the leaves and flowers, her mother took a knife from a drawer and stood with it hovering over the stem.

Diana didn't say anything, just watched. She didn't remember Lord Colburne saying anything about the stem. He had spoken of the leaves and the fact that you didn't use the flowers, but beyond that she had no idea how the medicine was made. When he'd given her mother instructions on how to prepare it, she hadn't been listening, so maybe he'd told her to use the stem as well.

"You're certain you remember—" Diana began.

"I do," her mother said, cutting her off.

Not wanting to antagonize her mother any further, or to distract her, Diana closed her mouth and watched.

After a moment, Lady Rivers cut into the stem and placed a couple inches of it, along with the leaves, into a pot. She added fresh water and then put it over the fire. They watched as it came to a boil, and then Lady Rivers moved it off to the side a little so that it would catch the heat of the flames, but not be at a full boil.

They both watched it simmer for some time, with Diana's mother giving it a stir now and then. She removed it and carefully poured the liquid into a teacup.

"How much are you supposed to give him?" Diana asked.

"He said not to give him too much, but, well, if a little medicine will make him a little better, then perhaps a lot of medicine will make him much better faster," she said with a shrug.

"I don't know, Mother, perhaps you should just give him a little at first," Diana said, looking into the cup. The smell of the concoction was harsh and bitter and an odd sort of pale green.

"Hmm...perhaps. Well, we'll let him decide how much to drink." She put the cup on a saucer and carried it up the stairs to Lord Rivers' chamber.

He was sitting in his favorite chair by the window with his broken leg propped up in front of him on a stool. "Ah, if it isn't my two beautiful ladies," he said, greeting them with a smile.

"We've got this foxglove medicine for you," Lady Rivers said, handing him the cup.

He sniffed at it, wrinkling his nose at the smell. "I'm to drink this?"

"We don't quite know how much," Diana started. She was shushed by her mother, though.

"Yes. Just have some of it. I don't believe you're supposed to have it all," Lady Rivers said. Diana was happy she wasn't pushing too much on him. She just wished her mother hadn't lost the instructions.

Her father gave a shrug, pinched his nose closed with one hand and tipped the cup back pouring the contents into his mouth. "Ugh! That's awful," he said. His face paled immediately and he began choking.

"No! I... I don't feel..." He sputtered, dropping the teacup to clutch at his stomach. It shattered as it hit the floor.

Diana ran for the chamber pot, but he was gagging by the time she got back with it. He seemed to be trying not to lose what he'd just consumed, but it was a losing battle.

Her mother's eyes were wide, and she'd starting wringing her hands. "Diana, maybe you'd better go for the doctor."

"Yes!" She pushed the chamber pot into her mother's hands and ran out of the room, just as her father started to vomit.

She didn't waste time, but ran straight to the stables. She grabbed Nike from her stall and hopped onto her back from the mounting block without even bothering with a saddle. She was well aware of the fact she was wearing an ordinary morning dress, so she sat with one knee up as if she had a sidesaddle. It was a precarious position, but for the few blocks to Lord Colburne's home she could manage it.

With one swift kick and a whisper in the horse's ear, they took off at a fast trot—a full gallop through the streets of Mayfair would have been impossible, and certainly not in her current position.

She reached the home of the Marquess of Darby quickly. She slid off the horse and ran to pound on the door. It was opened with frustrating slowness by an aged butler who stared at her malevolently. "Yes?"

"I need Lord Colburne immediately. This is an

emergency! My father is dying!" she said as quickly as she could.

The man recoiled. "And who are you?"

"Oh, my God! I'm Diana Hemshawe, Lord Colburne has been treating my father." She didn't have time for niceties. She barged into the house. "Lord Colburne!" she shouted up the stairwell. "Lord Col—"

"Miss! I must ask you to refrain..." the butler began in the most severe tones.

"What? What's wrong?" Lord Colburne appeared at the top of the stairs, and a moment later started running down them, taking them two at a time. "Miss Hemshawe, what's happened?"

"It's my father. Please, you must come immediately." She grabbed his arm, but he pulled back.

"Just a moment. Let me get my medical bag and I'll be right with you. Not a minute!" he said as he turned and raced back up the stairs.

He was true to his word, and a moment later, he was running down once more, his medical bag in one hand, his hat in another.

She rushed out to the street where she'd just left her horse standing. A footman in the Darby livery was standing at her head caressing her nose.

"Oh, thank you," Diana said.

"Wait," Lord Colburne said, "you have your horse? I can't—"

"You must, my lord, please! You must!" Diana pleaded. She'd completely forgot about his fear of horses. She turned to the footman. "Give me a leg up." He dutifully cupped his hands, and she placed her foot into them and then hopped onto the horse's bare back. "And now his lordship. Please, Lord

Colburne, just get behind me and I'll handle everything. It's not far and will be so much faster."

"Oh God," he whimpered, but he did as she said. She was momentarily distracted as she felt the warmth of his body press up against her back. She gave herself a good shake, however. "Put your arm around my waist and hold on," she instructed. This was going to be more than precarious, but they had no choice. She put the reins in one hand and held onto Nike's mane with the other. She settled herself as securely as she could, but still her breath caught when she felt his hand come hesitantly around her waist.

"Don't forget to hold on with your legs," she said, as she gave her horse the go ahead.

"Oh God," Lord Colburne said a little more strongly this time as they started into a slow trot and then sped up. "Oh, my hat!"

Diana took a second to glance behind them to see his hat tumble to the ground. "No time to retrieve it, my lord. I'll buy you a new one."

"It's not necessary. It wasn't a favorite. My life, however..." he said, his voice wavering with the motion of the horse.

"Your life is in good hands," she reassured him.

He didn't reply.

It took them only ten minutes to arrive back to her house, where there was a groom waiting for them.

Lord Colburne dismounted clumsily, but managed to stay on his feet. Diana slid off with grace, for once grateful for having to sit sideways, as it did make dismounting easier.

They both ran for Lord Rivers' chamber.

~*~

Lady Rivers was in hysterics, and Lord Rivers was on the floor in a near fetal position clutching his stomach when Andrew ran into the room just ahead of Miss Hemshawe. He would have been trembling and probably sick from that ride, but all of his focus was on his patient. He shoved aside all of his own emotions and narrowed in on what was directly in front of him.

"What happened?" he asked no one in particular.

When Lady Rivers didn't say anything, Miss Hemshawe strode forward and said, "My mother gave him the foxglove tea just like you told her."

Andrew stole a glance up at her from the floor next to Lord Rivers. "Tea? Tea! I didn't say to make tea! I said to make a decoction."

"How does one make a decoction?" Miss Hemshawe asked.

"It's… It's like tea, only more concentrated," he answered shortly. He didn't have time to get more detailed than that just now, he needed to know the particulars. He turned to Lady Rivers. "Did you use just the leaves as I told you?"

The lady burst into more tears but shook her head. "I lost… lost…"

"You lost my instructions?" he asked incredulously.

She could only nod.

"Then why didn't you—" There was no time to argue and point out that the obvious thing would have been for her to ask for them again before doing anything, but the man needed help without delay.

"She used some of the stem as well," Miss Hemshawe said. Thank goodness she, at least, was keeping a level head.

Andrew ground his teeth together to keep himself from saying something inappropriate. "And how much did he take?" he asked, kneeling down on the floor next to the baron. He put two fingers to Lord Rivers' neck to feel his pulse. It was pounding and, not surprisingly, rapid.

"He drank the whole cup," Miss Hemshawe answered.

"My God! Did you want to *kill* him?" Andrew snapped, finally unable to control himself.

Lady Rivers let out a wail.

Andrew reached into his medical bag and pulled out his bottle of ipecac syrup, which he always kept on hand. He measured out a dose and turned Lord Rivers over onto his back. "Here, my lord, this will make you vomit and get the poison out of your system." As he pried open his lordship's mouth, he noticed a chamber pot sitting nearby. It looked like he'd already lost some of what he'd taken in, but clearly there was more.

As soon as the syrup had been poured down his throat, the man started spewing. Andrew caught some on his clothes, but managed to get the chamber pot in place quickly and held Lord Rivers up so he could empty the contents of his stomach.

Within a few minutes he was coughing and spitting, but it was clear that most of the poison was out.

"Here." Miss Hemshawe handed him a wet cloth.

Andrew threw her a small smile of thanks as he took it and wiped her father's face clean. "Let's get you back to bed, my lord," Andrew said. He looked for some assistance, hoping there would be a footman nearby. There was only Miss Hemshawe.

"I can help," she said, stepping forward.

Andrew would have argued she wasn't strong enough, but she crouched down next to her father, grasped him under his armpit, and waited for Andrew to get on his other side. Between the two of them, they managed to lift and carry him to his bed.

Once he was settled, Miss Hemshawe smoothed back his hair from his eyes and adjusted his pillows so he was comfortable. "Is he out of danger now, do you think?" she asked.

Andrew realized she was talking to him and not her father. "Yes, I believe so. He may vomit again if there is any more of the poison in him, but other than that, he should be all right. I suppose I should see to your mother."

He could tell Miss Hemshawe didn't agree from her pursed lips.

"This is entirely her fault," she said, quietly, stepping away from the bed where her father was falling asleep. "She clearly didn't remember your instructions, but she went ahead and did whatever she thought might be right anyway."

Andrew sighed. "I don't understand why she didn't just ask me for the instructions a second time. I would have been happy to write them out for her again."

Miss Hemshawe just shook her head, her eyes glassy with unshed tears. She blinked and they were gone, but not before he reached out and gave her arm a gentle squeeze. He couldn't help but want to touch her. She was so good, so brave and levelheaded in the midst of a true emergency. "Thank you."

Her eyes softened as she looked up at him. She did such strange things to him, making butterflies dance in his stomach and heat go surging through his body all at the same time. He could stare into her beautiful eyes all day...but he had Lady Rivers to see to. She would probably need a dose of laudanum to calm her—she had been quite hysterical when he'd come in.

With a sigh, he said, "I should see your mother."

This time Miss Hemshawe nodded her agreement and showed him to her mother's room next door.

~*~

Diana, once again, had to force herself to attend her weekly meeting of the Ladies' Wagering Whist Society. After the scare they'd had that morning, she really didn't want to leave her father's side. He'd insisted, however, saying he was merely going to sleep and she needed the distraction.

That much was certainly true, she thought as she rode to Lady Norman's home.

She was one of the first to arrive. Only Lady Blakemore and Mrs. Aldridge were already there having tea with Lady Norman.

"Miss Hemshawe, how are you? And more importantly, how is your father?" Lady Norman asked as soon as she'd come in.

Diana curtsied to the ladies before joining them around the teapot. "I'm doing well. My father had been doing better but had a set back this morning when my mother inadvertently gave him too much medicine."

"Oh, dear! I do hope he's all right," Mrs. Aldridge said, allowing her sweet little dog to jump from her lap so the pup could greet Diana properly.

"He is, and he insisted I play cards this afternoon," she said, picking up the dog and putting her on her own lap. Her fur was so soft, it was lovely to stroke. She was the most affectionate little thing Diana had ever met. It calmed Diana just being able to sit and pet the dog.

"Well, I'm glad he did insist you come, although..." Lady Norman paused and looked from one lady to the other before lowering her gaze to the book in which she tallied their points won. The book sat ominously on the table just in front of her. "You may not be," she finished, as she pulled the book onto her lap.

"Oh, dear. I've lost this game, haven't I?" Diana said, playing with Duchess's long soft ears.

"I'm afraid you have," Lady Norman said.

# Chapter Twenty-Two

"I'm not surprised I've lost. I've been so distracted lately with my father's health, and well, I'm not a very good player to begin with," Diana said with a little laugh.

The other ladies smiled at her, but then they all looked to the door as Lydia, Lady Sorrell, and Lady Moreton all came in together.

After they'd all greeted each other, Lady Norman poured tea for all saying, "We only need the duchess and then Diana is going to talk to us—she has come in last in this past game we played."

"Oh, I'm so sorry," Lydia said, reaching out and putting a hand on Diana's arm.

Diana gave her a little smile. "It's all right. I knew it would happen." She continued petting the dog. After rubbing her soft little face under Diana's chin, the pup had settled down on her lap with her head resting on Diana's knees, facing the tea tray with her bottom tucked against Diana's torso. She fit the length of Diana's thighs perfectly.

The Duchess of Kendell came in while Lady Norman was handing out tea. Once everyone had been served, she called for attention. "Ladies, it is, unfortunately, once again time for one of our members to tell us her deepest secret. Miss Hemshawe," Lady Norman said, turning to look at Diana expectantly.

At first Diana wasn't exactly certain what secret to reveal. She really didn't have many. The only one she could think of at the moment was the one that had been preying on her mind almost non-stop for the past few weeks. So with a sigh, she said, "You might have all heard that I've been racing more recently."

"And winning!" Mrs. Aldridge added.

Diana gave her a smile. "Yes, and winning. Well, I've needed to win. It was imperative that I do so. I... I needed the money."

"I hope it wasn't for a gambling debt," Lady Blakemore said with a disapproving sniff.

"Actually, it is. But not one I made," Diana admitted. "I don't know why—truly, I have absolutely no idea what came over him—but before the relay race when my father became ill, he placed a wager for five thousand pounds that we would win the race. He's *never* placed so large a bet before. I can't begin to imagine what he was thinking when he did so," Diana said, shaking her head, still unable to believe her father's stupidity.

"I imagine he was thinking you would win," Lady Moreton said.

"Well, yes, and we probably would have if he hadn't become ill, but still, that's *a lot* of money!" Diana said.

"It's a huge amount," Mrs. Aldridge said nodding.

"Does he not have..." Lady Sorrell asked tentatively.

Diana looked over at her, continuing to pet

Duchess and working hard to keep from petting the dog too hard in her agitation. "No."

"Oh, dear. What's he going to do?" Lady Blakemore asked.

"He doesn't know about it," Diana admitted.

"What?" "How could that be?" a few of the ladies said at once.

"A few days after the race, the man with whom he'd made the bet came to ask for his money. I saw him and told him if he gave me a few weeks' grace, I would get the money for him. I didn't want to disturb my father, whose health was very fragile at that time, with such concerns, so I went to his solicitor on my own. He told me my father simply didn't have the cash. He *has* that much money, and more, but not in cash."

"Could you sell...?"

"I pawned my pearl earrings, but they only brought me a very small amount. I don't own any other jewelry—my mother has all the family heirlooms," Diana explained.

"Did you tell your mother?" Lady Norman asked.

"No. I didn't want to involve her, or... Or let her know what a silly thing my father had done," Diana said.

There was silence for a moment as all the ladies digested this.

"I've been riding in as many races as I can and having my cousin make wagers for me. I've earned three thousand pounds this way, so I just need another two, and then I'll be able to pay off the debt. But it's been..." Diana stopped and bent over the little dog on her lap, burying her face in the soft fur.

A hand rubbed up and down her back

consolingly.

"Miss Hemshawe, you only needed to tell us of this unfortunate circumstance and we would have been able to lend you the money," the Duchess of Kendell said.

"Yes! We could have pooled our resources and come up with the amount for you," Lady Blakemore added.

Diana sat up again, fishing inside her reticule for her handkerchief. Another was pressed into her hand before she could find her own. She gave Lydia a watery smile.

"Thank you. It was too embarrassing to admit to anyone. I'm sure you understand," she said to the kind ladies who offered their support.

"And the gentleman to whom you owe this money?" Lady Sorrell asked.

"He is no gentleman, I can assure you," Diana said, wiping away the tear that had slid down her cheek. "Oh, he is a peer of the realm, but at first he didn't want to give me any time at all to come up with the money—he instead said that I could pay him back by agreeing to marry him!"

There were gasps around the room.

"He has been pestering me since then with unwanted attentions," Diana added, "going so far as to corner me in the garden at Lady Middleton's ball. If it hadn't been for Lord Colburne coming along just when he did... Well, it would have been extremely unpleasant."

"My goodness!" Lady Blakemore said.

"Oh, how awful!" Lydia put in.

"He sounds like a cad," the duchess added.

"He is and it was awful, but very soon I'm going to be free of him," Diana said.

"Is there anything we can do to help?" Lady Norman said.

"No, thank you, my lady. As I said, I'm nearly there. One more race and I will have what I owe him and possibly more. Once he is paid off, I hope never to see the man again."

"Well, good for you, Miss Hemshawe, in managing this awful situation on your own," Lady Moreton said.

"Yes, indeed, you've clearly been very strong and clever in handling this," Mrs. Aldridge added.

"I don't think I would have been able to manage so well," Lydia put in.

Diana was finally able to smile and relax. She had friends. Good friends. And it made all the difference just knowing they were there for her should she ever truly need them. She didn't quite know why she didn't come to them at the beginning and admit the whole story to them then. They would have found a way to come up with the money, and then she and her father could have paid them back slowly once her father was better She would have been able to manage so much better without all of the stress she'd been under for the past few weeks.

Yes, that was what good friends like this did. Diana had never had such friends before, but she was very glad she had them now.

~*~

Albert was lying in his bed half reading, half dozing, that evening when there was a tap on his door. A moment later Sophia popped her head in. "Are you sleeping?" she whispered.

"No, come in," he answered.

She did so but stopped short of his bed. "I... I just wanted to apologize."

"For what?"

She dropped her hands to her sides. "For nearly killing you this morning? I assure you, Rivers, it wasn't intentional."

He gave a little laugh at the thought she might actually have meant to poison him.

"You're laughing?" she asked incredulously.

"I'm sorry, but it's just so funny. Come here, Sophie." He patted the bed next to him.

She came forward and sat gingerly on the edge.

He took her soft, small hand in his own. "We may not have had the happiest marriage. We may not be the most compatible couple. But I know with absolute certainty you would never intentionally try to kill me."

She breathed out a little sigh. "I wouldn't. And while it is true ours has been an unusual marriage, I still..." Sophie paused and turned her face away, looking like she was thinking hard about what she was about to say.

Albert waited patiently, wishing he had an inkling of what she might be thinking. They'd never been able to tell what was going through each other's mind. They were just such very different people. They had different interests, they thought differently... Truly, it was probably only because they'd spent so little time together that they were still as close as they were. It wasn't because he didn't care for her though. It honestly wasn't that—

"I still love you," she said, breaking into his thoughts.

That stopped him. "You what?"

She gave a little laugh. "I love you, Albert. I always have, ever since we met at that awful house party."

"Really?"

"You were so dashing and handsome. So very different from anyone I'd ever met. I was absolutely knocked flat by you—your charm and exuberance for life. You were so adventurous and passionate. I was just a quiet little mouse next to you."

"You were—are—sweet and gentle and yes, quiet, but I found that utterly charming," he said, remembering so well how enthralled he was with this soft-spoken, brilliant girl. "You were so clever. You saw everything and could interpret everything going on around you. And you are so lovely, still. You haven't lost any of your beauty, Sophia. How is it that when I'm so old and weathered, you've hardly changed a bit?"

She giggled. "I stayed home and protected myself while you were out gallivanting across Europe."

"Ah, yes, that's right."

They were quiet for a moment, each one remembering the past.

"I was so scared," she said quietly.

He looked up at her.

"When it looking like you were dying this morning. I mean, it was terrifying with you lying there curled up on the floor."

"I thought I was going to die too," he agreed.

"Thank goodness for Diana, who had the good sense to run for the doctor," she said.

"And Colburne, who was able to come right away."

"Yes. He's very good."

"I love you too, Sophie," Albert said, realizing he hadn't said so.

"Do you? Even though?"

He gave a little laugh. "Yes, even though."

She ran a hand down the side of his scratchy face. He turned so he could press his lips to her palm.

"I'm a very lucky man to have you, Sophia."

"And I am a very lucky woman—and I want to keep you around for a very long time."

~July 3~

Diana had just come in from a nice ride and was about to get changed when there was a knock on her chamber door. She opened it to find a footman there.

"There's a Lord Swindon here to see you, Miss Hemshawe," he informed her.

Diana took an involuntary step back. She did not want to meet that man alone; she didn't want him in her house.

"Tell him I'm not at home to visitors," she told George.

He bowed and went off to deliver the message.

She'd taken out the dress she was going to change into when there was another knock. George was there once more, this time looking uncomfortable.

"He says he won't be put off. He insists on seeing you."

"My word!" Diana exclaimed. The nerve of the man!

"What would you have me do?" George rolled his hands together as if he were readying for a fight. That wasn't the answer, though.

It looked like she had no choice but to meet the man. But if she had to meet him, she would do so on her own terms, and outside of this house. She couldn't stand the thought of him even being in her home. It would also be safest if neither her father nor mother were aware she was meeting him—there would be too many awkward questions she would not be able to answer.

She lifted her head and said, "Tell him I will meet him at the gate to Hyde Park in half an hour, and then show him out the door."

George looked slightly disappointed but nodded. "Very well, Miss. May I come with you to the park—just to make sure you are safe?"

Diana nearly laughed. "Yes, George, you can. I'd appreciate it greatly."

He smiled and nodded before going off to deliver the message.

Diana decided to wear a dress with a higher neckline than the one she'd originally taken out, and paired that with a navy blue spencer. She would probably be warm, but she wanted to get across the idea that she was doing all she could to make herself as unattractive to this man as possible. Maybe then he'd leave her alone—and, of course, she had to pay him what she owed, which she would be able to do soon enough.

She arrived at the gate to the park precisely half an hour later with George in tow.

"My lord," Diana said, striding up to where he was standing and looking at his watch.

He looked up and pocketed his watch. "Right on time. I do like punctuality," he said, meeting her. He took her elbow and guided her off to one side of the gate so they would be out of the way of traffic—foot and otherwise.

"You wanted to have a word, my lord?" Diana asked. She just wanted this over with as quickly as possible.

"Yes. As I believe I mentioned when we met the other night at the Middleton's ball, it's has been well over the two-week deadline I allowed you. When can I expect to see my money?"

Diana did her best not to wring her hands, keeping them firmly at her side. "I almost have it all. I'm nearly there. I just need one more week, my lord. Surely, you can be a gentleman enough to allow me that?"

She could see him clench his jaw, the sinews in his neck standing out. Clearly, she'd hit on a nerve with her comment. He regained control of his emotions and spread wide his lips in what she assumed was some sort of smile. Taking a step closer, he took hold of her hand in both of his. "Miss Hemshawe, this can all go away, you know. It can all be taken care of so easily and quickly if you'd just agree to marry me." He pulled her unwilling hand up to his lips.

Not wanting to cause a scene in public or alert George into action, she forced herself to stand there, unmoving, while he kissed the back of her hand, grateful for the glove between her skin and his lips. The moment she could do so, she snatched her hand back. "My lord, I have already given you my answer to that question twice. My response remains the same. I will have your money as soon as I can, I assure you. Good day."

She didn't wait for him to respond, and she didn't give him a chance to call her back. Instead, she jumped right out into the street and walked as quickly as she could to get as far away from the man as she could. She was nearly a block away when she heard footsteps running up behind her. She almost didn't turn, fearing that it was Lord Swindon following her, but curiosity had her glancing behind her.

She breathed easily when she saw it was merely George catching up to her.

"I beg your pardon, Miss Hemshawe," he said. "You slipped in between two carriages so quickly, I couldn't... I needed to wait for the traffic to clear."

"It's quite all right, George. I'm sorry I lost you for a moment there. I just... I needed to get away from that man. He gives me the chills."

"I understand, Miss. He does seem a bit...off to me as well."

She gave him a grateful smile, and they walked the rest of the way home in comfortable silence.

Diana just didn't know what she was going to do to get that money within a week. She could appeal to the ladies of the Whist Society, and she would if she absolutely had to. She just prayed that another race would come up so she could earn the money properly.

# Chapter Twenty-Three

"Well, my lady, how have you fared with your new diet?" Andrew asked, coming into Lady Buton's private sitting room.

She was sprawled on a gold damask sofa this time. Languidly, she raised a hand to Andrew, allowing him the pleasure of grasping her fingers. She might have intended for him to kiss it, but this was a professional visit, and he didn't feel it appropriate. Instead he took her hand, turned it over, and pressed two fingers to her wrist, feeling her pulse.

A vision flashed before his eyes—Miss Hemshawe's hand in that of the man he'd seen her speaking with on his way to this appointment. He wished he'd been able to see her expression better. He couldn't tell if she had been looking up at the man with affection, or something else. All he'd seen was the man taking her hand and pressing his lips to the back of it.

It was enough.

No, it was more than enough. Andrew's blood had boiled, but he'd immediately chastised himself. Miss Hemshawe was not his. He was not officially courting her, and she had no reason not to accept such a salute from another man. His jealousy was unfounded—or so he tried to tell himself.

"Are you listening to me? I said I'm doing ever so slightly better," the countess said, frowning at him.

"I do beg your pardon, my lady, my mind was wandering for a moment," Andrew said, giving himself a good shake. He was working. He couldn't be thinking about Miss Hemshawe.

"I could see that." She smiled slyly up at him. "So, who is she?"

He gave a little chuckle. "It is of no consequence. You said your diet was going better?"

"Well, I've been having the mint tea. It has been working wonders. Were you present at Lady Middleton's ball? I heard there was quite a to-do with Lord Bradmore collapsing. Someone said a young gentleman was there, and he brought his lordship back from the dead. That was you, wasn't it?"

Andrew should have anticipated his actions would make the rounds of gossip. "Yes, it was. How did you hear of it, dare I ask?"

"Oh, it was in the paper. But it seems as if no one knew your name. You were only listed as a handsome young gentleman. If I were you, I'd be sure to hand out your visiting cards to anyone and everyone within earshot at such an occasion. You could gain quite a lot of business from such actions."

"That's all right. I will count on you to spread the good word about. Would you do that for me?" he asked, giving her his most charming smile.

It worked as he'd hoped, and the lady was giggling away as he pulled out his stethoscope to listen to her heart and other internal organs.

"You still haven't answered my question,

though. How are your eating habits?" he asked again.

She waved a negligent hand in the air. "Oh, you didn't actually mean that I needed to change what I ate."

He knelt by her side and looked at her. "Yes, I did. I meant it very seriously, as a matter of fact. If you wish to stop having digestive discomfort, you need to eat better. Lighter food and more vegetables."

She made a moue with her lips, clearly not happy with his suggestion. "I want to hear more about your young lady."

Andrew had finally thrown his jealousy out the window where it belonged, but with the countess's comment, it came surging back, filling his chest with a tightness. In his mind's eye, Miss Hemshawe was standing there smiling up at that man as he kissed the back of her hand. She might have even been giggling, and she was *certainly* enjoying his attentions.

But he didn't know if that was what actually happened, Andrew reminded himself. All he knew was that a man had kissed her hand—and that it was none of his business.

### ~July 4~

Andrew was surprised to see his father sitting in the reading room at Powell's that evening. He'd come to the club to do as his father had suggested and meet more people, but, considering Lord Darby had made the first move in reconciling their relationship, Andrew felt maybe it was his turn.

"Do you mind if I join you?" Andrew asked, approaching his father.

Lord Darby looked up from his newspaper. "No, not at all." He carefully folded the paper while

Andrew caught the eye of a footman and ordered a bottle of rum for him and his father to share.

"All going well?" his father asked.

"Yes. I just came this evening to do as you suggested and meet more gentlemen, but actually, if you have the time, I'd appreciate a bit more advice," Andrew said, settling himself in the chair next to his father's.

Lord Darby raised his thick blond eyebrows. Andrew had gotten his coloring from him, while Ian had taken after their mother, with her darker, almost brown hair. "I don't know that I'll be able to help... What do you have on your mind?"

A footman came at that moment with their drinks. Andrew waited until he'd poured and then left them alone.

"I'm afraid I'm rather at a loss as to what to do about a young woman. Er, Miss Hemshawe, to be precise," Andrew began.

His father's pale blue eyes widened before he took a sip of his drink. "She's the young lady you were dancing with at the ball?"

"Yes."

"Who's her father?"

"Lord Rivers, one of my patients."

"Ah! Is that, er, allowed?" His father lowered his eyebrows over his eyes, peering at Andrew.

He could only chuckle. "Yes, I believe it is. At least, well, I've never heard of anyone saying it wasn't."

"Very well," his father nodded. "What about her?"

Andrew took a sip of his own drink while trying to form his thoughts into coherent sentences. "I like her."

"That's good."

"But I don't know how she feels about me." He continued before he could lose the nerve to spill his worries. "And today I saw her with another man at the park. He was standing very close to her, holding her hand—and then he kissed it."

"Her hand," his father clarified.

"Yes."

Lord Darby nodded and took another sip of his drink. "And you're jealous, is that it?"

"I was, but I had absolutely no right to be so. I haven't asked permission of her father to court her. I haven't said anything to her about doing so either."

"Well, you can feel jealous even if you have no hold over someone." His father paused. "Did I ever tell you how I got your mother to marry me?"

Andrew gave a little laugh. "No." His father would never have told him such a thing, or even had such a conversation with him, while his brother had been alive. Ian had been everything to his father. It was as if Andrew hadn't even existed. He hated it, but in a way, his brother's death had truly helped Andrew's relationship with his parents.

"She was being courted by someone else. Her father had set the whole thing up. He was your grandfather's choice, so there was no question about whether they would marry."

"So what happened?"

"I was jealous. I'd danced with Marietta at a number of parties, thought perhaps we had an understanding. I'd been all ready to go to her father and ask his permission when he strutted this other fellow out."

"Oh no! What did Mother say?"

"Well, she didn't have a choice, naturally. She

had to do what her father told her." He paused to take a drink. "But I wouldn't have it. I loved her and wanted her for my own, so I challenged the other man to a duel—pistols at dawn."

Andrew's eyes widened. He couldn't imagine his father behaving in such a passionate way.

"He accepted my challenge, and we set up a time and place to meet. I arrived and brought my dueling pistols."

"And what happened? You won?"

"No! He never showed up! Marietta was there, however," his father said with a laugh. "When I first saw her, I thought she had come to support her intended. But then she strode right up to me and said she would be my second if I needed one."

"Mother?"

"Yes. She'd even brought her own set of dueling pistols—her father's, of course, but she knew how to use them and was prepared to do so."

"But you had your own second, presumably," Andrew said.

"Yes, of course, but that's not the point. She was there and ready to do battle for me," Lord Darby said with a huge grin on his face. "Of course, then her father arrived and told us the fellow he'd chosen to marry her had backed out the previous evening. Wasn't willing to risk his life for the girl."

"What did he say when he saw Mother there?"

"Oh, he was furious," Andrew's father said with a burst of laughter. "But he did say if we both felt so strongly about wanting to marry, he wasn't going to stop us."

Andrew laughed and shook his head. "That's an incredible story!"

"Yes, but you see, sometimes it's all right to be

jealous even if there isn't a spoken understanding between you."

Andrew sat back cradling his glass of rum in his hands, thinking about what his father said.

"So, are you going to fight for this girl or not?" his father asked after a few minutes.

Andrew gave him a smile. "I think I might."

"I can lend you my pistols."

Andrew burst out laughing. "I hope it won't come to that, but I'll keep it in mind."

"At least you won't need to have a doctor on site."

"Well, I will if it's me who gets shot. I can't operate on myself," Andrew said, laughing.

"Oh, well, then you just have to make sure that doesn't happen."

They were quiet for a few minutes and then his father said quietly, "I don't think I ever gave you a fair shake, Andrew. Ian was the perfect son. He took an interest in the estate from a young age and wanted to follow in my footsteps."

"I never did."

"No. You were always rather contrary, needing to forge your own path."

"You hated that," Andrew said, pouring more alcohol for both of them.

"I did," his father agreed. "But now... Now I admire it, and I admire you for sticking to your own ideas. You wouldn't let anyone sway you from your path when you were younger, and you wouldn't do so when I told you to just last week. I respect that. You know who you are and what's important to you."

"Thank you, Father. I guess I've known since Grandfather died that I wanted to be a physician."

He paused to remember his grandfather's passing. It had been a sad occasion. He'd been there with his mother, visiting his grandparents, when it had happened, and he'd vowed then and there that he would do everything he could to save as many people from the same fate as he could. "Mother challenged me, you know. I told her I wanted to stop people from dying of heart conditions like Grandfather had, and she said she didn't think I could. I had to prove to her that she was wrong."

"And you have. You saved Bradmore the other night, and you're going to save your own mother from the same thing."

"Well, they probably have different problems with their hearts, but yes, that's the plan. I want to save her, and I want to save Lord Rivers, who also has a heart condition. I want to save as many people as I possibly can."

"It's a fine ambition, son."

"Thank you. Let's see if I can't make it come true."

~*~

Diana, Lydia, and Lady Moreton were riding back from the Dorothy School for Boys and Girls, an orphanage they visited from time to time, when Diana just couldn't hold her thoughts in any longer. "I just don't know what I'm going to do!" she said, realizing immediately how anguished she sounded. But in truth, it was how she felt.

Lydia nearly pulled her horse up. "About what?"

"My goodness, Miss Hemshawe, you must tell us what is wrong so we can help you make it better," Lady Moreton said.

"It's this debt," Diana admitted. "Lord... The man to whom I owe the money has been hounding me. He came to my house yesterday and once again told me that I could make it all go away by agreeing to marry him. But... I just can't! He's the most awful man!" Diana couldn't believe she was practically in tears. This was so unlike her, but she was just at such a loss.

"Come," Lady Moreton spurred her horse forward and led them into a small park by the side of the road where they could stop and speak properly.

They dismounted, allowing Diana's groom, who'd accompanied her, to take their horses for a walk while they talked.

Lady Moreton indicated they should sit on a bench, but Diana knew she wouldn't be able to sit still. "Please, let us walk, at least," she said.

"Very well," Lady Moreton agreed and arranged them so that Diana was in between the other ladies so they could both hear her. "You absolutely do not want to marry this man, correct?"

"Absolutely!" Diana agreed.

"And how much money do you need to pay him off?" Lydia asked.

"Two thousand pounds."

Lady Moreton choked. "That's a lot of money!"

"I already have three thousand," Diana pointed out.

"My goodness!" Lydia clearly agreed with Lady Moreton.

"Well, then," Lady Moreton began, thinking this through. She was truly a most down-to-earth, practical woman. Diana admired her greatly. "You've earned that by riding and wagering on yourself winning, isn't that right?"

"Yes."

"So, then it seems to me that you need to do that again, no?" she suggested.

"Yes, but as far as I know there are no more races coming up," Diana pointed out. "I have already asked my cousin, Lord Audley, to arrange one race for me. He was kind enough to do so, but I couldn't possibly ask him to do it again."

"Why not?" Lydia asked.

"Because he's already quite suspicious of why I asked him to do so the first time."

"You don't want to tell him about this problem?"

"No. He'd just tell his mother, who would tell my mother, who would tell my father, who would have an apoplexy and die," Diana said, trying not to sound overly dramatic. "Lord Colburne has specifically said my father could suffer no great surprises or stress."

"My goodness!" Lady Moreton said.

"That is difficult," Lydia agreed.

"You couldn't simply ask him not to speak to anyone about it?" Lady Moreton offered.

"No. He's never been very good at keeping a secret. I know him. Actually, I'm surprised he's kept quiet this long about the fact I've been making large wagers on the last two races I rode in. I couldn't tax him with this anymore."

"And there's no one else you know who could do this?" Lydia asked.

"No. Only my father and Audley," Diana said. She gave a heavy sigh. "There has to be some way... I'll... I'll think of something, or something will come up. It's just that this man wants his money next week."

"Well, you just have to put him off until something comes up," Lady Moreton said.

"You need to become too ill to see him until another race occurs. I would suggest the mumps," Lydia suggested with a big smile on her face.

Diana laughed. She couldn't believe she was laughing, but Lydia could always bring a smile to her face.

# Chapter Twenty-Four

~July 5~

"Good afternoon, my lord. Are you here to see his lordship?" the footman greeted Andrew at the door. "He's doing much better today."

"I'm very glad to hear that, and yes, I am here to see him, but first, I'd like a word with Lady Rivers if she's available," Andrew responded, the knot in his stomach tightening.

His evening with his father had been wonderful and informative, but he didn't think challenging the man he'd seen with Miss Hemshawe the other day was the right way to go for him. First of all, he didn't even know who the fellow was. The only other idea Andrew had come up with was to ask for more advice, so that's what he was here to do.

"Of course, my lord, right this way." The footman led Andrew up the stairs to a small, private sitting room. A few moments later, Lady Rivers came in.

"Lord Colburne, welcome. George said you wished to have a word with me before you go in to see my husband," Lady Rivers said after joining him.

"Yes, if you wouldn't mind—"

"I'd just like to apologize once again for my

awful mistake the other day. I should have waited and asked you once again for instructions on how to use the foxglove," she said, sitting gingerly at the edge of a chair and indicating he take the one across from her.

"I don't think it's *me* who you should be apologizing to, my lady, if you'll excuse me for being so blunt."

"No. And I have already apologized to my husband. He understands it was a mistake—an unintentional one," she said with much more poise than Andrew expected.

"Then the matter is closed and we'll move on from here. Today I've come with some of the medicine already prepared, and I will give him the proper dose myself," he said, giving her a polite smile.

"And you are certain that's still a good idea?"

"I am. I gave a dose to my mother a week ago, and she is doing much better."

"Oh! I'm sorry to hear she wasn't doing well to begin with," Lady Rivers said in all sincerity.

"Thank you. I'm sorry to say the death of my brother hit her particularly hard. I believe the shock of it damaged her heart. But, as I say, this medicine is making her feel much better. I think it will do the same for Lord Rivers."

"Well, that's excellent news," she said, standing.

"But actually, my lady, that's not what I wanted to speak with you about. If you don't mind..." he said, catching her before she walked away.

She sat back down. "Of course."

"I wanted to ask for your advice, if I may?"

"On what?" she asked, cocking her head to the side a little, clearly curious.

"Your daughter."

"Diana?"

"Yes. I... I wish to court her, er, with your permission, of course, and that of Lord Rivers."

"Really?" she asked, sitting back a little.

"We've met, not only here but on a number of other occasions," he started.

"And you've found her to be charming?"

"Very charming and fascinating, beautiful and incredibly intelligent, and understanding," he said, the words just slipping from his tongue before he could even give them a thought. He found himself blushing with his honesty.

Lady Rivers gave a laugh. "Well, it definitely sounds like you are besotted!"

He sighed. "I'm afraid I am. But what should I do about it?"

"You need an opportunity, that's all," she said, smiling at him.

"Yes, precisely!"

She thought about it for a moment, staring out the window as she thought. "How about a picnic?" she asked.

"A picnic?"

"Yes, at Kew Gardens. There are some lovely spots for a picnic, and then you can go for a walk with Diana and tell her how you feel. How does that sound?"

"Just the two of us, or..." he started, a little confused.

"No, naturally, we couldn't have that. No. I could arrange a little party. Actually, I've been wanting to meet all of her Whist Society friends, but I didn't bring any evening clothes with me to

London. A picnic during the day would be a wonderful opportunity for me to meet them and for you to get a little time alone with Diana."

"That's a brilliant idea," he agreed.

"I'm so happy you think so." She stood again.

This time he followed her the few steps to the door. With one hand on the handle, she turned and said, "I wonder if tomorrow is too soon."

"Tomorrow?" he choked on the word.

"Yes. A Sunday would be the perfect day to have such a thing, and I don't imagine you want to wait too long before speaking with Diana. Yes," she said, making up her mind. "I'll send 'round notes right away and make the arrangements."

She opened the door and headed toward Lord Rivers' room. "I'll just show you to Rivers and then get started."

Diana, Miss Hemshawe, was standing outside of her father's room with her hand raised to give a knock when they approached. "Oh, Lord Colburne! The footman informed me you were here. I was just going to see how you were doing with my father."

"Your mother and I were discussing our next steps. We've agreed that I will be giving him a dose of the foxglove I made myself."

"*You* made it?" she confirmed.

"Yes. And I will give him the correct amount," he agreed.

A smile spread on her beautiful face. "I am glad to hear it."

Warmth spread through him and Andrew knew for certain that he was very happy Lady Rivers had proposed having her picnic for the following day. An opportunity to speak with Diana in private couldn't come soon enough.

~*~

He liked her! He wanted to court her, or possibly even propose!

Diana felt bad for having overheard the conversation Lord Colburne had had with her mother in her private sitting room, but still...

Diana couldn't get the refrain out of her head the entire time Lord Colburne was explaining to her parents how the foxglove medicine worked. She hardly paid attention to a word he said but smiled and nodded every time he looked over at her.

He thought she was beautiful and intelligent!

How could she have been so oblivious to his feelings for her?

Well, perhaps because she'd been so busy trying to figure out her own for him. She liked him—a lot. She felt excited and happy every time they were together and always wished for more time with him whenever they had to part.

Did she love him?

"It is a very little bit," he was saying to her father after measuring out a dose of the foxglove. He gave her mother an apologetic look. "You only need a very small amount to have a strong effect. More than this is poisonous, as I'm afraid you have already discovered."

Her mother had the grace to blush.

He was so gentle and nurturing, how could Diana *not* love him?

Standing there, looking at him across the bed from her mother, Diana realized Lord Colburne was everything her mother wasn't. Warm. Loving. Caring.

Oh, her mother probably cared a great deal for her, but they'd never understood each other. They'd never gotten along.

With Lord Colburne, she felt comfortable. She could speak to him about anything, and she knew he'd either understand or sympathize.

Her gaze settled on her father, in between them. He was warm and loving in his own way. He was also self-centered, and too much of a dare-devil for Diana's liking. She had loved traveling around with him, and she completely understood his love of racing, his desire to see new places, meet new people, have new and interesting experiences. She loved all of that as well and wouldn't have passed up the opportunities he'd offered her for anything.

But he didn't take care of her—and never had. She'd been the one to take care of *him*, even when she'd been no more than eleven or twelve years old.

Lord Colburne, she was certain, wouldn't think twice about caring for her. He was that sort of man and she... Yes, she loved him.

~July 6~

Andrew couldn't believe Lady Rivers had actually come through and put together a picnic for the very next day. He wondered how many people were going to be there on such short notice. Although, perhaps she was right; because it was a Sunday, most people had had no plans.

Either way, he was thrilled to be able to have a chance to speak with Miss Hemshawe of his feelings. This was going to be a very good day.

He stepped out of his father's house and into the bright summer sunshine. He could only stand there for a moment and bask in the warmth and admire the beautiful blue of the sky.

"Are ye Lord Colburne?" a woman's voice asked tentatively.

He looked down from the top stair where he was

standing just outside of the door. "Yes. May I help you?"

"I'm Mary's neighbor. She sent me to find ye. Her baby's been cryin' and cryin' up a storm. Could ye come and see to 'er?"

"I was just..." Andrew stopped. If a patient needed him, nothing else mattered. And it was probably nothing. It wouldn't take him very long to see what the matter was, and then he could join the party at the gardens. "Very well, let me just get my medical bag. I'll be with you in a moment."

Thirty minutes later, he was climbing the stairs to Mary's flat. He'd taken the time to change into work clothes as well as collecting his bag—knowing babies, it was unlikely he would emerge from tending her as clean as he went in.

Indeed, the child was screaming when they went in. The poor thing sounded to be in great distress, and her mother looked like she was ready to pull her hair out.

"Oh, doctor! Thank the lord! I don't know what to do. She won't quit. It's been goin' on for hours this mornin' and then all last night."

"*All* night," her neighbor confirmed.

"Why didn't you fetch me sooner?" he asked, taking the baby from her.

"I didn't want ta bother you too early. I know you swells like ta sleep in," she said.

"We know you have wild nights and don't get ta bed till the wee hours of the mornin'," the neighbor said, nodding her agreement.

Andrew could only open his mouth and then close it again. "It is true a number of gentlemen do so, but I am not like that—I'm an early riser. And if there's an emergency you can come to me at any time."

"You are good," Mary said, tears slipping down her cheeks. She was clearly exhausted.

"It's quite all right. Why don't you sit down and relax for a moment while I examine the baby and see if I can't discover what's bothering her," Andrew said, putting the baby down on a blanket on the table.

The child only cried harder when he put her down, but he had no choice. He needed to listen to her lungs and feel her little belly. She looked healthy enough, aside from being red in the face from crying for so long.

He palpated her abdomen, but everything felt normal. He felt her arms and legs and checked her nappy. Andrew was stumped. She looked perfectly fine.

He picked her up again, but instead of putting her to his shoulder, he turned her over to take a look at her back and the back of her head. Holding the baby in his left hand, he ran his right over the back of her head and down her spine. It all seemed normal.

He gave the poor little thing a pat on her back and then was shocked to see liquid rolling out of her ear. He angled his hand so that her ear was tilted toward the floor. He gave her the gentlest of shakes and then rolled her the other way.

The baby gave a little cough and stopped crying.

Both Mary and the neighbor gasped.

"What did you do?" Mary asked.

He handed her the baby back. "She had water in her ear. Did you give her a bath?"

Mary nodded, dumbstruck.

"It's a very good thing to do, but be careful when

you do so."

"I washed 'em out," Mary said, her tears stopped and her eyes went wide. "I washed her ears."

"Ah. Best not to do that."

"No. I suppose not." She looked down at the child, who was now quiet and desperately rooting for her breast.

He gave her a smile. "I'm sure she's famished and exhausted after all that crying. I'll leave you to it. Good day." He nodded to the two stunned women and walked out.

He pulled out his pocket watch before setting out for Mayfair once more. He needed to change back into his nice clothes before he could go to this picnic. He'd been with Mary for nearly an hour and it would take him time to go home, get changed, and then drive to the gardens. He sighed heavily as he gave the signal to his tiger to let go of the horse, snapped the reins, and set off as quickly as he could.

~*~

Diana and her mother both burst into laughter at Lydia's description of Lord Westerland's dancing style. Even the Duchess of Kendell, sitting on Lady Rivers' other side, giggled and was in a good mood, enjoying the beautiful day and the lovely picnic Diana's mother had somehow managed to put together so quickly.

The only thing missing from the otherwise perfect day was Lord Colburne.

Diana had been on pins and needles waiting for him all through lunch and still the man hadn't shown up. Could he have gotten cold feet, she wondered? If he had, wouldn't it have been the gentlemanly thing to show up and then not pay her any special attention? But he hadn't even come!

She looked around once more, but Lord

Colburne was conspicuously absent.

"He's still not here," her mother whispered, leaning closer.

"No. I just can't imagine why he hasn't come," Diana said, looking at her mother.

"I'm sorry, Diana. He said he would. That's all I know," her mother said, before turning back to the ladies sitting on her other side.

Mrs. Aldridge's dog, Duchess, came sniffing around and begging for scraps. Lydia got up and beckoned the dog a little away from the tables where they'd been sitting. Diana, too, felt the need to get up and move, so she joined them, finding a stick to throw for the dog.

They were happily engaged in playing fetch with the pup, when Diana noticed a male-shaped shadow coming toward her from behind. At last, she thought, turning around happily to greet Lord Colburne... Only it wasn't his lordship. The welcoming smile dropped from her face, and her stomach clenched into knots immediately.

# Chapter Twenty-Five

"Miss Hemshawe, what a lovely surprise! Miss Sheffield, I believe?" Lord Swindon said, giving them both a bow.

Duchess barked at the unknown man.

"What a, er, cute dog," he said, stepping away from the animal with a slight sneer on his lips.

"Lord Swindon, what are you doing here?" Diana asked rudely.

"My, my, not at all gracious, are we? Must I remind you this is a public park, Miss Hemshawe?" he asked.

"No, you need not remind me. It's just a bit out of your way, isn't it?" Diana asked.

"I was here with another party and saw you. I thought it would be polite to say hello," he said, raising his eyebrows, as if to say *at least I know my manners*.

"Diana?" Lady Rivers said, coming up to greet the stranger speaking with her daughter.

Diana turned toward her mother and swallowed her groan. She did *not* want her mother to know who Lord Swindon really was or what he held over her. She had no choice but to be polite. "Mother, this is Lord Swindon, he, er, is an associate of Papa's."

Lord Swindon bowed as Diana's mother curtsied. "Oh, do you also race horses, my lord?" her mother asked politely.

"I own some race horses, my lady, but don't ride them myself as Lord Rivers and your daughter do," Lord Swindon said, giving Lady Rivers a charming smile. His voice was so smooth; it chilled Diana to the bone.

"Then you are wiser than either my husband or my daughter," Lady Rivers said with a little laugh. "It always makes me nervous when they race, I have to admit."

"Does it? But we almost never had accidents," Diana said. She hadn't known racing worried her mother.

"I think the key word here is *'almost',*" her mother said.

"I was happy to hear Lord Rivers is doing better," Lord Swindon said. "He has been missed at the track."

"Yes, he is, thank you. He is getting stronger every day," Lady Rivers said, looking truly relieved at the truth in her words.

"That is excellent." Lord Swindon smiled at her before looking to Diana for a moment. "I say, Lady Rivers, would you mind terribly if I took your daughter for a little stroll?"

"Oh, I don't know if that would be a good idea," Diana said immediately.

"Why? I think it is exactly what you need to keep your mind off other things," her mother said meaningfully. Diana knew her mother thought she was being clever, giving Diana a diversion from waiting for Lord Colburne, but she really didn't want to be in Lord Swindon's company for any longer than she had to, and definitely not alone.

"Excellent!" Lord Swindon said before she even had a chance to argue. He took hold of her arm, holding it tighter than necessary as he led her off, as if she would try to run away from him. Diana admitted the thought was tempting, but sadly impossible with the way he was grasping her.

She bit her tongue and walked away with him, not wanting to cause a scene.

They wandered into a stand of trees strewn with bluebells. The smell was heady, and any other day and with anyone else, she would have enjoyed it immensely—just as she had when she had gone looking for foxglove with Lord Colburne. But today, with this man, she could find no joy in this walk.

"So, this is how you raise the money you need to pay me, is it? By attending picnics in the park?" Lord Swindon said conversationally.

"Of course not. There weren't any races being run today. There is nothing I can do," Diana answered.

"But there was this morning at Newmarket."

"That's too far for me to travel—and clearly for you as well," she snapped.

"Do not assume, Miss Hemshawe. In fact, I *was* there yesterday and only arrived back in town early this afternoon."

"But then you weren't there for the race," she pointed out.

"Not today's. But there were others yesterday. Sadly, I had other commitments today," he said, stopping underneath a large oak and turning toward her.

"Like this other party you attended here at the gardens," she said. She turned to look back the way they had come, wishing with all her might that Lord

Colburne would turn up. Surely, if he arrived at the picnic, her mother would send him after them, wouldn't she?

"Yes, like that." He smiled.

He was still holding onto her arm, and she didn't like it. She moved to pull away. His grip only tightened however and instead of moving farther from him, she was pulled closer.

"My lord," she protested.

"Miss Hemshawe, I find I am extremely attracted to you," he said, leaning toward her.

"I am very sorry to hear that, because I am not at all attracted to you," she said, doing her best to hold her ground. Why *wasn't* Lord Colburne here?

"I'm sure that after a year or so of marriage, you would begin to find me tolerable." He bared his yellowed teeth in what she thought he meant as a smile. It looked more threatening to her than anything.

"I don't—" she started, but before she could finish her sentence, he moved to kiss her like a snake attacking suddenly when it was least expected. She managed to turn her head just in time so that his lips landed on her cheek rather than her lips.

He was put off balance by her move, giving her the opportunity to pull her arm out of his grasp. She turned and ran, lifting her skirts out of her way. As she neared her mother's picnic, she slowed to a fast walk so as not to alarm anyone. She didn't know where Lord Swindon was, but she resisted the urge to turn back to look. She just wanted to get back to safety, back to her mother... No, she wanted to go home!

She could see at a glance that Lord Colburne still wasn't there, and she feared Lord Swindon would follow her back to her own party. She couldn't risk it.

The day was ruined anyway.

"Mother, I'm going home. I'll send the carriage back for you," Diana told Lady Rivers, interrupting the conversation she'd been having with Mrs. Aldridge and Lady Moreton.

"What? You can't leave my picnic. That would be rude!"

"I'm sorry, but I just... I'll apologize to everyone properly on Wednesday. I'm afraid I can't be very good company just now. I'll see you this evening." Diana didn't wait for her mother's protests. She wasn't sure just how long she could hold back the emotions quickly swamping her.

~*~

Andrew rushed through his change of clothing, although he did briefly contemplate arriving at the picnic in his work clothes. If he hadn't been planning on asking Miss Hemshawe to marry him, he might have. But one did not propose wearing a threadbare coat and coarse cotton breeches. He also needed to pick up the ring he'd purchased first thing that morning—a beautiful diamond surrounded by blue sapphires. He'd noticed she wore blue frequently and figured it was a favorite color, so he'd been sure to get a ring to match.

When he arrived at the park, it had taken him another ten minutes to find where Lady Rivers' picnic was being held, but finally... Finally he strode quickly across the lawn, bypassing the winding path that led to the area where tables had been set up.

"I beg your pardon," he said to Lady Rivers as he approached her. She was speaking with Mrs. Aldridge, who Andrew had met a few times with Miss Hemshawe.

"Oh, Lord Colburne! *Finally*, you have come," Lady Rivers said, her eyes widening at his approach.

She excused herself and stepped away from the lady so they could talk in private.

"Yes, finally," he said with a heavy breath. "I am so sorry I'm late." He looked around but didn't see Miss Hemshawe.

Her mother clearly noticed him looking and said, "You've missed her. She returned home not thirty minutes ago."

"What? She left?"

"Yes. I'm so sorry. She waited for you." She gave a little laugh. "I don't know, but I think she might have known you might say something to her today, for she was constantly looking out for you."

"But then why did she leave before I arrived?" he asked.

"I don't quite know why. She went for a walk and when she returned, she insisted on leaving immediately."

Andrew ran his fingers through his hair, so frustrated he felt like pulling it out.

"You could try seeing her at home," Lady Rivers suggested.

Andrew gave a nod and attempted to give her a smile as he thanked her. He strode straight back to his phaeton, not wanting to be social with the others who were there. He simply wanted to be with Miss Hemshawe. To speak with her. To tell her how he felt about her and find out how she felt about him. Well clearly, however she felt wasn't nearly as powerful as his own emotions.

If she felt the least bit of affection for him, she would have waited, for surely her mother would have told her that he was coming.

On the other hand, if she didn't have the patience to wait, was she really the sort of woman he wanted to marry? The sort he *could* marry?

He was a doctor. He needed a wife who would wait patiently for him while he tended to his patients. Whether that meant he was late for dinner or for an evening's engagement, she had to be patient. If Miss Hemshawe couldn't do that, then she wasn't the wife for him.

He'd thought she was different. He'd thought she was patient and understanding. Clearly he'd been wrong, he thought with disgust. He gripped the reins in his hands tighter, feeling the leather straps biting into his palms.

Miss Hemshawe had seemed so sweet. She'd presented herself as a caring, thoughtful, patient woman. Clearly she wasn't.

How could he have been so taken in by her? How could he have thought she was the one for him?

He arrived home and slammed into the house.

"What the…" His father came out into the foyer as Andrew stood there pulling off his gloves. "What's gotten you into a tizzy? I thought you had gone to propose to Miss Hemshawe?"

"I'd thought so too, but she left the picnic her mother had arranged so that I could do so," Andrew said. He started toward his father, wanting nothing more than a tall glass of his father's excellent port. And then, maybe another.

But his father didn't move out of his way to allow him to come into his study. Instead he said, "So what are you doing here? Why aren't you chasing after her?"

Andrew stopped. "Well, clearly if she doesn't have the patience to wait for me, she isn't the right sort to be my wife."

"Don't be a fool! How late were you?"

"Over an hour, perhaps an hour and a half," Andrew admitted.

"An hour and a half! No wonder she left. If I had to wait an hour for someone, I would have not only gone, but left a scathing message for them."

Andrew tried once more to get past his father. "Well, she didn't. She simply left. Her mother said she went home."

"And why aren't you there presenting yourself? Because you're miffed she didn't wait around for you all day? Be reasonable, Colburne, really!" Lord Darby folded his arms across his chest and glared at Andrew. He was clearly not going to give an inch.

"Look, I just want a drink, Father," Andrew started.

"Yes, and I'm sure Miss Hemshawe just wants an explanation as to why you were so late. Go and give it to her. It's the least you could do."

"She's not the right one," Andrew argued.

"Are you absolutely certain? A few days ago you were mooning over her like a love-sick boy."

Andrew closed his eyes, hating the picture that came to his mind at his father's description.

"Now you go over to the Rivers' home and talk to the girl," his father said.

"Father, I'm really not in the mood."

"And I'm sure she's not either, but if you put it off, you'll be making things worse. Now go," his father pointed back to the door.

When Andrew didn't immediately move, he added more gently, "Andrew, just talk to her. If she's not the right one, then you never have to speak to her again. But if she is, then you will regret this for the rest of your life, because you probably won't get another chance."

It didn't look like his father was going to give up on this, so Andrew turned around, took back his hat and gloves, and left the house. He supposed he should at least have a word with her.

Ten minutes later, he was admitted into the Rivers' drawing room. Miss Hemshawe was standing, staring out the window. She didn't move for a moment after he was announced. And then suddenly she turned on him. "Where were you?" she asked accusingly.

"I was tending to a patient. Could you not have waited for me?" he retorted with just as much anger.

"I did wait. I waited and waited. All through lunch and then after..." Her eyes filled with tears.

Andrew had never seen her show anything other than strength, no matter what the situation. He was completely put off guard. Something was wrong. Something much more than him showing up late to a picnic.

He advanced toward her. "Diana." He took her hands as the first tear made its way down the gentle slope of her cheek. "Diana, what's wrong? What happened?"

"I needed you," she said, blinking furiously. "I needed you and you weren't there."

"Why? Tell me," he pleaded with her.

"It doesn't matter anymore. You weren't there." She pulled her hands away. "I don't think I want to see you any more, Lord Colburne. You... You're unreliable. You say you're going to be somewhere and you don't show—and this isn't the first time it's happened. So I... I think you should just go."

"There was an emergency. If you can't understand that, then maybe I *should* go," he said, his anger spiking again.

"I would have understood if you had informed me. But you didn't think I warranted that much consideration, did you? You don't show up when you say you will. How can I trust you? How can I rely on you?" She stepped away from him and turned back to the window. "Good day, my lord."

He turned and strode out. There was nothing further to say to her, and clearly, she had nothing to say to him. She wanted nothing more to do with him, and that was absolutely fine. He was right. He should have followed his initial instincts, simply had that glass of port and stayed at home.

But when he was sitting in his room later that night, thinking over what she'd said, he realized she'd been right. He *hadn't* given a thought to her when he'd been called to tend to Mrs. Small's baby. He'd never had to tell anyone of his comings and goings. But she'd been absolutely correct. He *should* have sent her a quick note. He could have even just sent a footman around with a message saying he would be late.

But he couldn't help thinking there was something more she wasn't telling him. Something else had happened at the picnic. Something had upset her.

Well, clearly she didn't trust him enough to tell him what it was. And he had no desire to be leg-shackled to a woman whom he would have to inform of his every move. No, he was well out of that trap, he decided as he finished off his second glass and started to pour another. Perhaps, with enough to drink, he might just believe it, too.

# CHAPTER TWENTY-SIX

~July 7~

Diana had stayed in her room the previous evening, not even coming down for dinner. In truth, she didn't have much of an appetite after the day she'd had. She went to sleep early and ended up sleeping on a pillow damp with her tears.

This morning, however, her mother didn't seem as if she was going to be as easy to dismiss as Lord Colburne had been.

She knocked on Diana's door over an hour after she normally had breakfast. "Diana?"

"Yes," Diana said as she answered her door.

"Are you feeling all right? George said you didn't come down for breakfast this morning, and Cook said you sent back your dinner untouched," her mother said. The worried look on her face nearly had Diana in tears once again.

"I... I'm not hungry," she admitted, blinking to keep her eyes clear. It wasn't working.

Her mother stepped forward and took Diana into her arms. "I don't know what happened yesterday between you and Lord Colburne, but I assume it wasn't anything good."

"No," Diana said, succumbing to her emotions.

"I'm sorry, dearest. Can you tell me what happened? George said he came over, but that he left again rather quickly."

Diana did the best she could to stop the flow of tears, taking in a deep breath to try to calm herself. "He...He's just not trustworthy. He says he'll show up and then he doesn't."

"I'm sure he had a reasonable explanation," her mother said.

Diana lifted and dropped one shoulder. "A patient. He said he was seeing a patient."

"Well then, I'm certain it was something very important that couldn't wait. He wouldn't have just not shown up."

"He didn't show up to the last race I ran. Was that a patient too?" Diana asked.

"Do you mean the one where the winning horse was disqualified?"

"Yes. You were there—although, you disappeared too."

"I was terrified of that horse, Diana. And yes, I left—with Lord Colburne, who was kind enough to see me home."

"He *was* there?"

"Yes, he was. And he was as unnerved by that horse as I was."

"He told me once he was afraid of horses. He...he had a bad experience as a child."

"My goodness! And he still came to the race?"

Diana couldn't answer that. Of course he'd come.

Her mother just looked at her. "I think you owe him an apology," she said after a moment.

"Well, even if he did come then, he didn't

yesterday," Diana said, beginning to realize her excuse sounded weak.

"He did. He was simply late. If you hadn't run off the way you did, you would have seen him."

"I don't know what I'm going to do," she admitted to her mother.

"Well, how do you feel about him? Do you love him? Like him? Hate him?" she asked, a little smile tugging up one side of her mouth.

Diana swallowed hard. "I... I thought I loved him... I guess I'm unsure."

"Well, think about it. Personally, I think he's quite wonderful for you." She gave Diana one more quick hug, and then left her alone to sort through her confused feelings.

~*~

It didn't take Diana long to get changed into her riding habit. She just couldn't think sitting in her room. She'd tried to do so the previous evening and even most of that morning, but her mother was absolutely right. She needed to work out exactly how she felt, and the only way to do so was on horseback.

She had just mounted her horse in front of her house when she heard her name being called. She turned and found Lydia, Lady Sorrell, and Lady Moreton all approaching her on horseback.

"I'm so glad we caught you!" Lydia said, walking her horse up to Diana as she sat atop her own.

"Are you ladies out for a ride?" Diana asked, looking from one to the other.

"Actually, we were just coming to ask you to join us," Lady Sorrell answered.

"Yes, we were going to go for a good gallop outside of the city," Lady Moreton said.

"You all want to go for a gallop?" Diana asked

suspiciously.

"Well, we figured you would need to do so..." Lady Sorrell started.

"Considering yesterday's events," Lydia finished for her.

"It was clearly a very difficult day for you," Lady Moreton agreed.

"And we know you..." Lydia said.

"We figured you'd need to ride it out," Lady Sorrell said, finishing Lydia's thought.

Diana burst out laughing at her friends. "You *do* know me!" she said. She tried surreptitiously to wipe away the tears that were trying to escape from the corners of her eyes. "And you are all the *best* friends a girl could have." She swallowed hard. "Please, let's go before I start to make a fool of myself." She gave Nike the signal to start, and together they all trotted through the morning traffic until they were finally free of the city.

"Who's game for a race?" Lydia asked.

"Me!" Lady Sorrell cried out with a laugh.

"I am!" Lady Moreton said.

"Are you truly going to challenge me?" Diana laughed.

"You'll go easy on us, Diana, we're not on thoroughbreds like you," Lydia said, laughing.

"All right. You all go ahead. I'll catch up," Diana said, moving her horse off to the side. The other three lined up their horses in front of her and Diana called out, "Ready? Steady! Go!"

They took off, leaving Diana in the dust. She held her own horse back until they were a good distance away before allowing Nike to follow her instincts.

As expected, she easily caught up and then passed her friends. A little down the road, she slowed Nike and waited for the others to catch up.

They were all laughing when they finally slowed their sweating horses.

"There's an inn not too far where our poor beasts can be watered and cool down," Lady Sorrell said.

"And *we* can be watered as well?" Lydia asked.

They all laughed, and Lady Sorrell said, "If you want to be watered, I'm sure you can be accommodated. Personally, I'd like a cup of tea."

"Oh no, tea sounds perfect," Lydia agreed.

They headed off to find this wonderful inn.

Diana's groom, who had followed at a discreet distance, took command of their horses as soon as they arrived at their destination, leaving the ladies free to see to their own comfort. They sat at a sweet little table in the corner of the tap room.

"Some tea, ladies?" the innkeeper asked, coming up to their table as they settled themselves.

"Yes! Thank you," Lydia said.

"Do you have breakfast?" Diana asked. "I'm famished."

"Yes, Miss. Eggs, ham, some toast and jam?" the man offered.

"Perfect, thank you." Diana agreed. Her stomach rumbled its approval.

Lydia burst out laughing. "You'd better make that as fast as possible," she said to the innkeeper.

The man gave a little laugh and went off to see to their order.

"I can't tell you how wonderful it is you came to ride with me. I feel so much better already," she admitted to her friends.

"We figured you would," Lady Moreton said with a smile.

"And we thought you could use an ear or six," Lydia said with a giggle.

Diana laughed. "Six is a good number of ears," she agreed.

Their tea was served and soon Diana's meal.

"As soon as you've satisfied your hunger, I want to know why you disappeared so quickly from the picnic," Lydia said.

"Was it simply that you were tired of waiting for Lord Colburne, or did something else happen we aren't aware of?" Lady Sorrell asked.

Diana's appetite began to wane, and she started to toy with her food rather than eat it.

"No, no, Miss Hemshawe, you cannot waste all that food you just asked for," Lady Moreton protested immediately.

"Oh, please call me Diana," she said, looking up at the three of them. "Really, it seems silly to be so formal when you've all been so wonderful to be here for me."

"Of course. We will all use our given names as well," Lydia said.

"My goodness, I don't even know your given names! Mine is Cynthia," Lady Sorrell said.

"Ellen," Lady Moreton said with a laugh.

Lydia and Diana likewise shared theirs.

"Good. Now, Diana, you are going to eat that breakfast while you tell us what happened," Ellen said.

Diana nodded before taking a bite of her food. By the time she'd chewed and swallowed, she'd summoned up the courage to tell them the truth.

"Lydia, yesterday when we were playing with Duchess, do you remember the man who came up to me?" she began.

"Yes, who was he? I thought it rather odd you didn't introduce him," her friend said. "Although he seemed to know who I was."

"Well, everyone knows you," Cynthia said with a laugh.

"You were playing with the duchess?" Ellen asked, already confused.

Lydia and Diana laughed. "No. We were playing fetch with Duchess, Mrs. Aldridge's dog."

"Oh!"

"That can be so confusing," Cynthia laughed.

"Yes. But that man was Lord Swindon," Diana said, getting back to the point. "The man who made the wager with my father," she explained just before taking another bite. Her friends all gasped, their eyes widening.

"That's who that was?" Lydia said.

"What was he doing at the park?" Cynthia asked.

"He said he was there with a party of his own," Diana told them. She then proceeded to tell them all that had happened between her and Lord Swindon, including his attempted kiss.

They were all suitably shocked and horrified.

"Why didn't you tell us?" Ellen asked.

"You should have said something," Cynthia said.

"Instead of just leaving," Lydia agreed as well.

"I just... I couldn't. I was so upset," Diana admitted.

"Well, I'm not surprised at that," Ellen said.

"Not only at Lord Swindon, but at the fact Lord Colburne wasn't there. The last time Lord Swindon cornered me, Lord Colburne was right there to protect me. But this time..." Diana pushed the food around on her plate.

"Eat," Ellen reminded her. Reluctantly, she took another bite.

"Have you spoken to Lord Colburne?" Cynthia asked.

Diana nodded and then swallowed her food, her mouth dry. "He came by yesterday afternoon to tell me he'd been with a patient. I was so upset, I didn't know if he was trying to apologize or not."

"What did *you* say?" Lydia asked.

"I told him to leave. I couldn't face him," Diana admitted. "I told him he couldn't be trusted and he should just go."

Ellen gasped.

"And he did?" Lydia asked.

Diana nodded before taking a sip of her tea.

"But it's really not his fault he had to see a patient," Cynthia pointed out.

"That's true. I'm sure that if he could have, he would have much preferred to have been there for you," Ellen said.

Diana took in a deep breath. Her friends were probably right.

"You're clearly in love with him, Diana," Lydia said quietly. "Don't you think you can forgive him this?"

Diana turned and looked at her friend. "Am I? I just don't know."

"Think about it, Diana. How does he make you feel when you're with him?" Ellen asked.

"Safe," was the first word that popped out of Diana's mouth. "And cared for." She fiddled with her fork. "Ever since I can remember, I've never really felt cared for. My mother and I never got along and then I left with my father to travel around the Continent. He was too busy to bother with a teenage girl, beyond taking me to the racetrack with him and teaching me how to race. I know he loves me, but I never felt..."

"Cared for," Ellen finished for her.

Diana looked up at her. "No. *I* was the one who cared for him, not the other way around."

"That must have been so difficult," Lydia said, putting her hand on Diana's arm.

"I didn't realize it until we came here and I met Lord Colburne," Diana admitted. "He was so thoughtful and caring. And... I don't know how or why, but even my mother has begun to be kind to me. Maybe she just couldn't deal with a little girl either, but now I'm grown it's easier for her."

"I'm sure she loves you," Cynthia said.

"And *I'm* sure Lord Colburne loves you, too," Lydia added.

Ellen gave a little laugh. "I'm pretty sure Diana loves him too."

Diana could only smile because deep down in her heart, she knew her friends were right—each one of them.

"So," Lydia said, clapping her hands together. "What are we going to do about this?"

"I say we have a dinner party," Cynthia offered.

Diana looked at her. "A dinner party?"

"Of course! So you can have another opportunity to speak to Lord Colburne," Cynthia said as if it were obvious.

"Oh, but I don't know..." Diana said.

"Well, I do. You take it from an old, married lady. You need to tell him the truth, and I'm pretty certain he'll have some things to tell you too," Cynthia said with absolute certainty.

# CHAPTER TWENTY-SEVEN

~July 9~

Andrew really wasn't certain this was a good idea. Accepting Lady Sorrell's invitation to dinner, when he'd been explicitly informed that Diana would be there, probably was not the right thing to do.

Lady Sorrell's note inviting him had been unusually explicit. She was holding the party for the express purpose of giving him an opportunity to work things out with Diana, and he'd been stupid enough to accept. Why? The last time he'd spoken with Diana she'd been absolutely certain she never wanted to have anything to do with him.

Could she have changed her mind?

The only reason he accepted the invitation was that he knew Lady Sorrell was a particular friend of Diana's. They must have spoken, which meant that Diana had said something to Lady Sorrell to indicate she was at the very least open to discussing what happened between them.

Yes, he was an idiot who still held out hope.

"Lord Colburne, I am so glad you could make it," Lady Sorrell said, greeting him at the door to the drawing room.

He bowed. "Of course. I would never miss an

opportunity to attend one of your parties," he said politely.

She gave a little giggle and brought him farther into the room. Lord Sorrell stood up and shook his hand. "Good to see you, Colburne."

"Thank you, and you," Andrew said. He turned and nodded to the other ladies and gentlemen present. Those present this evening would be very much the same group as had been at the picnic the other day, although not everyone had arrived yet. Still, he supposed he owed them all an apology.

"I, er, am horribly embarrassed by my behavior on Sunday," he started.

"Oh, do you mean when you came to the picnic and then didn't greet or even say a word to anyone but our hostess, Lady Rivers?" Lady Blakemore asked. She was clearly a stickler for proper behavior.

"Yes," Andrew admitted. "And I wished to apologize. Such behavior was completely uncalled for."

"Oh, pish-posh!" Miss Sheffield said. "Of course you were put out that Diana wasn't there. It's completely understandable."

"He should have at least greeted everyone," Lady Blakemore said.

"But he—" Miss Sheffield's argument was interrupted by the entrance of Miss Hemshawe and her mother.

She was beautiful. She was always beautiful, but this evening she looked especially well. Her dress was pale blue with light orange—peach-colored, he supposed— ribbons that brought out the red of her hair and the pink in her cheeks. She might have even put a touch of color on her lips, because her face looked brighter, and she looked so kissable. If only...

Andrew shook himself free of such thoughts and actually looked at the expression on her face, not just the beauty of it. It wasn't an encouraging one. No, he was definitely an idiot for thinking this might not be a lost cause.

"Miss Hemshawe," he said, bowing to her and her mother. "Lady Rivers, it's a pleasure to see you again."

"And you, my lord." She gave him a significant look as if to say, *You'd better make this right.*

He nodded to let her know he got the message and would do all he could but didn't hold out a lot of hope.

Miss Hemshawe had barely curtsied to him before immediately turning to the other ladies and began chatting with them, effectively cutting him. He didn't know if it was intentional or if she was just being polite to the others. He was trying very hard not to look like a desperate fool, but he wasn't so certain he was succeeding. Meanwhile, she looked so cool and uncaring, as if nothing had changed at all.

He was debating his next move when the butler announced the next guests. "The Duke of Warwick, Lord Ayres, Lady Norman, and Miss Ayres."

Lady Sorrell clearly moved in excellent circles—a duchess and a duke. Andrew was impressed. Of course, he would one day be a marquess, but after years of being plain Dr. Crowther, he was still getting used to being in such exalted company.

He turned to bow to the newcomers. "Binny, is that you?" The words popped out of his mouth before he realized they were even there. He was just so surprised to see his old school mate.

The man in question turned Andrew's way. "Crow?" A huge smile spread across his face, and he slipped from behind the two ladies and came forward with his hand outstretched.

Andrew grasped it and pulled him in for a brief hug. "My God, it's good to see you!"

"Where have you been, old man? Didn't I hear you were in France?" his friend said.

"Yes, yes, I was. After medical school, I went to work and do research there. Back here now," Andrew finished, trying not to take on too sober a note.

"Yes," Binny's eyes saddened momentarily. "I heard about your brother. My sincere condolences."

"Thank you."

"Adler's not here too, is he?" Andrew asked, looking toward the door.

"No. I heard his father died. He's probably at Vineland Hall taking care of matters," his friend said.

"Warwick? Would you introduce me?" a lovely young woman said, joining them.

"Oh, yes. I do beg your pardon. Er, it's Lord Colburne now, isn't it?" Binny asked.

At Andrew's nod, he continued. "May I present my fiancée, Miss Tina Ayres?" He turned to the young woman. "Crow, er, Colburne was my closest friend in school. We roomed together for, what? Three years, wasn't it? Or four?"

"Four, actually," Andrew said with a laugh. "But wait, is it Warwick now? I'm afraid I haven't kept up on the news here."

"Yes. My parents were both taken by influenza a few years ago," Binny—no, Warwick, said.

"Oh, I am sorry! But congratulations on your engagement. That must be a new occurrence?" Andrew asked, turning a smile onto Miss Ayres.

"Yes," she said with a broad smile, slipping her

hand through Warwick's arm.

"It's been a whirlwind of a season, but a wonderful one," Warwick agreed, giving his fiancée a warm smile.

"You both look very happy," Andrew said.

"We are, thank you," Warwick said.

"We should probably greet the others," Miss Ayres said tactfully.

"Yes, er, you go on ahead and I'll join you in a few minutes." Warwick placed a kiss on the back of her hand after he unwound it from his arm. He then placed a strong hand on Andrew's shoulder and said, "Let's get a drink."

They walked over to a sideboard where there were decanters and glasses waiting for guests to help themselves. Warwick poured them both something that was a beautiful golden amber.

He then held up his glass and said, "Here's to beautiful women and old school chums."

Andrew lifted his glass to that and took a sip. The liquor was intense, burning its way all the way down his esophagus.

"Ah! Sorrell does like his whiskey," Warwick said with satisfaction.

"Yes. My father drinks port, so that's all I've been having recently. In France, we only drank wine," Andrew said. He took a sniff of the whiskey, and then another sip. It wasn't half bad.

"Has it brought from Scotland," Warwick said. "So, I hear this little gathering is for you."

Andrew sighed. "Did Lady Sorrell share my woes with everyone invited?"

"There isn't much these ladies *don't* share," Warwick said with a little laugh. "My Tina isn't an official member of the group, but her, ah, Lady

Norman is, and she's engaged to Tina's father, so we get kept up to date on all the gossip they share."

"Is there some that they don't?" Andrew asked, intrigued at Warwick's careful explanation. There was clearly something more going on there, but it was none of Andrew's business. And he had enough on his plate already.

"Yes. Do you not know what the Ladies' Wagering Whist Society does?" Warwick asked, lowering his glass.

"Play whist, I imagine?" Andrew answered.

"Yes, but it's the stakes they play for that's most interesting."

Andrew just cocked his head a little, waiting for elaboration.

"Secrets, old man. They play for secrets. And then, once the secret is known, they do something to help fix whatever it is."

"Assuming the secret is something that can be fixed?" Andrew asked.

"So far it has been. They put Tina and me together and helped Miss Sheffield become engaged to Lord Welles. It's your turn now, I'm afraid." He gave a little laugh before taking another sip of his whiskey.

"Really? How did they help you?" Andrew asked, and then added quickly, "If you don't mind my asking."

"No, not at all. They sent the Duchess of Kendell and my sister after me when I retreated to my estate after making the stupidest mistake known to man— I asked Tina to marry me at exactly the wrong time. She took it the wrong way and eviscerated me with her words."

"My goodness! How did the duchess and your

sister help?”

“They told me the circumstances I wasn’t aware of, and then escorted me back to London so I could have another go at it.” He gave Andrew a broad smile. “It worked the second time. It’s all in the timing and knowing exactly how to ask.”

Andrew laughed. “I suppose it was my timing that has caused me problems as well.”

Warwick just smiled.

“The thing is, I’m not sure Miss Hemshawe is interested in me trying it again. She was pretty upset.”

“Do you love her?” his friend asked sincerely.

“Yes,” Andrew answered without hesitation. “But...” he continued, “I’m not certain she’s the right one for me. The reason my timing was bad was because I needed to see a patient. If she’s going to be upset every time I’m late because someone needs me, it’s just not going to work.”

Warwick frowned. “You were seeing a patient when you were supposed to be seeing her?”

“Yes.”

“Did you inform her of this?”

Andrew opened his mouth and then closed it again.

“Ah, I see.”

It was Andrew’s turn to frown. “She said I should have done so, but it didn’t even occur to me. I’ve lived on my own for so many years now, I’m not used to having to report my whereabouts to anyone.”

Warwick placed a hand on his shoulder. “And here we come to the crux of it, my friend. If you want to be with her, you need to think of her first. Yes, tend to your patients, but you can’t just forget about her.”

Andrew sighed and nodded. "Yes. Yes, I think you're right. If I'm going to marry anyone, whether it be Miss Hemshawe or someone else—and I sincerely want to do so—then I suppose I am going to have to stop thinking of only myself, my schedule, and my patients. I have to think of her as well."

"You're getting it," Warwick said with a laugh. "And now I'm going to go and be polite to the ladies."

Lesson learned, Andrew thought to himself as he too went to be social with the others. Now he just needed to find a time when he could get Diana off into a corner to have a private word with her—which was the point of the entire evening, after all.

~*~

Diana couldn't eat a bite of the delicious dinner Cynthia served. She was much too nervous. She knew what was to come—somehow Lord Colburne was going to pull her aside and talk to her about what had transpired between them. But Diana just didn't know whether he was going to apologize or if it was up to her to do so.

She did notice that Lord Colburne didn't seem to have much of an appetite either. He very efficiently shoved the food around on his plate, loaded up his fork, but only once in a while did he actually take a bite. It was reassuring to know he was as nervous as she.

When the ladies rose after dinner to withdraw from the table, Lord Colburne stepped in front of Diana as she was about to pass him.

"Would you mind if we spoke?" he asked quietly.

"No, not at all," she answered. She indicated he should follow her. She had been to Cynthia's home enough times to know that Lord Sorrell's study was across from the dining room, so she led the way there instead of going upstairs to the drawing room with the other ladies. Someone had kindly left a small fire burning in the grate, even though the temperature outside was quite mild. The house did still retain some of the winter's chill, so she was happy with the cozy warmth.

She sat on the sofa, and then wondered if she should have taken a chair as Lord Colburne sat directly beside her.

"Diana—you don't mind me using your Christian name, do you?" he asked, interrupting himself before he'd even gotten started.

"No, not at all," she answered.

"Good. You should call me Andrew," he said.

She smiled and nodded.

He took in a deep breath and started again. "I've been thinking about what you said—that I should have informed you I would be late. You're right. I should have. I didn't even stop to think about it, though, because I've never had to."

"I should have been more understanding," she admitted. "I know your patients come first. They need to. It could be a matter of life or death."

"Thank you." He took her hands in his. "I feel much better already, and I hope you do as well?"

"Yes."

"There's just one other thing that's bothering me," he admitted before she could say much more.

"Oh?"

"You were very upset on Sunday and I... I could be wrong, but it seemed to be more than the fact that I was late. Your mother said you went for a walk and when you came back you insisted on leaving right away. What happened on your walk?"

Diana looked away toward the fire. She'd apologized. He'd apologized. They'd come to an understanding. Did she need to divulge all of her secrets to him as well?

She thought about exactly what it was that so attracted her to him—that he was caring. If she truly wanted him to care for her, shouldn't she be open and honest with him? He couldn't look after her if he didn't know the truth, and if she were being completely honest with herself, she could use someone's help at this point. There was no one she wanted to help her more than Andrew.

"Honesty is the basis of a good relationship," she said, half to him, half to herself.

"It is. Can you be honest with me? Can you trust me?" he asked quietly.

She looked up into his light green eyes. They were filled with concern, and she knew she truly *could* trust him. She gave a slight nod.

"Lord Swindon insisted I go for a walk with him," she started.

"Lord Swindon? I don't know him," Andrew interrupted.

"He's the man who was bothering me at the ball, in the garden. You joined us at just the right moment and saved me from his attentions," she explained.

"Oh, yes. What was he doing at your mother's picnic? Is he a friend of hers?"

"No. He's an acquaintance of my father's. He said he was at Kew Gardens attending another party and he saw me, so he came over," she said.

"And asked you to go for a walk with him."

"Yes. I didn't want to, but my mother was there and she encouraged it. There was nothing I could say without being rude, although now that I think back on it, that would have been preferable to what—" She couldn't go on.

Andrew took her hand, sensing her distress. "What did he do?"

She turned her head away, not able to look him in the eye. "He tried to kiss me."

Andrew was up and standing in front of her. "And I wasn't there," he said bitterly.

"No. I wanted you to be. I *needed* you." Diana felt the tears pricking at her eyes once again, but she'd already cried over this once, and she refused to do so again.

"Oh, Diana," he said, sitting back down. "I am so sorry! I *should* have been there."

She shook her head. "No, it's not your fault. I should have known better than to be alone with that man."

"He's bothered you before—at the ball and then again another time. I saw you with him at the park," Andrew admitted. "I didn't know if you were pleased with his attentions or not."

"Most decidedly not!" she answered quickly.

"Who is he and why does he keep pestering you? I assume you've let him know you're not interested in him?"

"A number of times. The thing is…" Diana swallowed as she got to the hardest part to admit.

"You can tell me, Diana. Please, trust me," Andrew nearly begged.

# Chapter Twenty-Eight

Diana explained to Andrew about her father's debt. It wasn't easy and she felt terrible for opening up her father's folly, but she had to be honest with him. She had to trust him.

He nodded throughout her explanation. When she got to the part where Lord Swindon had insisted she marry him in order to get him to forgive the debt, his lips pinched together, and she could tell he was holding back his ire.

"And so he keeps on bothering you for this money?" he finally asked, once she was finished with her tale.

"Yes. I've almost got all of it. I've got three thousand pounds. It's just the last two thousand I need to somehow earn—and no, I refuse to borrow from you or anyone else. The ladies have all offered," Diana said before he could even offer.

His face relaxed into a smile. "I wasn't actually going to offer. I don't think I've got that much money just laying around. I'd have to ask my father, which would lead to all sorts of awkward questions."

Diana gave a little giggle of understanding. "But I've got to think of something, some way to earn that money. One more race would do it, but I don't know if there are any more scheduled, and I've got less than a week to get it. To be honest, I should have paid him back last week. He's been remarkably patient, allowing me to take the time I need."

"Patient isn't the word I would use, but yes, it is good he hasn't pressed you harder for the money."

Diana could only sigh. It was clear that Andrew was as stumped as she was as to how she was going to get this money. "I'm so sorry to burden you with this," she started.

"What? No, don't be! I want you to be honest and open with me, and you have been. I appreciate that."

She nodded. "It's been so awful having this debt hanging over me. I haven't been able to sleep properly. I haven't been able to fully enjoy hardly anything because it's been constantly weighing on me. If only my father hadn't been so stupid." She sighed again. "If I could only turn back time and make it so that he'd never made this wager..."

"I'm so sorry, Diana. This has been truly awful for you. I wish so much I could think of a way to help." He paused, thinking about this, and then said, "So the other man, the one at the track who tried to give you money. Was that someone with whom you've been wagering to earn the money you need?"

"No, he's my cousin, Lord Audley. He arranged the first race I rode in and has been placing my bets for me."

He nodded. "Ah, your cousin. It did look like you knew him well. So he's a part of the racing scene also?"

"Yes. He's been wonderful in helping me, although I have to admit, I've not been completely honest with him. I haven't told him about my father's debt, for fear he would tell my father."

Andrew frowned. "I don't know that would be a good idea. With the delicate condition of his heart—"

"Precisely! That's why I haven't told him."

"That's wise. But I also have to admit that between Swindon and Audley, I've been working very hard not to feel jealous. It hasn't always been easy, nor entirely successful, but I've been trying."

Diana laughed. "I appreciate your efforts. There is really no reason for you to feel jealous, however. Swindon I truly want nothing to do with and Audley is a close relation, like a brother, really."

He nodded. "Good. Let's keep it that way. I don't want to have to duel anyone for your hand."

"What? Duel anyone?" Diana was shocked. Never would she even think of anyone having to fight for her!

"No, no, it's just something my father told me once. Pay no attention," he said, laughing. "Let me think about this. Perhaps I can come up with an idea for you."

"I would appreciate it. I'm out of them. I've been so focused on this problem for so long now, I can't even bear to think about it anymore."

"It's a lot for one person to deal with. You are an incredibly strong woman, Diana. I can't tell you how much I admire you for that."

Warmth filled her chest at his words. "Thank you."

"Well, if I'm being completely honest, there is a great deal more than simply your strength I admire." He turned toward her and ran his fingers lightly down her cheek. "I also admire your intelligence, your incredible talent with horses, and of course, your beauty."

Diana could feel herself begin to flush. "You are too kind—"

"I'm just being honest, as we said we would be," he said interrupting her. "And I want you to be happy."

"I am happy when I'm with you. You make me feel cherished."

"That's precisely how you should be." He leaned closer. She was sure he was going to kiss her, and liked that he gave her a moment to move away if she didn't want him to. Oh, but she did want him to, so she moved herself a touch closer as well.

A smile spread slowly across his face. With the lightest of touches, he feathered his lips across hers. A chill of desire shot through her, followed by a moment of disappointment when he moved away. But before she could say or do anything, he was pressing his lips to hers once again, this time with more urgency and intent.

She could only melt into him, feeling as if her bones had turned to putty. But he was there, strong and secure and supporting her, and she knew without a doubt she wanted to be with this man for the rest of her life.

~*~

Andrew went home that night and thought through the eventful evening. From seeing his old school friend, to the wonderful stolen kisses, to the gentle teasing from the ladies after he and Diana had rejoined the party. There was something nagging at him though—a thought just at the tip of his mind he simply couldn't capture. He was probably too tired. A good night's sleep and it would come to him, he was certain.

Andrew bolted awake. He had it! He knew exactly how he was going to help Diana. The clock in the hall began to chime. Andrew paused to listen.

Three.

He flopped back down in his bed. It was three in the morning, which meant there was nothing he could do for hours—except go back to sleep. He closed his eyes, determined to do so. And first thing in the morning, he would go see Lord Audley about arranging a re-running of the relay race where Diana's father had made that stupid bet to begin with.

~July 13~

"Rivers, just what do you think you are doing?" Sophia's voice stopped Albert short the moment his foot crossed the threshold of his room.

He turned to face his wife. "I'm getting out of this room. I can't stand it anymore. I've been in that room for longer than I've been in some cities. If I don't move to another room... Well, let me just say I won't be responsible for my actions."

She came and placed a hand on his chest, standing so close their breath mingled—hers smelled of mint and tea, not an unpleasant combination. Smiling up at him she said, "I'm so happy you're feeling better."

He chuckled and placed a kiss on the tip of her nose. "I am, you minx. Now, come with me to the drawing room."

She took a step back and laced her arm through his, giving him a bit more support than the cane he had found in the back of his closet. He still wanted to keep one hand ready to lean against the wall to balance himself, but it felt good having her arm as well. Slowly they walked to the end of the corridor and into the drawing room.

She helped him to the sofa and saw him seated.

He took in a deep breath, feeling winded just

from the very short walk. "How ridiculous. I'm as shaky as a newborn colt."

"It's not surprising at all. You've not moved so far in a very long time," she said.

She started to sit on a chair across from him, but he stopped her. "Wait, before you sit down. Open up that window." He pointed to the one directly across from him overlooking the street.

"Are you sure?"

"Absolutely! I'd go outside if I could, but since I can't I'll take what fresh air I can get."

She gave a nod and did as he asked. A breeze fluttered the curtains and brushed against his cheeks. It felt incredibly good.

"Now, come over here," he directed her. "Sit with me." He patted the sofa next to his good leg.

With a smile twinkling in her eye, she did so. "Yes?"

He ran a finger down her soft cheek. "I just wanted to thank you," he said quietly.

Her eyes widened. "For what?"

"For being here. For taking such excellent care of me over the past few weeks. I know Diana would have done so if you hadn't come, but... It wouldn't have been the same," he said.

She leaned her face into the palm of his hand. "Of course I came. It's not only my duty as your wife, but it's my great pleasure to see you well." She paused. "The past few weeks have been important. It's been wonderful having you captive so we could spend time together."

He burst out laughing. "Captive, eh?"

"Well, it has been nearly impossible to keep you in one place for very long before this," she said, defending her choice of words.

He had to admit she was right, so he nodded. "And?"

"And this time has allowed me to become closer to Diana, which is also important. We missed out on a great deal of time together. She grew up with you, and has become a responsible, clever, sweet girl. I would never have known this if I hadn't come."

"It's true. I'm very happy you've mended that relationship," he agreed.

"And I'm happy we've had a chance to work on ours as well," she said. A soft smile graced her beautiful lips.

She might now have a few more and deeper lines on her lovely face than she did when they first married, but she was still the most beautiful girl he'd ever seen. He leaned forward and captured her lips with his own—and she still tasted like honey to him.

He deepened his kiss, reveling in the feeling of her arms winding around his neck. He pulled her closer and ran a hand up and down her back and then, as their tongues intertwined, around her front to feel the fullness of her breast.

"Oh! I beg your pardon!" A man's voice made Albert and Sophia jump away from each other.

Albert looked over his wife's head, which she'd ducked down to his chest, and saw his doctor standing there looking awkward. "Lord Colburne, were we expecting you?"

"Er, no, my lord. I just thought I'd come by and check to see how you were feeling," the young man said, coming farther into the room. "Your footman simply told me to come up. When I found your room empty, I thought I'd see if you were here, but I didn't mean to interrupt..."

"No, no, it's quite all right," Sophia said, standing up. She flushed prettily. "As you can see,

Lord Rivers is feeling much better."

Lord Colburne smiled. "Yes, indeed. The fact that he is here and not in his room says a great deal," he said tactfully.

"And tomorrow I plan on venturing out into the garden," Albert announced.

"An excellent idea!" the doctor said, opening up his medical bag and pulling out that damned tube he like to press against Albert's chest.

He took a seat next to Albert and did just that. After listening silently for a moment, he pulled away and put two fingers on his neck to feel his pulse. "Your heart is going a little fast, but at the moment that's not unusual. It sounds so much better."

"It feels better too," Albert admitted.

"This is very good news."

"And you think it will be all right for him to go out into the garden?" Sophia confirmed.

"Oh, absolutely. I think he should get up and about as much as he can over the next few days. He needs to rebuild his strength so he can go to the race next week," Lord Colburne said.

Albert perked up. "Race? What race?"

"There's going to be a re-running of the relay race where you had your cardiac event," the doctor said.

"Really? But I won't be—"

"Oh, no, my lord, *you* are not going to be riding. Your nephew will ride in the first length and Diana in the second," Lord Colburne informed him.

"Audley?" Albert thought about it for a moment. He wasn't certain Audley was good enough to win. "Well, then, I'd better call that boy over and give him some pointers. We can't have him losing this race for Diana."

"It's an excellent idea, because, yes, they do need to win." And with that cryptic remark, he packed up his tube, bowed and let himself out.

# Chapter Twenty-Nine

Andrew didn't leave the Rivers' home after he left Lord and Lady Rivers to their previous occupation. He was very happy Lord Rivers was feeling so much better, although it had been rather embarrassing to just walk in on their amorous activities. He started to wonder if his parents still engaged in—no, he just couldn't think about such things.

Changing the direction of his thoughts, he strode back to the front door and asked the footman where he might find Miss Hemshawe.

"I believe she is in the study, my lord," the man said, nodding toward the closed door across from where they stood.

"Thank you." This time, Andrew knocked before walking into the room.

"Yes," Diana's voice called out.

"I was wondering if you had a minute," Andrew said, coming into the room.

"Oh, Andrew," Diana rose from the large desk on the far side of the room. A smile brightened her face.

"Good afternoon. I have good news," he said, approaching her.

"Good news is always welcome," she said. She came around the table and indicated they sit in the seating area by the fireplace.

"Two pieces of news," Andrew said, sitting on the sofa after she had taken a chair across from him. "The first is that your father is doing very well. He and your mother are in the drawing room, and he seems to be in excellent spirits." There was no way he could tell her what her parents were doing in the drawing room, but at least she should know he was doing well.

"That's wonderful!" Diana said. "It's amazing how well that foxglove medicine is working."

"I agree." It was a relief to him that it had worked on both his mother and Lord Rivers. It was a potent tool to keep in his medical bag.

"And the other piece of good news?" Diana asked.

"I had an epiphany last night—or, well, early this morning, to be precise."

"Oh?"

"And I acted on it this morning," he continued.

"And what was it? What did you do?" she asked, her curiosity obviously piqued.

"I went to see your cousin, Audley. Nice fellow."

She lost her smile. "Yes, he is. You didn't—"

"Tell him about your father's problem? No, I didn't. I think we both agreed that would not be a good idea. Although, you are going to have to come clean soon. He tried five different ways to wheedle the information out of me."

She truly began to look worried.

"I didn't say a thing, I promise," he reassured her.

"Then what did you talk about?"

"I asked him to arrange another race. This one as a celebration of your father's recovery," Andrew said, smiling at her. "It's to be a relay exactly like the one you raced in before—only, this time no one is going to have a cardiac event, I hope!" Andrew said with a little laugh. "I've even asked Audley to see if he can't get exactly the same people to participate."

"What a brilliant idea!" Diana looked truly shocked, which pricked at Andrew's pride for a moment before he shoved it aside. "Why didn't I think of that?"

He shrugged. "I don't know, but you said yesterday you wished you could turn back time. This doesn't exactly erase what happened, but it certainly makes it so that everything that did can be set right."

"Yes! Yes, it does! But... but my father can't possibly ride in this race," she said, growing worried again.

"No, he can't. Audley offered to ride in his stead. Actually, he offered to ride in your place and for you to ride in your father's. Something about you being a stronger rider?"

"Yes, I'm much better at racing than he is," Diana agreed. "And you need the better rider to finish the race."

"Yes, so he said he'd ride first. When I told your father about this just now, he said he'd call Audley over to give him some pointers." Andrew gave her a smile and wondered if such good news might win him another kiss.

"You told my father? And he was all right with it?"

"Of course. He was thrilled to be able to go to the races and see you and Audley ride."

"And he didn't insist on riding himself?" she asked, looking at him skeptically.

"Not at all. He knows his own limitations," Andrew reassured her.

She stood, so Andrew followed suit. "I don't believe this. I'm actually going to get a chance to earn the rest of that money," she said, coming forward.

"You are. Audley even said he would place your bets for you," he agreed, also stepping closer. He could feel his heart speed up at the anticipation of what was about to happen. Heat rushed through him and it took all of his self-control to keep himself from reaching out for her.

"That's wonderful, Andrew," she said, moving very close to him. "I don't know how to thank you."

"Oh, I might be able to think of a way," he said with a smile. He leaned down and kissed her sweet, upturned lips. He didn't hesitate a moment this time but deepened his kiss right away.

Diana wrapped her arms around him and pulled him close, and he was more than happy to do likewise.

~July 20~

"Your biggest problem, Audley," Diana's father said, leaning toward his nephew, "is that you need to be in tune with your horse. You need to talk to him. Coach him. Encourage him."

"You talk to your horse as you are racing?" Audley asked with a lift of one eyebrow.

"I do! I lean right over his neck and whisper in his ear," Lord Rivers said, lifting his lips into an encouraging smile.

Audley sat back and narrowed his eyes at him, clearly thinking about this. "Now that you mention it, I have seen Diana do that when she's racing. I thought she was just leaning over the horse's neck to reduce wind resistance. A lot of jockeys do that."

Diana's father gave a little laugh. "The result might be a reduction in resistance, but what they're doing is talking to their horses."

"Do you talk to Nike?" Audley asked Diana, turning toward her.

"I do. I always do. And my father's right. It helps," Diana said. "Don't think me mad—she listens to me and is encouraged to run faster when I whisper in her ear."

Audley gave a little nod. "All right. It certainly can't hurt—" He was interrupted by a knock on the drawing room door.

"I beg your pardon, my lord," George said upon entering. "There's been an urgent message for Miss Hemshawe from the stables. Her presence is required immediately."

Diana jumped from her chair, her heart suddenly pounding in her chest. A message from the stables the day before the race was never a good thing. Her groom was supposed to be taking Nike down to Epsom Downs today in preparation for the race the following day.

"I'll go with you," Audley said, also standing.

"And I," her father said, getting up more slowly.

"No, Papa, you should rest before the excitement of tomorrow," Diana said.

"I want a trial run. I haven't been out of this house, except for brief excursions to the garden, for a month," her father stated.

"But then you'll be too tired—" she started.

"You let me worry about how tired I am. I'll be careful, I promise. Just give me a few minutes to dress." He walked slowly out of the room, leaning on his cane.

She turned and gave a nod to George. "Send back a message saying we'll be on our way soon, and make sure his lordship's valet is in his room to help him dress."

"Yes, Miss," George said.

A quarter of an hour later, during which Diana didn't sit down once, her father was ready. He went slowly down the stairs and paused just outside the front door to take in a deep breath.

"Ah, it feels good to get out of the house," he said, hardly having taken one step out.

"Please, Papa, I'm worried," Diana said, encouraging him as gently as she could.

"Right." He continued down the few steps to the footpath and then led the way to the stables, which was just half a block away. He walked slowly and steadily. Diana had to resist the urge to take his arm and support him.

Instead, Audley took hers and held her back, forcing her to allow her father to walk on his own.

At the stables, all was too quiet. Diana's groom greeted them at Nike's stall. He doffed his cap and shuffled some loose hay around with his foot. "I... I don't know 'ow to tell you this, Mademoiselle, and honestly, I don't quite know 'ow it happened..." he said slowly in his halting English.

"Just spit it out, man," her father said sharply.

The groom looked up at his employer and nodded. "I was checking Nike before taking 'er down to Epsom and discovered that she's got a... an inflamed hock. She must 'ave strained it yesterday when I exercised her. I... I don't quite know 'ow. I am always very gentle, never pushing 'er to do more..."

"She must have come down awkwardly on a bit

of uneven ground," Audley suggested.

"Oui, my lord, that must be it," the groom said with some relief.

Diana didn't wait to hear more but went into the stall with her horse. First, she offered her the sugar cube she'd brought, and then went to feel the horse's hind legs. Indeed, one was clearly swollen and the horse was favoring it, not putting all of her weight down on it. Diana went back up to her head and stroked her soft nose before coming back out and rejoining the men.

"Well?"

"She can't run. She can't even stand on one leg fully," Diana said.

"That is not good news," Audley said.

"No," her father agreed.

"We'll have to drop out of the race," her cousin added.

"No! No, we can't do that. This entire race was organized so that…" She paused—she'd been just about to reveal the true reason for the race. Her mind was so scrambled. She was so upset. She had to think. She had to…

Audley looked at her closely, waiting for the truth to be spoken, but her father cut in first, thank goodness. "To honor me, which is incredibly kind, but if your horse is lame, Diana…"

"She can't run," Diana said, suddenly having a brilliant idea. She turned to the horse in the stall next to Nike. "But Goliath can."

"You absolutely cannot ride your father's horse!" Audley's protest was loud and firm.

"Why not?" she immediately threw back him.

"He's enormous and much too strong for you. You would be like an annoying gnat on his back," her cousin said.

Her father laughed but shook his head. "She's ridden him before."

"What?" Audley turned to look at Lord Rivers.

"You heard me. She's ridden Goliath before. Did quite well, actually."

Diana could hardly believe her father was defending her ability to ride his horse.

"But you've told me that no one rides Goliath but you," Audley protested.

"I told you because I didn't think *you* would be able to control him. Diana can, however," Rivers said. He put a hand on her shoulder. "What you don't understand, Audley, is what will keep you from ever becoming a brilliant rider. It's what makes Diana better than half the riders out there. There's a connection. She talks to the horse. She gets inside their head. She understands them and they, in turn, understand her." He turned to her. "You can do that with Goliath, right?"

"I've done so before," she said with a nod.

"Then it's Goliath you will ride. But I want you to take him down to Epsom today. I want you to work with him this afternoon and then, personally, I want you to rub him down and groom him."

She nodded, fully understanding what her father was saying. "We'll become very close, I promise."

"Good." Her father gave her cheek a little pat. "I have full confidence in you, my girl. And now I really must return to the house. Audley, give me your arm." Her father took a shaky step forward and Diana worried he'd overdone it with this outing. He needed to be there the following day, since he truly believed the re-running of this race was for him.

"And you, Papa," Diana said, following behind, "will spend the rest of the day in bed resting up for tomorrow."

"Yes, ma'am," he said, not even turning around.

She paused to have a quick word with the groom, assuring him that she'd return within the hour ready for the trip down to Epsom Downs. When she returned to the house, she'd dispatch her maid with a valise and preparations to stay the night there. It was going to be a long day for her and Goliath. They both had a lot of work to do, and then a lot of resting up for the race the following day.

# Chapter Thirty

~July 21~

The only person Diana had time to speak to before the race was her cousin, Audley. He'd come down early to prepare himself and his horse. She quizzed him about how her father was doing, but he hadn't spoken to him since handing him off to Diana's mother after they'd returned.

Diana looked about the throngs of people, trying to spot him or their coach, but she hadn't been able to find them anywhere. She sincerely hoped he hadn't had some sort of relapse.

The announcement that the race was being run in his honor wouldn't come until afterward, but still Diana worried he wouldn't make it. He *had* to be there. Surely, he would? What made her even more worried for his health was that she hadn't seen Andrew either. If her father had needed him, he would have gone without question, which meant he wouldn't be here for the race either.

"Diana, stop pacing, you're agitating the horses," Audley had finally said, placing his hands on both of her shoulders to keep her still.

"I'm sorry. It's just that I haven't seen my father or Lord Colburne. I don't know where they might be."

"They will be here. Don't worry." It wasn't much comfort, but they didn't have any more time to discuss it further as the riders were called to put their mounts into place for the race.

Diana took in a deep breath and mounted Goliath. They had had some good runs the day before, but she knew he still wasn't fully comfortable with her slight weight on his back. That, combined with her own agitation, had the horse prancing as she tried to guide him to her spot where she would wait for Audley to give her the go-ahead to start the second length of the race.

She noticed a good number of the people riding in this race were, in fact, the same who'd ridden in the first race. There weren't many people who would ride in such an unusual race. It had been the brainchild of Lord Bunbury, and so far she'd not heard of anyone who had jumped forward to mimic it. She supposed she should be grateful so many who participated the first time were back to try it again.

She watched as the race was started, holding Goliath as steady as she could. It wasn't easy. He could sense there were other horses running, and he wanted to be one of them. He was a born competitor. Luckily, she wasn't the only one who was having trouble keeping their mounts steady as they waited for their team member.

Diana did take one quick glance toward the rails to see if her father or Andrew had shown up, but she still didn't see them. Goliath quickly recalled her attention, however. No, there was nothing she could do but keep her focus on the race and the horse. To do anything else was courting trouble.

Horses from the first length of the race were coming toward her and the other riders, but she didn't see Audley among them. Where... oh, there he was, in fourth place sitting tall on his horse! Clearly he hadn't listened to what her father had told him the day before. There was clearly no communication going on between man and horse. And because of that, she was going to have a lot of catching up to do to win this thing!

He finally approached and gave her the go-ahead to start. She gave Goliath a swift kick, and he took off like the thoroughbred he was. Still, she was stupid enough to look toward the rails, still looking for her father and Andrew as she passed. The horse faltered.

"No, no, no," she whispered. "We've got to win! I've got to pay off that debt! And what would Andrew think of me, if after all, this I lost. Would he still want to marry me? Would he still love me?"

Such thoughts were not going to help her, she realized. Nor would worrying about her father's health or her mother's control of the household, although, happily they'd come to an agreement on that one. She shook her head. Thinking about everything that had plagued her for the past few weeks was not helping.

No, Diana had to focus on winning. If she didn't, the horse wouldn't.

She took in a deep breath through her nose and leaned down over Goliath's neck. The horse was so much bigger than her Nike, she hardly came close to his ears. Still, she didn't let that stop her from saying aloud all the encouragement and endearments she could think of.

"Come on, old boy, you can do this. We can do this. You are the horse to beat. You are the greatest racer on this field, if not in the country. Spread your wings, Goliath, fly! Fly!"

The horses sensed her determination, her focus. He smoothed out his gait, lowered his head, and flew. Within moments, she was passing the horses ahead of her. As they came neck and neck with the horse in the lead, she renewed her determination. "Come on, Goliath. This is an easy one for you. You show him what you've got." She gripped his sides even harder, encouraging him, pushing him with everything she had in her.

"It's Goliath by a nose!" she heard someone shout as she crossed the finish line.

She slowed the heaving horse. Her own heart was pounding, and she had to work hard to keep herself from just slipping off the horse. She'd put everything into this race.

She sat up as she slowed Goliath and moved him into the center of the course where Audley was waiting, still mounted on his own horse.

"That was too close, Diana," he called out as she came near. "And I'm afraid that was my fault."

"It's all right. We made it." She reached out and he took her hand, placing a kiss on the back of it.

To Diana's great relief, she saw her father, followed by Andrew, come forward on the course along with Lord Bunbury. At first Andrew held back, and she thought that maybe he was allowing her father his limelight. But then she remembered his fear of horses.

She started to dismount, but before she had both feet on the ground, Andrew was at Goliath's head, one hand on the reins to keep the horse steady for her. She looked up at him and smiled. "Thank you."

He nodded, but she could see the fear in his eyes as he gave the horse a sidelong glance.

"It's all right. My groom will take him," she said, putting her hand on top of Andrew's. He gave her a smile and released the reins. As soon as the groom had come and taken control of the horse, Andrew finally found his voice. "That is a very large beast."

"It is," she agreed.

"I can hardly believe you could ride him. What happened to your horse?"

"She was injured and couldn't run."

"Oh, I am sorry." At least he understood the importance of what she'd said, but before they could talk further, Lord Bunbury called out for all to hear. "Gentleman and ladies"—the man started with a nod toward Diana—"we are here to re-run this race in order to honor Lord Rivers' return to health."

There were shouts of approval as well as polite applause.

"A vital member of the racing community for several years, we are very pleased and relieved to see his lordship back amongst us, and hopefully, back on horseback soon."

There was some laughter and a little more applause.

"And to honor him with all that he has done for the community and for racing, we hear by announce his acceptance into the Jockey's Club. Congratulations sir, and congratulations on your daughter and nephew's remarkable win today."

Diana's father's face glowed with pride and happiness. He shook Lord Bunbury's hand and then gave a short wave to the crowds.

As they all moved back to the rails, Diana noticed Audley had disappeared. She was sorry to see that Lord Swindon had somehow slipped in to take his place.

"Well, well, congratulations, Miss Hemshawe," he said.

"Thank you, my lord," Diana said, taking a slight

side-step closer to Andrew.

"You have finally achieved what I suppose was intended all along," Lord Swindon said.

"As I knew I would, given the chance," Diana answered.

"I would suggest you find someplace else to gloat, Swindon," Andrew said.

"Swindon? Didn't we have a bet?" Diana's father said, just now noticing the gentleman.

Lord Swindon turned to her father. "We did."

Audley rejoined them just then with a large purse in his hand.

"That wouldn't be..." Diana started, looking at it and then up to her cousin.

"It is. This is all of your winnings in total. Six thousand pounds," he said, handing it over.

"Six?" Diana repeated. She couldn't believe she actually earned a thousand pounds more than what she owed.

He nodded. "When it became known you would be riding Goliath instead of your own horse, the odds increased."

"You won six thousand pounds?" her father repeated, astounded.

"Five thousand is mine," Lord Swindon said, holding out his hand.

"What?" Lord Rivers nearly shouted.

"We had a wager, if you remember, my lord. Five thousand pounds for you to win the first relay race. You lost," Lord Swindon reminded him. "Hasn't your daughter told you of this all these weeks?"

"No, I hadn't. His heart—"

"Blast my heart!" her father snapped. "You've

known that I owe this man five thousand pounds all this time, and you never said anything to me?"

"Papa, Andrew said you might not be able to take the strain," Diana said as calmingly as she could.

"It's true, my lord. I told her not to burden you unduly," Andrew said, backing her up.

"And so instead, you'd been lying to me and... and... What? How have you gotten this much money?" her father asked, beginning to quiet.

"Racing," Diana admitted. "With Audley's unknowing help."

"She never told me why she needed to race and place bets at each one," Audley said quickly.

"But you aided her nonetheless?" her father said, turning on him.

"Yes. I will always help my cousin when she's in need. Although she wouldn't tell me why, I was determined to help," he said, standing straighter.

"My money," Lord Swindon prompted.

Diana glared at him then opened the purse and counted out one thousand pounds, turning to her father to hold the money for her. With five thousand left in the purse, she handed it over to Lord Swindon. "There is your money, my lord. It has *not* been a pleasure, and I hope never to see you again. Good day," she said, dismissing him.

He gave a little chuckle as if he didn't care one whit what she thought. He took his money and left.

Lord Rivers handed the extra money back to Diana. "That is yours to do whatever you like. I just... I wish you had been honest with me, Diana."

"I'm sorry, Papa, but I was concerned with your health," she said, accepting the money back.

"I understand that, which is why I'm not furious

with you," he said.

"And now you are free," Andrew pointed out.

"Yes, thanks to you and your wonderful idea to re-run this race," she said, smiling up at him.

"What are you going to do with that money?" Andrew asked.

"Oh, I've got an idea, but it depends upon a certain gentleman." She glanced up at Andrew from under her eyelashes.

"Oh, ho!" her father said with a laugh.

"I think you've been caught, Colburne," Audley said with a laugh.

Andrew laughed. "I think you may be right," he said to her cousin. He then turned back to Diana. "Miss Hemshawe, would you happen to be free tomorrow afternoon for an outing?"

"I believe I may be available," she said saucily.

"Excellent. I'll pick you up at three."

~July 22~

The following day could not have passed any slower for Diana. At one point, she was absolutely certain the clock in the drawing room had actually stopped. She tried winding it, but found it was already fully wound.

"You need something to occupy your time," her mother had said after laughing at her. "Why don't you sew?"

"I never learned how," Diana admitted.

"Paint? Play the piano forte?" she persisted.

"No and no," Diana answered. "I was too busy riding and running the household."

"Well, you know how to read," Lady Rivers said with a touch of exasperation.

"Yes, that I know how to do, but I can't

concentrate. Maybe I'll go for a walk." She got up and headed out the door.

It didn't take her long to fetch her maid and put on a pelisse. By half past one, she was heading out the door, but she was stopped the moment she started toward the park.

"Diana," Andrew called to her from his phaeton as he slowed to a stop right next to her.

"Andrew! I thought you said three," she said, smiling up at him.

"I did, but then I got impatient and decided I didn't want to wait that long."

She burst out laughing.

"Can you come now?" he asked, reaching down a hand to help her up.

"Of course!" She quickly told her maid to go back home and inform her mother she'd gone out with Lord Colburne. The girl bobbed a curtsy, gave his lordship a sly look, and ran back to the house.

"I have no idea why I said three," he admitted as soon as they were on their way.

"It seemed like a good time, but I agree it's a very long time to wait."

"I saw some patients this morning, but then I had nothing to do but wait for the appointed time this afternoon," he said.

"But then you found you couldn't?" she asked with a giggle.

"Yes," he sighed. "What about you?"

"I attended to some correspondence in the morning, but by one I was checking to see if the clocks were wound, time was moving so slowly. I was just going for a walk to pass the time when you drove up."

He laughed. When they needed to stop for traffic, he handed over the reins. "I have to admit, I prefer it when you drive. Do you mind?"

"Not at all! Where are we going?"

"Kew Gardens."

"Ah, the meeting we never had," she said, understanding immediately.

He just looked at her and smiled. "That's one thing I really admire about you—you are incredibly intelligent and quick."

She just smiled and drove.

They reached the gardens and decided to walk along the same paths as they had the first time they'd come.

"I did so like that big field of flowers," Diana admitted.

"It was pretty," he agreed.

"And we can collect some more foxglove to make more medicine for my father and your other patients," Diana offered.

He laughed and pulled her hand through his arm. "I'd rather just focus on what's important here—you. So actually, if you don't mind, I'd prefer to go to the area where your mother's picnic was held to do just what I'd been planning on doing that day."

She nodded. "I don't mind at all."

They wandered the beautiful paths and reached the area where her mother had held her picnic.

"I'd rather not go walking through those woods, if you don't mind. They don't hold very good memories," she said, indicating the way Lord Swindon had led her the last time she was here.

"I don't mind at all. What I'd been planning on doing that day was meeting you right here and telling you…" He paused and took her hands. "I want you to know that I… I love you."

She smiled right back. "I love you too, Andrew," she responded immediately.

His smile grew even brighter before fading a touch. "But you should know I'm a doctor first and foremost. When a patient calls, I'm going to go, no matter what else I have planned or what time of day or night it is. Can you live with that?"

She too became more serious. "I've been thinking about that, and the answer is that yes, I can. The reason I left the picnic before you arrived is not because I was tired of waiting for you—although, as I said, it would have been nice if you'd informed me that you had to attend to a patient—but because Lord Swindon had accosted me, and I was upset."

He nodded. "I am so sorry I wasn't here to protect you from him, but he's gone now—out of your life forever."

"I certainly hope so!"

"Well, he certainly has no more hold over you," Andrew pointed out.

"No, he doesn't.

"And I assure you, the next time I've promised to be somewhere with you, if I can't make it I will inform you."

"Thank you."

"So… Diana Hemshawe, will you marry me?"

"I will, Lord Colburne."

He bent down and was about to kiss her when she heard a terribly familiar voice call out. "There they are!"

Andrew stood up and moved a step away as all of the ladies of the Wagering Whist Society descended on them.

"Diana! Lord Colburne! What a lovely surprise," Lydia said, giggling.

"What are you all doing here?" Diana asked, trying not to sound as frustrated as she felt.

"Oh, we just came to decide if this would be a good place to hold our weekly card games during the summer," Lady Norman answered.

"Yes. We enjoyed your mother's picnic so very much," Lady Blakemore added.

"We thought it would be lovely to hold our card games outdoors," Mrs. Aldridge said. Her dog, Duchess, barked her approval as she ran around all of the ladies, weaving in and out amongst them.

"Mrs. Aldridge, if you cannot control that dog..." the Duchess of Kendell said, clearly upset.

"But that is one reason why we wanted to have our games here, outside," Lady Sorrell said. "So that Duchess could run around to her heart's content."

"But must she run around us?" the duchess protested. There was no answer to that one.

"We hear congratulations are in order," Lady Moreton said, giving them a big smile.

"How could you have heard that? He *just* proposed!" Diana protested.

All of the ladies burst out laughing, but Diana had no idea what they found so funny.

"Then we must congratulate you twice," Lady Norman said.

"We were talking about your win yesterday," Lady Sorrell said.

"I'm so sorry we couldn't come down for your race," Mrs. Aldridge added.

"Yes, we had thought to make a day of it, but, well, the organization was just a little beyond us that day," the duchess said.

"Oh! That's all right," Diana said, now certain she was blushing furiously for her faux pas.

"But we absolutely must congratulate you now on your engagement! That's wonderful," Lady Moreton said.

"You paid that awful man back his money?" Mrs. Aldridge asked.

"Yes, and even had money left over which my father gave me to keep," Diana said.

"What are you going to do with it?" Andrew asked.

"I'm going to buy you a wedding present," she said, smiling up at him.

"Oh?"

"I'm going to buy you a horse!"

# Author's Note

Medicine in the early 19th century was more a practice of hit or miss than it was a science. There were a great number of developments later in the century, but in the early 1800's, doctors were still experimenting with a great number of possible remedies for various ailments. Most doctors still believed that cupping, or bleeding, patients was the best way to cure them—by bleeding out the "bad humors" causing the illness. Sadly, this practice did more harm than good.

According to legend,

*John Hunter, a brilliant English physician of the eighteenth century, was probably the first in Western medicine to paint the clinical picture of chest pain, called angina pectoris, and sudden death. Noting that his own symptoms were aggravated by anger, he complained that his life was "in the hands of any rascal who chose to annoy or tease" him. He proved the case by dying abruptly after an argument with–we know not whether a rascal–a fellow member of his St. George's Hospital board (Liebowitz 1970, 102).*

How to treat this condition was still unknown, but in 1785, one physician discovered how to make digitalin from foxglove and learned of its amazing ability to treat heart conditions, although he mainly believed it to be useful for kidney problems as it was a diuretic.

A few years later, Andrew Duncun published an

article in the *Edinburgh New Dispensatory* on the remarkable ability of the drug to slow the heart and therefore treat diseases such as dropsy (what we now call congestive heart failure) and *angina pectoris* (chest pain that often precedes or follows a heart attack). It was still being used experimentally at the time this story is set, in 1806.

I *have* shifted actual history around just a touch (call it fictional license, if you will) regarding the invention of the stethoscope. It was actually invented by the French physician Rene Theophile-Hyacinthe Laennec in 1816, a good ten years *after* my story. My apologies, but I just couldn't resist having my hero using this wonderful new technology.

And finally, Andrew performs CPR with chest compressions on Lord Bradmore. This technique was first documented only in the 1890s, although, as Andrew notes, people had known to put pressure on the abdomens of drowning victims to expel water, since the 1740s.

# ABOUT THE AUTHOR

Meredith Bond's books straddle that beautiful line between historical romance and fantasy. An award-winning author, she writes fun traditional Regency romances, medieval Arthurian romances, and Regency romances with a touch of magic. Known for her characters "who slip readily into one's heart," Meredith's heart belongs to her husband and two children.

Meredith loves connecting with readers. Sign up for her monthly newsletter at http://meredithbond. com/blog/newsletter-sign-up/ to receive free short stories and get all her news before anyone else. And don't forget to find her on-line:

**Website**: http://www.meredithbond.com
**Facebook**:
https://www.facebook.com/meredithbondauthor
**Twitter:** https://twitter.com/merrybond
**Pinterest**:
http://www.pinterest.com/merrybond/
**Amazon**:
http://www.amazon.com/Meredith-Bond/e/B001KI1SNE
**Instagram:**
https://www.instagram.com/meredith_bond/
**Bookbub**:
https://www.bookbub.com/authors/meredith-bond
**Newsletter:**
http://meredithbond.com/subscribe/

Please don't forget to leave a review wherever you buy books.

# Follow all of the women of the Ladies' Wagering Whist Society

***1806 Season***
***A Hand for the Duke***
*Featuring Christianne Norman, Lady Norman*
***The Jack of Diamonds***
*Featuring Miss Lydia Sheffield*
***The Games She Played***
*Featuring Miss Diana Hemshawe*

***1807 Season***
***A Trick of Mirrors***
*Featuring Claire Tyne, Lady Blakemore*
***A Bid for Romance***
*Featuring Alys Russell, Duchess of Kendell*
***An Affair of Hearts***
*Featuring Mrs. Penelope Aldridge*

***1808 Season***
***Love in Spades***
*Featuring Cynthia Montley, Lady Sorrell*
***A Token of Love***
*Featuring Ellen Aston, Lady Moreton*
***The King of Clubs***
*Featuring Joshua Powell, Lord Wickford*

# Other Books By Meredith Bond

**The Merry Men Series**
*An Exotic Heir*
*A Merry Marquis*
*A Rake's Reward*
*A Dandy in Disguise*
*My Lord Ghost*
*My Gentleman Thief*
*Under the Mango Tree*
*A Spanish Dilemma*
*When Hearts Rebel*

**The Storm Series**
*Storm on the Horizon*
*Bridging the Storm*
*Magic in the Storm*
*Through the Storm*

**The Children of Avalon Trilogy**
*Air: Merlin's Chalice*
*Water: The Return of Excalibur*
*Fire: Nimuë's Destiny*

*The Falling Series*
*Falling*
*Falling for a Pirate*
*Falling Through the Air*
(in the Love Gone Viral Anthology)

*Chapter One: A Fast, Fun Way to Write Fiction*
*Self-Publishing: Easy as ABC*
*"In A Beginning"*, a short story featuring Lilith

www.ingramcontent.com/pod-product-compliance
Lightning Source LLC
Chambersburg PA
CBHW071525120726
47907CB00013B/666